Anne Allen lives in Devon by her beloved sea, near her daughter and grandchildren. Her restless spirit has meant a number of moves, the longest stay being in Guernsey for fourteen years after falling in love with the island and the people. She contrived to leave one son behind to ensure a valid reason for frequent returns. Another son is based in London, ideal for her city breaks. A retired psychotherapist, Anne has now published eight novels. Find her website at www.anneallen.co.uk

PRAISE FOR ANNE ALLEN

Dangerous Waters - 'A wonderfully crafted story with a perfect balance of intrigue and romance.' *The Wishing Shelf Awards, 22 July 2013 – Dangerous Waters*

Finding Mother - 'A sensitive, heart-felt novel about family relationships, identity, adoption, second chances at love… With romance, weddings, boat trips, lovely gardens and more, Finding Mother is a dazzle of a book, a perfect holiday read.' *Lindsay Townsend, author of The Snow Bride*

Guernsey Retreat - 'I enjoyed the descriptive tour while following the lives of strangers as their worlds collide, when the discovery of a body and the death of a relative draw them into links with the past. A most pleasurable, intriguing read.' *Glynis Smy, author of Maggie's Child.*

The Family Divided - 'A poignant and heart-warming love story.' *Gilli Allan, author of Fly or Fall*

Echoes of Time - 'Not only is the plot packed full of twists and turns, but the setting – and the characters – are lovingly described.' *Wishing Shelf Review*

The Betrayal - 'All in all, totally unputdownable!' *thewsa.co.uk*

The Inheritance - 'A gorgeously intriguing story set in a beautiful location. I completely identified with contemporary heroine Tess and Victorian heroine Eugénie.' *Margaret James, author of The Final Reckoning.*

Also by Anne Allen

Dangerous Waters

Finding Mother

Guernsey Retreat

The Family Divided

Echoes of Time

The Betrayal

The Inheritance

Allen Anne

Her Previous Self

The Guernsey Novels - Book 8

Sarnia Press
London

Sarnia Press
London

ISBN 978 0 992711276

Typeset by Sarnia Press

This book is a work of fiction. Names, characters, businesses,
organisations, places and events are either the product of the author's
imagination or are used fictitiously. Any resemblance to actual persons,
living or dead, events or locales is entirely coincidental

To my mother, Janet Williams, with love

"The web of our life is of a mingled yarn, good and ill together"

William Shakespeare

(All's Well that Ends Well)

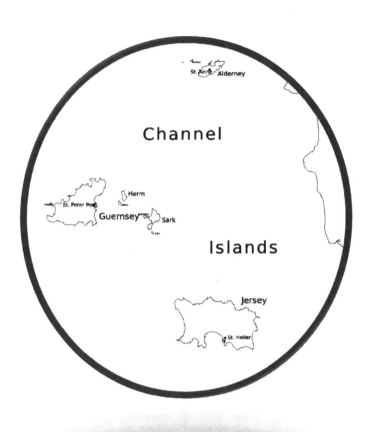

Chapter 1

'You're going away for how long?' Lucy's voice rose an octave as she stared at her parents in disbelief.

Her mother shifted in her chair, not meeting Lucy's eyes. Her father, however, stared back.

'I know three months sounds indulgent, but remember your mother and I haven't had a proper holiday in the three years we've been with your grandfather. We had always planned to take a world cruise when I retired, but it hasn't been an option. Until now, with your…return.'

'Dad, my return as you put it, was meant to be a chance for me to heal, in the bosom of my family, not to enable you to clear off and leave me babysitting Grandpa.' Lucy fought hard to breathe, gulping in air like a drowning swimmer. And drowning was what it felt like. Back on the island a mere two weeks, she had hoped to be cossetted by her parents, not abandoned for the call of the high seas. Although experience should have warned her against such expectations. When had they ever truly been there for her? Even when her baby, Amber, had died eighteen months ago, they hadn't exactly rushed over to console her and Hamish. The memory of that terrible, terrible time rushed to the surface, making her gasp.

'Lucy, come quickly! There's something wrong with Amber, I…I can't wake her.' Hamish shouted from the nursery as Lucy tried to pull herself from the deep sleep she'd been in for what felt like five minutes.

'Wha…? I'm coming.' She registered the panic in her husband's voice as she shook her head to clear it, but wasn't with it enough to feel afraid. Not then, anyway. As soon as she shuffled into the nursery and saw Amber lolling like a rag doll in Hamish's arms, fear sliced through her and she let out a scream as she lunged for her precious child. Afterwards everything was a confused blur of paramedics, an ambulance ride to hospital and the final confirmation by a paediatrician that Amber had died; a suspected cot death. Then the police. Was it a natural death or had she been mistreated? Until all the test results came back, proving it was a natural death, Lucy saw doubt in everyone's eyes. Or was it her imagination? Either way, those first days and weeks were a living nightmare and she and Hamish had retreated into themselves, not able to comfort each other. His parents were too frail to travel down to London from Scotland and hers didn't arrive until the funeral, offering the excuse of being unable to leave her grandfather for long. And now they had the cheek to dump him on her!

Her mother, Marian, cleared her throat.

'I know it's not ideal, but this cruise was a last-minute deal, which we couldn't afford to miss. And we thought you were looking so much better since we last saw you and you have friends here, after all. You'll be able to pop out when the carers are here and see them.' She waved her hands as if to indicate how free Lucy would be.

Gazing first at her mother's thin-lipped smile and then her father's pursed lips, Lucy knew they wouldn't change their minds and she wondered when the last-minute deal had been booked. Probably before she had even arrived, she guessed. Dennis and Marian hadn't been over to London to see her since the break-up with Hamish, six months ago. So how could they judge if she were well enough to cope with a frail old man of ninety when she had suffered a double loss? Her tearful phone calls must not have registered with them.

Lucy, knowing full well how close to tears she was much of the time, stood up. They were seated in what was once an elegant sitting room, complete with intricate cornicing and an imposing marble fireplace, but was now as faded as the curtains and Turkey carpet. Her grandfather was in the common position of being asset rich and cash poor, whereas her parents' house was more modest and their bank balance, she assumed, quite healthy. They planned to return to their home when the old man died, and sell the desirable Georgian mansion to swell the pension fund.

'It seems I have no choice, but don't blame me if anything goes wrong while you're away.' Lucy attempted a glare, but tears threatened to spoil the effect and she rushed out of the room and up the stairs to her bedroom. Flinging herself on the bed, she let out a muted scream, wondering what she had done to deserve such unfeeling parents. Lying on her side, Lucy hugged herself as the tears slid down her cheeks. The bereavement counsellor had said she must cry whenever she was overwhelmed, and that it was a necessary part of the grieving process. No trying to keep up the proverbial stiff upper lip nonsense, she said and Lucy had been relieved to know she wasn't being a silly, weak female as Hamish had implied. An unemotional Highlander, he hadn't cried when Amber died, but Lucy saw the tension around his jaw and the pain in his eyes and knew he suffered as she did. It made it difficult for her, watching him throw himself into his work as a self-employed electrician, working long hours while she barely made it out of bed some days. The anti-depressants helped, but until she was eventually offered counselling, Lucy had struggled, riven with feelings of guilt. As the counselling began to help, Hamish left, leaving her to spiral downwards again.

The tears slowed and Lucy fell asleep. She woke with a start and for a brief moment thought she was back in the flat listening to Amber crying. Switching on the bedside light she was relieved to find herself in her grandfather's house, although unhappy when she recalled her parents' desertion. For some reason her eyes were drawn to a portrait of a couple hanging on the nearby wall. She had hardly spared it a second glance since arriving, as the house was full of family portraits going back yonks. Standing up, she moved nearer. There was something familiar about the woman... Wearing a high-waisted pale blue gown covered in embroidered flowers, with dark hair piled on her head in a profusion of curls and carrying a small dog, the woman's brown eyes were staring straight at her. Or so it seemed. Lucy stood rigid with shock as she watched tears begin to fall down the woman's face. A memory surfaced. She had seen this woman before, in this room, when staying there as a child. And she had walked through the wall and out again.

Chapter 2

Lucy stepped back, holding her breath, and although the tears slowed, the painting seemed to emit such waves of grief she felt as if she had been struck.

'Who are you? What do you want?' Lucy whispered, not sure why she was talking to a painting, but the compulsion was too strong. As if the woman had somehow got inside her mind.

'Mary Carre.'

The mournful voice sounded in her head as the woman's face returned to its usual pose. Was she descending into madness? Or was the house haunted? Neither option was any comfort and made the prospect of three months in the house with only her grandfather, the visiting carers and a possible ghost seem the stuff of nightmares. And "Mary" appeared to be an ancestor, sharing the family surname. Lucy turned to study the man, presumably the husband. Tall and broad-shouldered, he was wearing a velvet knee-length coat with exquisite embroidery edging the front, cuffs and stand-up collar with a white neck-cloth flowing over a heavily embellished waistcoat. His dark hair was pulled back into a velvet bow and steely blue eyes looked down a straight nose over thin lips. His legs were encased in matching velvet pantaloons and white stockings and his right hand rested on a walking cane. Neither of them looked particularly happy.

Suddenly feeling unutterably drained, Lucy peeled off her clothes and slid into bed.

After a fitful night, Lucy joined her parents for breakfast in the kitchen. This used to be the domain of the family cook and her grandmother only ventured there to discuss menus and other domestic matters, the family eating in either the breakfast room or the formal dining room. Since the death of her grandmother, the daily help Meg, had been employed to prepare meals for her grandfather and do a spot of cleaning. He rarely left his room, unable to cope with the stairs.

'Morning. Meg's prepared scrambled eggs for you and there's fresh coffee in the pot,' Marian said, looking up from *The Telegraph*. Dennis grunted a greeting and went back to his *Financial Times*.

Lucy collected her plate from the Aga and sat down at the scrubbed pine table. Desperate for caffeine after the lack of sleep, she poured a large mug of coffee and took a deep swallow before tucking into the scrambled egg on toast. Her parents remained lost to their newspapers which suited her mood. Finishing the last mouthful, she pushed the plate away and said, 'Dad, do you know if this house is haunted?' That caught his attention, his head snapping up as he lowered the paper.

'Haunted? Why do you ask? Haven't seen a ghost, have you?' He gave a short laugh and her mother looked at her, wide-eyed.

'Not sure. Might have. When I was a child. A woman in an old-fashioned dress, probably Georgian, and there's a portrait of her and her husband in my room which I haven't seen before. So, is it?'

'Well, *I* don't believe in ghosts but my father did say something about one having been seen by the cook years ago. Apparently she only appears to women, which says it all, doesn't it?' He rolled his eyes and Lucy's face reddened with anger. Her mother looked thoughtful.

'Was there a Mary Carre in the family about two hundred years ago?'

'I've no idea. Don't tell me she spoke to you?' Her father's jaw dropped.

'I remember now, Lucy, you did tell me about seeing a woman in a strange dress when we spent Christmas here once. You must have been about seven or eight and I thought you were making it up,' Marian interrupted, with an apologetic smile to her daughter. 'I found the portrait in the attic recently and hung it in your bedroom to replace a drab painting of a cow. I liked the colours.'

'That's okay, I understand.' Lucy smiled back before turning to her father, who was becoming puce. 'In a way she did speak to me. I heard the name in my head as I looked at her portrait. Perhaps Grandpa will know, I'll ask him.' She poured another mug of coffee, and taking it with her left the kitchen before her father could reply. Gregory Carre, her grandfather, had a suite of rooms on the first floor which he refused to leave for the more convenient ground floor. His bedroom and adjoining sitting room both had views over the gardens and down towards Havelet Bay, offering a glimpse of the sea and the nearby islands; a view he would not sacrifice for convenience. Lucy sympathised with him as he had little else to enjoy these days.

Standing in the grand, but shabby entrance hall, she gazed around at the family portraits gathering dust on the walls, wondering why Mary's had been banished to the attic. There seemed to be no particular chronological order; contemporary portraits mingled with those from the eighteenth century and as she made her way slowly up the winding staircase, Lucy studied the older portraits in more detail. Until now she hadn't given much thought to her family history, or any history come to that. Not an academic, she had left school after 'A' Levels and taken time out to travel before deciding she wanted to be a gym instructor cum personal trainer. This had horrified her father who had tried to steer her into law or accountancy. He had followed his father into the family firm of advocates and Lucy was made to feel she was letting the family down, but she didn't waver. Marian's support had been lukewarm, but at least she had been on her side.

Marriage and motherhood had given Lucy a different view of family and after losing her child and the subsequent breakdown of her marriage, her view had sharpened. The faces staring down from their ornate frames were her ancestors; she carried their blood in her veins. Draining her mug, she put it on a side table outside her grandfather's room before knocking.

Meg opened the door, a tray balanced in one hand and beckoned her in, her face puckered in concern.

'I hear you've been told about the cruise. I'm so sorry, your parents could have waited a bit longer.' She paused. 'I could try and work a few extra hours…'

'No, it's okay, I'll manage.'

'If you're sure. Gregory will be ready in a minute, the girl's dressing him now. Make yourself comfortable.'

'How is my grandfather today?' Lucy held the door for her.

'Not bad, considering. That cold really took it out of him, but he's on the mend. See you later.'

Lucy closed the door after Meg and began studying the various portraits adorning the walls. The early spring sun illuminated the room, picking out the cracks in the ornamental plaster and highlighting the worn upholstery. In spite of this, Lucy thought it a beautiful room; high ceilinged with golden coloured walls setting off the solid mahogany furniture. She moved to the window where her grandfather's big high back chair was ready for him. This was where he would spend most of his waking day, either reading the papers, a book or gazing out of the window over the now neglected garden. Lucy remembered how lovely it was when she was a girl and a gardener was employed to keep it in tip-top condition. Now, like the house itself, the air of neglect was palpable, thanks, she understood, to some unwise investments and the cost of the nursing home for her grandmother and now her grandfather's care. She sighed. Although not materialistic like her parents, Lucy still felt sad her once successful family of merchants and more recently advocates could no longer afford the upkeep of their grand old house. And her grandfather flatly refused to sell it and move into an easy to maintain apartment.

'Good morning, Lucy. Come to check up on me, have you?'

Lost in thought, she hadn't heard the door open and the electric wheelchair glide across the wooden floor. She turned to face her grandfather, a shrunken shell of the man he once was.

'Of course. How are you, Grandpa?' She bent to kiss his papery cheek, noting the bloodshot eyes still held their old glimmer. She helped him into the armchair, checked he was comfortable and pulled up a chair beside him.

'Oh, could be better. Don't get old, my girl, it's not what it's cracked up to be.' He heaved a deep sigh as she patted his hand. Looking at him now, Lucy found it hard to believe she used to be scared of him. A tall man, he had a commanding presence befitting one of the island's senior advocates, complimented by a deep, mellifluous voice which must have been used to good effect in a courtroom, she thought. Not a cuddly type of grandfather, he had been a remote figure in her childhood and Lucy felt they hardly knew one another. It didn't bode well for the next three months of close contact.

'At least you've had a fulfilling life, Grandpa. Must be loads to look back upon and feel a sense of achievement.' Unlike me, she thought bitterly, a catch in her voice.

He pursed his lips.

'Sounds like you're feeling sorry for yourself, young lady. I can see we're going to make quite a team.' His voice, though not as deep as before, still had the power to unsettle her.

'Yes, well, life hasn't been rosy for me, either. And I'd hoped for some...' she stopped, realising she couldn't say what she really felt. That her father, his son, didn't see it as a problem to leave her to cope with the old man while she was grieving.

'Tea and sympathy? We don't go in for that in this family. I'd have thought you knew that by now.' He frowned. 'If it's any consolation, I do think your parents are being selfish going off on a cruise when you're clearly not recovered from your loss. Ah, you didn't think I notice these things, but I do,' he added as her mouth dropped open in surprise. 'You probably don't know, but your grandmother and I lost a baby before we had Dennis. And the look in your eyes is the same my wife had at the time. A bleakness.' He leaned forward and caught her hand in his mottled claw. 'It will get better, I promise, but in the meantime you and I have to navigate the next few months as best we can. And I'll try not to be too much of a burden if you promise to get out of the house as much as possible and do whatever young people do these days. What do you say?'

Lucy could only nod, too overcome to speak. She had thought him as hard and unfeeling as her father but he was showing her a softer side. No-one had ever told her about the lost child and she wondered if her father knew. Taking a deep breath, she said, 'I'm sorry about your baby, Grandpa, I...I didn't know. And I do realise I should be doing more, but it's been...hard.' An image of a gurgling Amber lying in her arms popped into her mind and she brushed away a threatening tear. 'I promise to make an effort.'

'Good, then we should jog along together. Which reminds me, isn't physical exercise supposed to be good for depression? And you are a gym instructor, aren't you? So, why not join a gym? They might even need another instructor.' He clapped his knees.

'I'm not ready to work yet, but I will look into joining a gym and perhaps do some swimming. See my friends.' The thought both scared and excited her. She had been a hermit for so long, shunning her London friends and barely leaving the flat after Hamish left. Perhaps it would be easier to see her old school friends, who would know little of her life over the past ten years. But would they see her as a failure? The one who chose to skip uni and "find herself" before deciding what to do. As she wrestled with these thoughts her grandfather asked her to rearrange his seat cushion, which she did. Sitting down again she remembered what she had wanted to ask him.

'Do you know if this house has a ghost? Because I think I saw one as a child and her portrait's hanging in my room.'

His eyes lit up.

'Ah, now that is interesting. A woman you say?'

'Yes.'

'Then you might well have seen one. She only appears to women, I believe, and our cook at the time saw her and promptly gave notice.' He chuckled, before looking more serious. 'Your grandmother saw her some months after we'd lost our daughter and at the time I thought it was grief playing tricks on her mind.' He gave her a penetrating look. 'But then she saw it again when Dennis was about five so that didn't fit. Can you describe her?'

Lucy closed her eyes in concentration.

'Average height, long dark hair loose around her shoulders, brown eyes and wearing a dress or nightdress in an old-fashioned style, covered with a shawl.'

'I see. Sounds similar to what my wife said, but it was a long while ago.' He clenched his hands in his lap.

'And she spoke to me.' Lucy didn't think it wise to mention she had been watching a portrait cry and then hearing a voice.

His eyebrows shot up.

'What!'

'Well, sort of. I heard the words in my head, "Mary Carre."'

Her grandfather paled.

'You know the name, Grandpa?' Lucy leaned forward, a buzzy feeling flowing through her body.

'I've heard a story that my – our – ancestor, one Mary Carre, went missing in mysterious circumstances. Apparently something to do with her husband, although nothing was ever proved. But there was a black mark against our name for a while.'

'When was this?'

'Oh, she died around eighteen ten, I think. We're descended from her son.'

Lucy sat back, taking it all in.

'Shall I fetch the portrait for you? See if it rings any bells?'

He nodded.

'Yes, do, my dear. We need to find out more about this poor woman. This ghost.'

Chapter 3

'Here it is,' Lucy said, holding the painting carefully as she returned a few minutes later.

'Ah! And you think this is the ghost you saw as a child?' Gregory peered closely, his brows pinched in concentration.

'Yes, I'm positive it is, although she looks different in this portrait. Presumably the man is her husband. Do you recognise the portrait? Mum says it was in the attic and she brought it down to replace another painting.' She balanced it on the table for him.

'There is something familiar about it, but I can't be sure. I do recall my father having rather a sort out of portraits when I was a lad, saying we didn't need to be reminded of all our forebears, or words to that effect.' He frowned. 'Something about black sheep in the family. Sorry, I don't remember any more. But did you notice the background? It's the drawing room.'

She had been so focused on the woman she hadn't registered the setting. The couple were standing in front of a carved marble fireplace and Lucy recognised it as the one downstairs. Above it, clearly visible, was a painting of a ship with the island of Herm visible in the distance.

'You're right. And do you think the ship's significant?'

He nodded.

'It's likely to be his clipper, quite a fast ship.' Gregory continued to stare at the portrait. 'The painting of the ship should be in the house somewhere. I'm sure I've seen it before.'

'I'll look for it, Grandpa. I'm determined to find out as much as I can about my ghost and her life. Don't fancy the look of her husband, do you? Looks a cold fish.' She wondered if he was the cause of Mary's distress.

Gregory grunted.

'It would have been an arranged marriage, purely for business. There's something niggling me, though. About the marriage. Damn this memory of mine! I used to have everything at my finger- tips.' He clicked his fingers, annoyance flashing across his face. Then he brightened. 'My father drew up a family tree but I've no idea where it is now.' He tapped his head with a grimace. 'Memory again! And I haven't been in some of the rooms for years.'

'Don't worry, I can look for it if you like.'

'Of course. The best place to start will be the library which my father used as a study. Like other rooms it hasn't been used for years so you might find it a bit chilly and somewhat dusty. Oh, and if you find a stash of money hidden away, please let me know won't you?' he said, a twinkle in his eye.

'For a small finder's fee!' She grinned, getting up to leave.

Lucy was sitting in the garden on a bench under an old apple tree decorated with a mass of blossom. Wearing jeans and an old wool sweater against the cool of late March, she hugged her knees as she replayed the conversation with her grandfather. It had been an eye-opener in more ways than one and it dawned on her it might not be such a bad thing if she were to be alone with him after all. And she was looking forward to trying to find out more about Mary once her parents left. She didn't want them to think she was obsessing about a 'ghost'.

'Ah, there you are, I've been looking everywhere for you,' her mother said, somewhat breathless from the long walk down to the bottom of the garden. Lucy sat up, allowing room for her to sit beside her, surprised Marian sought her out. Her mother had hardly spent any time with her since her arrival.

'Anything wrong? It's not Grandpa, is it?' Her heart quickened at the thought.

'No, no, nothing's wrong. I just thought we should talk before your father and I leave tomorrow.'

Better late than never, Lucy thought, summoning a half-hearted smile.

'Right. Anything in particular?'

Marian avoided her eyes, aiming her glance midway down the sweater.

'Yes. I know I…we haven't spoken much about what happened with Amber and then Hamish, but, to be honest, I'm not good about such things. And neither is your father. But it doesn't mean we don't care. Far from it, it's just not easy for us.' She was gripping her hands in her lap and Lucy was surprised by her nervousness. 'Do you remember Molly Ogier? Natalie's mother.'

'Of course, I was often at her house in the holidays. She was always very warm and welcoming. Lovely lady. Why?'

'We've kept in touch over the years, being members of *La Société Guernesiaise* and you may remember she was a psychotherapist.' She cleared her throat. 'I happened to mention you had come home after…what happened and you were holding the fort while we go away. And were still grieving. She said if you'd like to talk about it she would be happy to help. Molly works part-time now but would see you as a friend, not a client. What do you think, dear? Didn't the doctor suggest you continue with the counselling?' Marian sat back, looking relieved.

Lucy sucked in a deep breath. Her mother was right; her Guernsey GP had recommended further counselling while continuing with the anti-depressants in the short-term.

She had resisted so far, feeling she should be able to cope now. She saw the admission of needing more help as a sign of weakness. Contrary, she knew, considering she thought depression was a lack of mental strength. However, talking to Molly as a family friend might be different.

'It's generous of Molly to offer, Mum, and I'll certainly think about it. Where's Natalie these days?'

'Oh, she came back in twenty ten and bought a beautiful renovated farmhouse above Rocquaine and has married recently. Stuart, a teacher at the grammar school. I'm sure she would love to hear from you.'

She nodded. Although they had attended different schools, she and Natalie had become good friends after meeting one summer at Kings Health Club, where their parents were members. It would be good to catch up, if only she could motivate herself to see people.

'Let me have Molly's phone number, Mum, so I can ring her if I feel ready. And I was wondering about joining a gym.'

'Good, I'll feel happier knowing you're doing something while we're away. Why not join Kings? We're still members and you used to like going along for a game of tennis and a swim with your friends. They have a gym and we'll pay the membership fee. It's the least we can do.' Marian leaned forward. 'I…I wasn't entirely happy about leaving you on your own so soon, but you know how stubborn your father can be when he has his mind set on something,' Marian said, shrugging her shoulders.

Lucy wasn't entirely convinced her mother had raised much of an objection, but merely nodded in agreement. At least she had shown some awareness of their selfish behaviour, something her father never did. And paid membership of Kings was not to be sniffed at.

The following afternoon Lucy drove her parents to the airport for their flight to Gatwick. They were flying on to South Africa the next day to join their cruise ship. Lucy drove off after leaving them at departures, none of them being fond of drawn out goodbyes. Her mother had given her a big hug and her stomach clenched in fear. Would she cope without her? Dennis simply pecked her cheek before striding off for a trolley. Driving back to the house in Queen's Road Lucy forced herself to concentrate on the driving. The dark clouds scudding across the sky reflected her mood and she switched on IslandFM for some light relief. Katy Perry's upbeat but inane song didn't cut it for her and she switched it off. Lucy had promised both her mother and grandfather she would get out more, but the thought was scary. And then there was the weird portrait of Mary…would something happen again? From what her grandfather had said, there was likely to be a tragic story involved and although Lucy wasn't sure if she could cope with more tragedy, she was intrigued to know more.

Before she knew it, she was home and signalled to turn right into the drive of the impressive three-storeyed Georgian mansion. Even with peeling paintwork, the cream and white stucco frontage oozed the class and wealthy background shared with the other properties in the area. Lucy knew it had been built by her ancestors, successful merchants of the eighteenth century and lived in by the family ever since. But probably not for much longer. Neighbouring mansions were now medical centres, hotels or divided into apartments and Lucy hoped *Carreville* didn't meet the same fate. She ran upstairs to check on her grandfather and, opening the door quietly, saw he was fast asleep in his armchair. Disappointed, as she would have liked company, she went down to the kitchen to make a cup of tea. The sensation of solitude heightened and Lucy felt a lump in her throat. She had to do better than this. Her poor grandfather was nearing the end of his life and she had many years ahead of her. Hopefully better than the last few. Gripping her mug she paced around the kitchen, coming to rest in front of the noticeboard. Her eyes were caught by a bright pink post-it note bearing Molly's phone number. Taking a gulp of the tea, she lifted the phone off the wall and dialled.

'Molly? Hi, it's Lucy Stewart, was Carre. I believe Mum spoke to you…'

After a quick chat, they arranged for her to call at Molly's the following day at five. Making the call made her feel less alone and, after finishing her tea, she went upstairs to see if her grandfather was still asleep. He wasn't. As she opened the door he lifted his head from a book and smiled.

'Did they get off all right?'

'Yes, so now it's just us. Can I get you anything?' She sat down beside him.

'No, thank you. I want for little, except perhaps a new body,' he said, ruefully.

'Sorry, I can't offer one of those,' she grinned.

He gave her a keen look.

'Something's changed. You're a bit brighter today. Why?'

She told him about Marian's suggestion to see Molly and she now had an appointment.

'Good. We didn't have such people as counsellors in my day, and I probably wouldn't have seen one anyway, but it may have helped my wife. Women are better at talking things through than us men. We just pretend we're fine. Is that what happened with Hamish?'

She thought back to the days and weeks after Amber died and how quiet and detached her husband had been. Grief-stricken like her, but wouldn't talk about it. Whereas she had been a sobbing wreck and wanted to talk to him about their daughter. She had sought reassurance, hugs but Hamish barely acknowledged her. Their separation became inevitable.

'I guess.' She stared out of the window, her attention caught by the distant waves crashing into Havelet Bay as the wind intensified ahead of an approaching storm. She shivered.

'Someone walk over your grave?' Gregory asked, touching her arm.

'No, it looks like a storm's imminent. Talking about a grave, I'm looking forward to finding out more about our ancestor.'

'Ah, yes, thought you might be. Off you go and look for that family tree and I'll try and conjure up old memories.'

The library was on the ground floor, adjoining the drawing room, both no longer used with dust sheets covering the furniture. Lucy remembered as a child perched on a stiff brocaded sofa with her mother and being admonished to stop fidgeting while the grown-ups took tea and made, to her ears, boring conversation. She shivered at the chill air and the atmosphere of neglect, briefly picturing Mary playing hostess in similar fashion two hundred years before. Rubbing her arms, she went on through the panelled double doors to the library, which proved to be equally as cold. Lucy couldn't remember ever venturing into this room before and gazed with interest at the glazed book cases lining the walls. Shuttered full height windows kept out natural light and Lucy moved across to open them. The darkening sky meant there was little improvement, but now she could see the garden. Shrubs and trees bent in the wind and the spring flowers struggled to remain upright. Turning back to the room she began to pull the covers off what turned out to be a huge partners desk and chair and a couple of armchairs set near the windows. An old wooden filing cabinet nestled against the desk.

'Right, where to start?' Lucy muttered to herself as she ran her fingers across the leather topped desk. Finding the filing cabinet locked, she sat at the desk and began opening drawers, looking for the keys. Various sets came to light and she began trying them. The fourth attempt proved successful and she pulled open the top drawer, sighing as she found it stuffed with thick files. The other drawers were equally full and her heart sank. This could take some time…

Two hours later Lucy hadn't found anything remotely connected to a family tree and was in need of a break. She found Meg in the kitchen preparing dinner.

'Hi, I understand you and Gregory have spent some time together today. I'm so pleased and he seems much brighter for it. I think he needs younger company, take him out of himself a bit.' Meg grinned at her over the chopping board and a pile of veg.

'Well, I enjoy his company, too, which surprised me given I was scared of him as a child,' Lucy said, switching on the kettle. 'Want a cup?'

'Please. Shame you weren't close as a child, specially considering you're the only grandchild.'

'I was closer to my maternal grandfather, but Grandpa Carre was more distant and didn't seem to know how to be with me, not having had a daughter.' Lucy bit her lip, recalling what he'd said about losing a baby girl. Had that been why he hadn't been as warm as her grandmother? She had been happy to cuddle her. Lucy made two mugs of tea and sat near Meg.

'You're chopping an awful lot of veg, surely Grandpa can't eat all that.'

'No, I've been asked to cook for you as well, which makes sense with only the two of you now. Hope you like chicken and vegetable casserole?' Meg pointed to chopped chicken breasts in a pan.

'Lovely, thanks. No-one told me.' She sipped her tea, wondering if her parents hoped cooked meals would sweeten the pill of Grandpa sitting. 'Meg, you've been here a few years, haven't you?' She judged Meg to be in her fifties and was one of those unflappable women who got on with whatever life threw at them. Married with grown-up children, she had a disabled husband at home who, although mobile, needed her to nip home during the day at regular intervals. This fitted in well with the Carre household while carers were on hand for Gregory's more personal needs.

'Must be five, since your grandma passed away. Your grandpa was much fitter then, but couldn't cook to save his life. Why?'

Lucy cleared her throat.

'I wondered if you'd ever seen a ghost here? A woman.'

Meg's lips formed an O shape.

'No, I haven't and wouldn't want to. But I'm not usually here at night and that's when they appear, isn't it? Have you seen this ghost, then?' She stopped chopping, and stared at Lucy, frowning.

'When I was a child, and it was at night, so there's no need to worry.' Lucy wished she hadn't said anything, all she needed now was Meg to give notice because of a ghost.

'What happened?'

Lucy told her what she remembered from so long ago, mentioning only that she could well be an ancestor from a portrait in her bedroom.

Meg pursed her lips.

'Oh, I remember your mother going up to the attics to find a new painting and she came down with that unhappy looking couple. Wasn't impressed, actually, but she thought it more colourful than the old one and that were true enough. There's still loads more up there if you want to change it.'

Relieved Meg didn't seem to consider leaving and, in fact, was being helpful, Lucy leaned forward and kissed her. 'Thanks, Meg. I might take a look sometime as there's a painting of a ship I want to find. Now, can I do anything to help with dinner?'

The next morning Lucy woke to the sound of rain lashing down and turned over with a groan. She was not a lover of rain, or high winds, both seeming to affect her mood, particularly since the depression had kicked in. She had read somewhere that this was a known phenomenon and it was something to accept as part of her personality, but it could change with time. Since a child she had loved the sun and Guernsey was known for its sunny, balmy weather and she had loved growing up on the island. Days of wind and rain only figured occasionally, even winter days offering sun if not warmth. Not being able to ignore the noise, Lucy stretched and sat up. Eight o'clock blinked the bedside clock. She remembered the appointment with Molly and the search for Mary. Good, worth getting up for, she thought, padding across the room to stare at the portrait. No sign of tears and there hadn't been any the day before. Perhaps she had imagined it. But Mary still looked sad…

Brushing aside such thoughts she went into the tiny en-suite shower room. The mirror reflected back her pale, thin face dominated by large brown eyes and framed by short mousey hair in need of a wash. Molly would remember her as a girl with a good figure, long hair and a ready smile. Definitely room for improvement, then. After a shower and shampoo Lucy dug out clean jeans and an unworn red sweater. A Christmas present from her parents, it was a beautiful soft cashmere and she hadn't felt ready to wear it. Until now. The transformation was immediate. The sweater bestowed a gentle flush to her cheeks, now framed by bouncy hair. Satisfied, Lucy went in search of breakfast.

'Morning. Oh, I love your top. Suits you. Hungry?' Meg was frying a full English for her grandfather and the aroma made her stomach rumble.

'Thanks. I am rather and would love a fry up instead of my usual, please.'

Meg grinned.

'No problem. I'm glad your appetite's improving. We need to put some flesh on those bones of yours, young lady. Help yourself to coffee.' She waved the spatula in the direction of a cafetiére on the worktop.

Lucy watched as Meg deftly stirred eggs, bacon, mushrooms and tomatoes for two, enjoying the easy companionship between them.

Placing a plate of sizzling food in front of her, Meg said, 'Been up to those attics yet, eh?'

'No, thought I'd go up this morning. Will be easier to see what I'm doing.'

Meg nodded, filled up a tray for Gregory and left with a 'back in a minute.'

It didn't take long for Lucy to clear the plate and drink a mug of coffee. She popped some bread in the toaster and poured more coffee. Meg returned as she was chewing the last of the toast.

'Your grandfather was asking if you were up and when I said you were, says would you mind calling in a bit later when he's ready.' She sat down and poured herself some coffee. 'He seems a bit perkier today, just like you. Must be something in the water,' she said, laughing.

'I don't think it's the water, it's more likely that we have found someone to talk to.' She paused. 'Oh, that must sound odd. My parents…'

'You don't need to explain. The tension between you all's been obvious, if you don't mind my saying. Not been a very close family, have you?' Meg said, with a sympathetic look.

'Ah, well…' Lucy hesitated, knowing her parents would be mortified to hear her and Meg, the paid help, talking like this. Especially as it was true. 'I…I suppose not.'

Meg nodded.

'Your parents made no secret of the fact they didn't want to move in here three years ago, but it was kind of forced on them. Did you know your grandfather was so ill he wasn't expected to live more than a few weeks?'

'I was told he was ill, but I was about to get married so perhaps they didn't want to worry me.' She recalled her father saying it would be best if they moved in to supplement the professional care, but not that he might die.

'They thought it would only be for a short time and then they could move back home. But Gregory's made of sterner stuff and he made a good recovery, except for his loss of mobility. So they had little choice but to stay and weren't too happy about it, I can tell you.' Meg's pursed lips portrayed her scorn.

Lucy felt a flash of anger against her parents. They had expected to inherit her grandfather's estate within a few weeks and she could imagine her father making his plans for a wealthy retirement once *Carreville* was sold. Her mother, no doubt reluctant to leave their home in the first place, would have been dreadfully upset not to return. Their house was now let on a short-term basis while they waited for Gregory to die. Lucy did have a little sympathy with her mother as it would have been simpler for her grandfather to move in with them, but he had insisted on staying put.

Not wishing to criticise her parents to Meg, she merely nodded and drained her coffee.

'I'll have a quick look in the attics and then pop in to see Grandpa,' she said, taking her plates to the dishwasher.

'Okay, see you at lunchtime.'

The flights of stairs to the attics seemed never ending and the final flight was the steepest. Once the servants' bedrooms, this part of the house had not been touched for many years and the low ceilings seemed to push down on Lucy as she arrived at the top. Another part of the house she had never seen, she opened the first door not knowing what to expect. The grey light filtering through the small window allowed her to find the electric light switch. A not much brighter light emanated from the single bulb hanging from the ceiling but it was enough to see stacks of paintings amongst the usual accumulation of once loved but no longer needed items.

Lucy began checking the paintings, a mix of portraits, landscapes and seascapes. Then she spotted it. Blowing off the dust, she held it under the light and saw the lines of the clipper in the portrait downstairs. Another piece of the jigsaw.

Chapter 4

Excited, she rushed downstairs with the painting.

'I've found the ship, Grandpa,' she said, handing him the picture.

'Good girl. Hand me that magnifying glass, would you?'

Lucy watched as he examined the painting, focusing on the hull.

'Yes, it's what I thought. *The Mayflower*, one of the most successful privateers at that time and part-owned by our family and the Mourant family.' He pointed out the name painted on the hull.

Lucy was shocked.

'You mean this house was built with ill-gotten gains?'

'Not exactly, privateering was legal, with letters of marque issued by the king, and Guernsey and Jersey were well placed to watch out for French ships, in particular. Unfortunately, when the wars were over, the merchants found it hard to give up the practice and carried on intercepting what were then friendly ships.' Gregory smiled at her look of disgust. 'Everyone was doing it, not just our family, and it's why we have so many Georgian mansions around here,' he waved his arms, 'including the Governor's House up the road. It was once owned by the most successful privateer of all, Jean Allaire. Without the merchants and their privateering, Guernsey would not have been the successful and wealthy free port it was. And they weren't averse to some smuggling on the side,' he said, chuckling.

'Oh, they certainly didn't teach us that at school!' She found it hard to equate the beautiful, elegant houses of this part of Town with the type of seamen, rough and coarse she associated, thanks to books and films, with pirates and smugglers. And that snooty man in the portrait was one of them!

'Don't take it to heart, Lucy, times were different back in the eighteenth and early nineteenth centuries. And other countries had their own privateers pushing the boundaries of legalities,' he said, patting her hand.

'I suppose so. Just a bit odd to think I'm descended from someone little more than a pirate,' she said, with a rueful grin. 'Would you like to keep the painting here, Grandpa?'

'Yes, thank you, I would. What are you going to do now?'

'I'm off to look for the family tree again.'

By lunchtime Lucy was feeling disheartened and bored. Most of the paperwork was the everyday domestic stuff such as bills, receipts and letters, covering the past twenty years or so. Obviously a family of hoarders, she thought, ruefully. With one drawer left, she decided to take a break after lunch and go and check out the gym at Kings. Only a recce, not to actually get physical, she told herself, although conceding she should start soonish. The storm had blown itself out and a watery sun was reflected in the puddles in the drive. The club was less than a ten minute walk and wrapped up in a waterproof jacket and scarf, she set off along Queen's Road before crossing over to Belmont Road, leading to King's Road. Crossing the road again she arrived at the driveway curving around the tennis courts where she used to play with friends from school during the holidays. Puddles and leaves lay scattered across the courts, giving them a forlorn appearance. The old oak tree set like a sentinel in the drive made her smile. Leaning tight up against the chain-link fencing around the tennis courts its trunk caused cars to slow down in order to pass.

Approaching the main entrance from the car park, old memories began to surface. The excitement of meeting up with friends for a swim or a game of tennis during the summer. It seemed a lifetime ago to Lucy, not having lived on the island since she was nineteen. She pushed open the door and approached the reception desk. A man bearing a badge proclaiming him to be Sam Norman, Assistant Manager, beamed at her.

'Hi, can I help?'

'Yes, my parents, Mr and Mrs Carre, have set up a membership for me, Lucy Stewart.'

'Right, let me check.' While he tapped away on his keyboard Lucy found herself looking at him. His muscled arms and flat stomach were a good advert for the club. In his thirties, she guessed, his glowing health made her more self-conscious of how much she had let herself go.

Sam looked up and smiled, his eyes crinkling.

'Found you. Welcome to Kings. Is there anything in particular you're interested in?'

'Yes, the gym. I…I've not been keeping it up for a while now, which is heresy for a trainer and gym instructor like me.' She managed to smile, even though she felt intimidated by him.

'Well, let's see if we can help you get back into it. You're not working at the moment?'

'No, I've been ill and just returned to Guernsey after living in London. Perhaps in the future…'

Sam's smile slipped, replaced by a look of concern.

'Oh, sorry to hear that. Perhaps gentle workouts initially?' He looked back at the computer screen. 'I notice you haven't been here for some years, would you like me to show you around? Bring you up to date with the changes and what we're planning for the future?' His warm smile was so enticing she couldn't refuse even though part of her wanted to run away, not sure if she could cope with being with people after all.

'Okay.'

'Great. Let me get someone to cover me.' A quick phone call brought a young woman from a hidden office and Sam came round the desk and led the way. Starting upstairs, Sam pointed out a gym, changed little since she had been a member, then downstairs to another gym, a new indoor pool and the squash court before ending up in the bar and lounge area, which had undergone some changes and overlooked the outdoor swimming pool. Overall, it looked smarter than she remembered, but according to Sam, was due for an impressive refurb and upgrade.

'We've big plans for the future, but in the meantime I hope you like what you see and are keen to come back,' he said, offering her a hot drink as they sat at a table. Being mid-afternoon, there were only a few members relaxing nearby; a mix of young mums and retirees, she guessed. A good time to come for a work-out if she didn't want to mix with others. He ordered two teas from the bar.

'Yes, it looks great, thanks. I'm only looking to use the gym and possibly the indoor pool initially, as I'm not much of a social person at present.' Sitting close to Sam, she couldn't help being aware of how attractive he was as well as a great advert for the club.

'Understood. Before anyone starts using the gym, it's standard procedure to spend a preliminary session with an instructor to make sure you know how to use the equipment. I know you're a professional, but would you mind booking such a session? It covers us for insurance purposes and gym equipment can vary.' Sam smiled, displaying perfect white teeth.

'No, that's fine. I'll book a session today.' She sipped her tea, still unsure if she would cope.

'Good, when you're finished I'll check the diary.'

Minutes later she followed him back to reception where he logged into a computer. 'I can fit you in at three o'clock tomorrow if that suits?'

'Fine by me.'

He tapped in the details then presented her with a membership card and a note of the session, saying, 'Look forward to seeing you tomorrow, Lucy.'

'Yes, see you tomorrow. Bye.' Once out of the club, she took a deep breath to calm her nerves. Not sure if she had made the right decision, even though her body was telling her it was, Lucy returned home in time to check on Gregory before her meeting with Molly.

'Well, Grandpa, you'll be impressed to hear I've joined the gym, starting tomorrow.'

'Good girl. Can't have you moping around here all day, can we? I'm the one who's supposed to do that,' he said, straight-faced.

'I hope you're not really moping, are you? Aren't we supposed to be cheering each other up?' Lucy felt a twinge of guilt knowing she was about to go out again soon.

'Not actually moping, no. Just fed up of being old and useless, waiting to kick the bucket so my son can inherit this,' he waved an arm around the room, 'and then sell it.'

'Oh, Grandpa! I'm sorry that's how you feel, although I do understand. You're not useless and I…I love you.' She threw her arms around his neck, sniffing back a tear. Her declaration of love had surprised her, but she realised it was true. He was no longer the grandfather who scared her as a child.

'There's no need to get soppy, girl. But thank you, anyway. Now, didn't you tell me you're seeing some woman this afternoon? Mustn't be late.' He gently pushed her back and she saw his lips wobble.

'I'm leaving now but I'll pop in later. Bye.' Planting a quick kiss on his forehead she left, the sudden emotion unnerving her. Back in her room she splashed her face with cold water before touching up her makeup and combing her hair. Feeling more in control she nipped into the kitchen to tell Meg she was going out and then headed for her car. Turning right out of the drive she then took the left into Les Gravees in the direction of L'Aumone and on towards the west coast. The drive reminded her of the times she used to ride her scooter from the family home in St Andrews to Perelle to visit Natalie. The Ogiers were a complete contrast to her own parents and Lucy loved spending time with them. Completely unstuffy, unlike her parents who she considered snobby.

As Lucy drove with care through the granite archway she smiled at the memory of how she used to whizz through on her bright blue scooter. Ah, happy times!

'Lucy! How delightful to see you again.' Molly threw her arms around her as soon as she stepped out of the car. Murmuring a hello, she allowed herself to sink into the embrace, taking her back to her youth. 'Now, let me look at you.' Molly dropped her arms and studied her closely. 'You've lost weight, but that's to be expected. Come in and I'll make us some tea.'

Molly led her through to a small, book-lined room overlooking the garden and indicated an armchair. 'Make yourself comfortable and I'll be back in a minute.'

Settling into the chair, Lucy took a moment to get her breath back. Molly was even more exuberant than she remembered and hardly changed, except for being a little plumper and with salt and pepper hair. And the little of what she'd seen of the cottage looked different. Not surprising, as it had been nearly twenty years.

'Here we are. And I've made some gâche, as I seem to remember it was a favourite of yours,' Molly said, placing a tray with a large plate of the buttered fruit bread and two mugs of tea on the table.

Lucy grinned with pleasure.

'Fancy you remembering, lovely.' After taking a sip of tea she helped herself to a slice.

'Now, when you're ready, and in your own time, tell me what's been happening the past few years and how you're feeling now.' Molly patted her arm encouragingly.

Slowly, between sips of tea and bites of gâche and starting with Amber's death, Lucy recounted what happened, tears never far from the surface. It was like scratching at a sore, never allowing it to heal. She wished she never had to tell the story again, but knew no-one could help her without knowing how it had affected her. By the time she had described how Hamish had walked out the tears were streaming down her face. Molly silently handed her tissues.

'Sorry,' Lucy mumbled, blowing her nose. 'I know I'm pathetic…'

'No, you're not, it's a perfectly normal reaction to what's happened,' Molly interrupted, touching her arm. 'You've been through an extremely traumatic experience, and it sounds as if you had little in the way of support. No wonder you're still struggling, Lucy. But I'm sure we can, together, help you to come out the other side of this painful time and move forward with your life.' Molly smiled encouragingly. 'Now, how are you coping with being back and looking after your grandfather?'

Twisting a shredded tissue, Lucy forced herself back from the pain of the past and considered the events of the last few days.

'It's not as bad as I expected as Grandpa is proving to be nicer than I remembered. He's even urging me to get out more and I'm joining the gym at Kings although I'm still hesitant about mixing with people.'

'Well done on joining the gym, that's a great step forward. We can focus on improving your self-confidence until it becomes easier for you. Anything else?'

Lucy had a sudden vision of Mary's portrait and the tears.

'You might think I'm mad, but I think I saw a ghost when I was a child and my grandmother also saw her, and her portrait's turned up in my room, so perhaps I'm not going mad.'

Molly chuckled.

'I'm the last person to think you're mad! Natalie had quite an experience with a ghost in her new house along at Rocquaine. In fact, I was going to suggest you two met up as you were once such friends. Now there's even more reason for you to do so, if you wish.'

'Yes, I'd like that. I was so pleased to hear she was back and married. But I didn't expect we'd have a ghost story to share,' she said, with a small smile.

'I'll pass on your phone number. So, do you know anything about this ghost?' Molly topped up their mugs of tea and settled back to listen as Lucy explained she thought she was an ancestor called Mary who lived about two hundred years ago and she was trying to find out more.

Lucy was both relieved and amused at Molly's positive reaction to her story. She seemed as eager as she herself was to learn more about Mary. Although it shouldn't have been a surprise to her. Guernsey folk were known for their superstitions and ghost stories as well as the tales of 'faeries' and sea monsters which formed part of the island psyche.

Molly, with Lucy's agreement, spent a few moments taking her into a relaxed state using hypnosis.

'Oh, that was lovely.' She hadn't felt as relaxed in a long while and it was definitely better than the prescribed pills she had been loath to take.

'Good. We can use hypnotherapy to help you release past trauma and become more confident again. Are you happy to continue coming along? We can talk about anything you want and use the hypnosis if you wish.'

She was only too happy to agree and they settled on weekly visits.

'Good, I look forward to seeing you next week, Lucy. And, in the meantime, if you find you're not coping with anything, please feel free to ring me.' Molly led the way back to the front door and gave her a hug.

'Bye, Molly, and thanks.' Lucy floated to the car, smiling broadly. At last, she could see the proverbial light at the end of the tunnel and drove home humming to the radio.

After dinner Lucy went up to her room to fetch a book to read, the television being dire. Opening the door, her eyes were drawn to the portrait of Mary and her husband and she moved to stand in front of it.

'What happened to you, Mary? I wish I knew what made you so sad,' she whispered, looking at the woman's mournful eyes. Suddenly it felt as if she was being drawn downwards and glancing down, the carpet had morphed into a wooden floor and her feet were encased in embroidered satin slippers peeping out from under a long, full silky skirt. What on earth…?

Chapter 5

Mary – Guernsey 1800

A maid was tying her into a blue embroidered gown which looked familiar when there was a pounding at the front door, followed by the sound of men talking. She wondered if her betrothed, Nathaniel, had come to see her without warning. He must not see her in the wedding gown!

'Quick, Jane, go and see who has arrived. If it is Mr Carre, I will need to change.' She shooed her out the door, while trying to compose herself. Normally she would be happy to see her beloved, but it would not be appropriate while the wedding gown was being fitted. Catching sight of herself in the long mirror nearby, she caught her breath. It was indeed beautiful. A French blue sarcenet covered with exquisite embroidered flowers, it was cut low across the bosom as was the fashion, and high-waisted above a full skirt. The thought of Nathaniel had brought a blush to her cheeks and made her eyes sparkle, and at that moment she looked quite beautiful. It was not considered seemly for a lady to have such thoughts, but surely a bride may be forgiven…

The door burst open and her father strode in followed by a pale-faced Jane. Whatever can have happened to cause this lack of manners?

'Papa, my gown ¬–' she cried, alarmed by his stern expression.

He waved his arm in a dismissive manner.

'The gown is of no consequence, my dear. I'm afraid I have ill tidings and ask you to sit down. Jane,' he turned to her maid, 'fetch your mistress a glass of cognac.' He guided her to the sofa and sat beside her, holding onto her trembling hands. Taking a deep breath, he continued, 'Mary, I have just been informed Nathaniel has been missing since last night, and it is feared he may…he may have drowned.'

Mary heard an animal cry out in pain and wondered what could have made such a noise, then realised it came from her own lips. She sagged towards her father. A glass appeared by her face and she was persuaded to drink. Gasping as the fiery liquid seared her throat, all she could think of was her darling Nathaniel. Missing, feared drowned! Such terrible words to hear days before their wedding.

'But, Papa, how can anyone be sure he has drowned? Could he not be simply at the house of a friend or colleague?' she managed to say through her tears.

'It was Thomas who brought the news. And he said his brother was going to check on the captured French ship last night and there has been no sign of him since.' His face was grave as he patted her hand. 'The possibility is Nathaniel missed his footing in the dark while preparing to board. Thomas said he had imbibed much wine.'

'No! I do not believe it! Nathaniel drinks sparely, as you know, Papa. It is Thomas who is often inebriated.' Anger rose within her at the blackening of her betrothed's name.

'You're right, my dear, I have never seen Nathaniel in his cups.' He shrugged, adding 'but it does not mean he never drank to excess. However, what is important is finding the poor fellow as soon as possible, and, we must pray, in rude health.'

Her father took his leave and within minutes her mother arrived, fussing over Mary enough to set her nerves on edge. She begged leave to retire to her bed and her mother withdrew reluctantly, after admonishing the maid to take especial care of her mistress.

Jane helped her out of the gown she had been delighting in so happily only moments ago and Mary slipped into bed and curled up like a child, waving her away. She needed to be alone with her grief, gnawing at her insides like a disease. Part of her was desperate to believe Nathaniel might still be alive, as without a body there was indeed some hope. But surely Thomas would not alarm them so if he thought his brother could be alive? The thoughts whirled around her head until it was pounding and she rang for Jane.

'Please tell my Mama I am in need of one of her powders for the headache and to help me sleep.'

Her mother, of a nervous disposition, had long been prone to headaches and always kept a supply of powders from the apothecary. It was rare for Mary to suffer so, but today she wished to blot out the terrible thoughts. 'Oh, Nathaniel, where are you, my love? Please be safe and return home so we may be married.' She whispered the words into the empty room laying curled like a child in her bed.

'My poor girl!' her mother cried as she appeared at her side and bade her drink the powder dissolved in a glass of water. She stayed with her awhile until she was sleepy.

* * *

Lucy opened her eyes, finding herself lying on her bed, wearing jeans and sweater, and with her heart full of sadness over the missing Nathaniel. What happened? Surely she couldn't have slipped into Mary's life? But it had seemed so real! Even now she could smell Mary's perfume, recognising it as Lily of the Valley, a favourite of her grandmother's. Was she losing it big time? Checking her watch she saw only fifteen minutes had elapsed since she came up to her room.

Dragging her fingers through her hair, she stood and moved towards the portrait. Was that a slight smile on Mary's face? Lucy blinked. The smile had gone. Oh, God, what on earth has happened to me? Could it have been some fantastical dream brought on by the hypnosis? Reaching for a notepad and pen she jotted down all she could remember from the "dream". The room she had been in was not this bedroom, it had been furnished with old-fashioned furniture, including a curtained four-poster bed, and there had been a fire burning in the grate. But it wouldn't have been this bedroom as Mary would have been at her parents' house until her wedding. And the clothes! Lucy recalled the tightness of what she guessed was a short corset over a full-length petticoat and then finally the gown itself over the white silk stockings held up with garters…. It was all so *real!* And when she had looked in the mirror she had seen Mary's face, not hers. And the thoughts had not been hers, but Mary's.

'Well, Mary, I did say I wanted to know what happened to you, didn't I? Did you make this happen? But you couldn't, you've been dead for nearly two hundred years,' Lucy muttered out loud in front of the portrait. Confused and scared, she turned away and went downstairs to make a cup of tea. Camomile for calmness. Accompanied by half a packet of chocolate biscuits. Feeling only marginally better, she turned to the television for diversion. Anything to stop her thinking. As she tried to follow the intricacies of a crime series set in Scotland, Lucy felt desperately alone. Was there anyone she could confide in who wouldn't think her mad? The only possibility was Molly, but it was too late this evening. She would phone her tomorrow. Pleased to come to a decision, she managed to watch the programme until the end before going to bed and drifting off to sleep.

The next morning, Lucy, relieved to find she was still in her own body and in her own room, wasted no time in getting showered and dressed before joining Meg in the kitchen.

'Morning, Meg. I'm starving, could I have another of your full English breakfasts, please?' She gave Meg, standing ready with the frying pan, a hug.

'Good morning. Of course you can, only too glad to see you eat more. Any plans for today?'

Lucy poured a mug of coffee and sat down.

'I'm off to Kings for an initial gym session this afternoon, otherwise not a lot.' She took a gulp of coffee, trying to quash an image of herself/Mary being fitted into the wedding gown. How on earth was she going to stop thinking about it? Hopefully, Molly might help. It was going to be hard to pretend all was normal, when she felt she had been an unwilling participant in an episode of Dr Who with possibly more to come.

'Here you are, eat up, my girl. You're looking a bit peaky this morning. Bad night?' Meg frowned as she put a full plate in front of her.

'No, not exactly. I'm sure your delicious food will soon have me feeling more with it, thanks, Meg.' Lucy smiled, the aroma making her stomach gurgle in anticipation. While Meg took her grandfather's breakfast upstairs, she tucked into her own with gusto. With her plate cleared, she felt more herself and went back upstairs to call Molly

'Well, I don't know what to think, Lucy,' Molly said, after she had described what had happened. Or thought had happened. There was a pause. 'It could be a genetic memory, sparked by the portrait of your ancestor, and such occurrences have been recorded. A genetic regression if you like. It may have been partly triggered by the hypnosis, but that was only a mild relaxation session, with no suggestion of regression. You must be particularly susceptible, possibly due to your recent loss and the consequent depression.

I don't think you're mad, my dear. It could be your vivid imagination playing tricks, weaving a story from the little you know about Mary, creating a waking dream, or…or you slipped into her life for a short time.'

'Could it happen again?'

'I honestly don't know. I would think it less likely if it's purely your imagination. A one-off dream. From what you've said, all the ingredients are there for a regression: you are not only living in her marital house, you are possibly sleeping in her bedroom and you have her portrait right by your bed. And you "asked" her what had happened to her. You could try sleeping in another room without the portrait and see what happens. And we don't have to use the hypnosis again if you'd rather not.'

Lucy chewed her lip as she took in Molly's words. It was a comfort to hear other people had had similar experiences but did she want to in effect re-live Mary's life? It was already clear the poor woman hadn't been happy in her marriage, but who was this Nathaniel she was meant to marry? The thought of regressing again, if that is what it was, was both scary but intriguing. To see at first-hand how the Georgians lived!

'Lucy? Are you still there? I do have to go soon –'

'Sorry. Was just thinking. Obviously, there's no guarantee it will happen again, anyway, but if I didn't try to stop it, could it be harmful to me? If Mary was badly hurt, for example, would I be hurt too?'

'Ah, as I haven't personally worked with such cases, I can only surmise that your physical body couldn't be hurt as it would still be here, but you may briefly remember the impact of any injury. To be honest, Lucy, I'm not sure I should encourage you to want to regress as you have your own problems to deal with without adding Mary's. Look, I do have to go, but please phone me later if you want to discuss it further.'

Clicking off the call, Lucy decided not to dwell on it for the moment. Perhaps finding the family tree would provide enough answers to satisfy her curiosity. Molly was right, she had enough problems of her own right now. After checking in with her grandfather she returned once more to the library and the pile of unchecked files in the last drawer.

There it was, a sheet of copperplate handwriting, headed The Carre Family Tree, dating back to the eighteenth century.

Chapter 6

Guernsey 2013

A quick glance showed a Mary Mourant married a Thomas Carre in 1800 and Lucy wasted no time in running upstairs to her grandfather's room.

'Morning, Grandpa. How are you today?' She kissed his cheek, barely able to contain the bubbles of excitement wanting to burst out.

'Quite well, thank you. And you're looking quite flushed. What's happened?'

'This,' she waved the sheet of paper, 'I've found the family tree. And Mary's mentioned.'

A gleam appeared in his eyes.

'Well done, my dear. Let me take a look.' She spread the paper on the table and sat beside him as his fingers traced the entries, beginning with Henry Carre 1746-1799. 'Ah, I remember something about this. He had two sons,' pointing to the next line, 'Nathaniel born 1775 and Thomas in 1778. But see Nathaniel died young, in 1800, not long after his father. And Thomas married the same year – Mary Mourant – she must be the woman in the portrait. The ghost. But there was something about the marriage, I can't quite recall what.' He tapped his forehead.

'Could it be that Mary was meant to marry Nathaniel, but he died, so she married Thomas?' Lucy wasn't sure how to tell him she had seen with her own eyes how Mary learned about Nathaniel going missing, presumed drowned. And that for Mary it was a love match.

Gregory frowned.

'Rings a bell, although I seem to remember there's more to the story. Oh. Did you notice there's no date of death for Mary. Odd.' He continued following the tree, pointing out that they were directly descended from Mary and Thomas's son, born in 1803 and the last entry was the birth of her own father, Dennis in 1949.

'We should bring it up to date for future generations,' he added, smiling.

'If there are any, Grandpa,' she muttered, her stomach clenching at the unbidden image of the small white coffin being lowered into the ground.

'Oh, my dear! Forgive me. How insensitive of me.' He gripped her hand. 'But you're young, and may remarry and have more children, surely? What happened to Amber was, I understood, a terrible fluke and not likely to happen to another child.'

'That's true, but I still have to take a risk with choosing the right partner and then hope I'll become pregnant again, which at my age is not exactly guaranteed.' She sighed. Was there a chance she could meet someone else and have a child together before her biological clock imploded? Though another child would never replace her beautiful Amber …

'Don't give up, you never know what's around the corner and remember your grandmother and I went on to have another child and she was in her late thirties by then.'

Lucy managed a smile.

'All right, but even if I do have a child, I'm afraid it won't be a Carre, so it's still technically the end of the family tree,' she said, tapping the document in his hand.

'True, but the blood of our family will flow in their veins.' He continued looking at the sheet of paper with a faraway look in his eyes.

'You all right, Grandpa?'

He blinked.

'Sorry, I was trying to recall what my father had said concerning a story passed down the generations of events around the time of Nathaniel and Thomas. Of course, it was so long ago, it might well have been just a silly rumour and nothing to concern us. At least you've found Mary, your ghost.'

'True, but isn't it odd there's no date of death? I'd like to find out more about her, although I'm not sure how.' As she said it, the memory of her slipping back in time, if that's what it truly was, reminded her of a way...

Later that afternoon Lucy retraced her steps to Kings for her first gym session. Winter was loosening its grip and daffodils and crocuses brightened the gardens, shielded by bushes of camellias and rhododendrons showing off tiny buds. Drawing in a deep breath, Lucy smiled, a feeling of anticipation flowing through her. Spring, the time of new beginnings, fresh starts after the long winter and her favourite time of the year. Straightening her shoulders, she walked briskly down the entrance road to the club, giving the oak tree a quick pat.

'Hi, I'm Lucy Stewart and have a session booked with Sam.'

The girl on reception checked her membership card and waved her through to the changing rooms, saying Sam would meet her in the gym. As she hung up her coat in a locker, butterflies started beating a tattoo in her stomach at the prospect of being with strangers after more than a year of hiding away. 'Come on, girl, you can do this,' she muttered to herself as she headed for the gym, the place where she used to feel completely at ease and confident.

'Hi, Lucy, how are you doing?' Sam's smile was warm and reassuring.

'Okay, thanks. A bit nervous as it's been so long.'

'I'm sure you'll be fine once you get going. But first I need you to fill in this health questionnaire, so let's pop into my office.' He waved her to what was little more than a cubbyhole and she was conscious of their knees touching as they sat down. He handed her a clipboard with the form and a pen. Lucy hated filling in forms at the best of times and could feel her cheeks reddening as she answered the questions about her medical history. Suffering from "depression" hardly described what she had endured over the past year. Handing it back, she couldn't face Sam in the eye.

'Okay, so there's no physical problems limiting exercise, right?'

'No, just lack of motivation.' She glanced up to see him smile and relaxed.

'That's something we can work on. Now, if I can just check your height and weight and then we're good to go.'

He kept up a cheerful dialogue as she stood on the scales and he noted her height and weight.

'Hmm, a bit underweight, but hopefully your appetite will return once you start regular exercise. We'll be aiming at increasing core strength rather than muscle development so don't worry about ending up like a female wrestler!' He laughed and she managed a grin.

By the time Sam had taken her through the programme he recommended, Lucy felt energised, more her old self. And she hardly noticed the few others in the gym.

'You've done really well, Lucy. To be honest, I was a bit nervous of working with you, being a pro yourself.'

Disarmed by his frankness, she laughed.

'Me too! But you made me feel totally at ease, Sam, and I'd have chosen the same workout if I'd been in your shoes. I've enjoyed it, thank you.' And she had, the endorphins were flowing nicely and she was pleased with herself.

'Great stuff. Another satisfied member, I hope,' he said, his head on one side.

'Oh, yes, I'm looking forward to coming back. Do you think three times a week will do to start?'

'Absolutely. Even a couple of times if you find your muscles are aching too much. And some swimming afterwards would ease any tightness.'

'Exactly what I thought. You're not a mind reader, are you?' she teased him. It had been a long time since she had felt so at ease with a man her own age and it felt good.

Sam laughed.

'Don't think so! I guess we're just two professionals with similar ideas.' He coughed. 'I've enjoyed working with you today, Lucy, and if at any time you want to discuss making changes to the workout, I'd be happy to help. And no doubt I'll see you around.'

He offered his hand and, as she took it, was aware of a tingling warmth flowing from his hand to hers. Startled, she quickly let go, gave a brief nod and strode off to the changing rooms. She was in desperate need of a shower.

Walking back home gave her time to think. On the one hand she was happy with how she had coped with the session and hadn't disgraced herself. On the other hand, she had been disturbed by her reaction to Sam. Yes, he was good-looking and easy to talk to, but her body had reacted in a way that hadn't happened for years, not since she had been with Hamish. Still, Lucy reassured herself, she wouldn't need to spend much time with him from now on.

Once home, Lucy called in on her grandfather, then went into her room to change. Immediately her eyes were drawn to the portrait. It seemed to have an hypnotic effect on her, pulling her closer. It was Mary's eyes…so sad, so beseeching. Before she could turn away, she was once more overtaken with a sensation of falling as her bedroom disappeared and she was once more in Mary's room – and in her head.

* * *

Mary opened her eyes and the faint light filtering through the curtains proclaimed it was the next day. For a glorious moment, she had forgotten what had happened. Then the memory flooded in and she cried out.

'Are you all right, ma'am?' Jane's voice floated up from the end of the bed and it would seem she had been sleeping there on her cot.

'I…I have just woken and remembered the events of yesterday. Is there any news?'

Jane appeared by her pillow, her hair awry under her mob cap and her eyes bleary. Mary pulled herself up and Jane adjusted the pillows.

'Not as I know, ma'am. But I can ask when I fetch your hot chocolate. Do you wish to have breakfast here as well?'

'No, I am not ill and will join my parents at the normal time. Once I have had my chocolate you can help me wash and dress.'

She bobbed a curtsy and left Mary to her thoughts. These were irrevocably drawn to Nathaniel and the first time they met, at a ball in the Assembly Rooms, and her first to launch her into society. Mary knew the aim was to attract a wealthy husband although her parents had already informed her they had someone in mind. Her father was a successful merchant in Town, with shares in local privateers and wished to cement his business relationship with another firm, Carre and Sons. The senior Carre had died recently, leaving the elder son to inherit the bulk of his fortune. She had not met the gentleman and was inclined to not like him because her parents wanted the marriage for purely business reasons, while she wanted to marry for love. At seventeen, Mary's head was filled with romantic love, devouring the novels by Fanny Burney, among others, and seeing herself as another Evelina, overcoming much before marrying for love.

Her stomach fluttered with nerves as she arrived, excited about her entry into Guernsey's polite society as a young woman and no longer to be treated as a child. Her hair was elaborately coiffed in the latest fashion, with tiny curls framing her pointed face, and her mother had spared no expense with her gown. White, as became her youth, but an expensive French satin embroidered with pink rosebuds with a low neckline emphasising her bosom. Even her father had expressed how becoming she looked.

Chandeliers filled with dozens of candles cast a bright light over the ballroom and Mary's eyes widened as she admired the decorations and the flowers while the orchestra tuned up before the dancing began. The sight of so many young men, resplendent in close-fitting breeches and cut-away coats, brought a flush to her cheeks. Being an only child and schooled at home, she was unused to male society and felt a little lost as her parents stopped to talk with friends. Her gaze was drawn to a particular group of men where an acquaintance of her father, a fellow Freemason, was in earnest conversation with a tall young man. Hiding behind her fan, she thought him about twenty-five years of age and admired his dark good looks and merry smile. He happened to turn and look in her direction, catching her staring at him, and his smile widened. Lifting her fan higher to hide her blushes, she wished the ground would swallow her up, but he approached them, bowing to her parents, then allowing his gaze to settle on her.

'Ah, Nathaniel, my boy, we were hoping to see you this evening. May I present my daughter, Mary, who is just come out into society.'

As she dropped a curtsy, her eyes lowered, he lifted her gloved hand and kissed it. Daring to look up, Mary saw the gleam of appreciation in his eyes and fell hopelessly in love.

And now he was missing! Mary paced up and down while waiting for Jane to return with her chocolate, and hopefully some good news. Since that first meeting with Nathaniel she had been convinced they were meant to marry, and he had been equally enamoured. With his father only recently deceased the courtship could not be hurried and it was now a year on from the ball. But what a year! There had been more balls, carriage rides suitably chaperoned by her mother or maid, promenades along Havelet Bay and supper parties held in the homes of their families. The only discomforting aspect of their courtship had been Thomas, Nathaniel's younger brother. Mary found it hard to believe they were kin, so different were they in temperament and behaviour. Whereas her beloved was hard-working, respectful of all he dealt with, but also good-natured and fun, Thomas was lazy, uncouth in his manner and was a known gambler and heavy drinker. Nathaniel had often confided in her his despair of him.

'For all he is my brother and I love him dearly, he brings shame on our family with his riotous behaviour with the rougher elements of Town, particularly the seamen.' Nathaniel shook his head as they walked his puppy, Storm, a lively Bassett Fauve de Bretagne, and her engagement present to him, around Havelet recently. Her maid Jane a discreet distance behind. 'I almost wonder if it is to spite me, as the elder brother, the one who has everything while he has nothing, as he tells me often.'

'Oh, that is not fair! You have ensured he has a prominent position in your family firm, even though he rarely seems to do any meaningful work, from what you have told me. And you have offered to let him live with us after we are married until a suitable house becomes available,' she replied, giving his arm a squeeze. Mary had disliked Thomas on sight, recoiling from his glazed eyes and the overpowering smell of brandy on his breath as he took her hand to kiss. But she had said little to Nathaniel, not wanting to appear critical of one who might one day, she hoped, be her brother-in-law. It was different if Nathaniel were to berate Thomas, it was his right as a brother. Mary had always avoided Thomas whenever possible, but made an effort to be polite when they had to meet.

Nathaniel sighed.

'I don't think anything I do will satisfy him, my love. I know he yearns to be at sea and would like nothing more than to captain our ship, *The Mayflower*, but he hasn't the experience and skill needed and likely as not, would drink himself senseless while in a foreign port. And what an example to the men that would be!'

Mary hated to see him so downhearted and managed to lighten the mood by throwing sticks for Storm to chase, some too large for him to manage, his antics causing them both to laugh. It had been a good choice of a present, as these French hounds were adept at scenting small prey such as rabbits and birds and Nathaniel was looking forward to spending time hunting on the cliffs when Storm was older.

'Ma'am, I have your chocolate but there's no more news, I'm afraid,' Jane said, carrying a tray and setting it down on the bedside table. Mary slipped back into bed as her maid poured the thick chocolate into a cup. She had drunk only a little when there was a knock on the door and Jane went to answer it. It was her father, his face sombre. Mary's throat constricted as he walked to her side.

'Mary, my dear. You must be strong. Nathaniel's coat, recognised by Thomas, was washed up in the harbour some half hour since.'

Chapter 7

Lucy came to with cheeks wet with tears. Nathaniel was dead! It took her some minutes to realise she was not Mary as she pulled herself up off the floor, now covered in the familiar fitted carpet and she was again wearing leggings and not a nightgown. Collapsing onto the bed, her head was full of vivid images, chasing each other across her inner vision. Dressed for her – Mary's – first ball, the feel of silk stockings on her legs, the tightness of the matching shoes, the intricate up-do kept in place by sharp hairpins and ribbons. The brightness of the Assembly Room and the crush of people gathered in the entrance. The overpowering smell of perfumes attempting – and failing – to mask the smell of infrequently washed bodies. Nathaniel, so handsome, so gallant. Then Mary's memory of walking with him and the puppy – Storm, wasn't it? A gorgeous, fawn coloured dog with a rough coat and big brown eyes. The sailing ships anchored in the harbour and the cries of sailors dressed in little more than rags. The pungent smell of fish and seaweed. And then, then Mary's father – the awful news.

She dragged herself into the bathroom for a glass of water. Catching a glimpse of her face in the mirror, Lucy was relieved to see it was her own, even though pale and with glazed eyes. Bewildered, she was convinced now she must have slipped back in time and was, for a while, Mary. Time! How long had she been gone? Her watch showed only thirty minutes since she had arrived home, and some of it was spent with Gregory. How weird! Time had virtually stood still. Hesitantly, Lucy retraced her steps into the bedroom and walked towards the portrait, but stood to one side to avoid Mary's eyes. The dog! It was Storm, the dog she had given to Nathaniel. And presumably now hers since his death only a short time before. No wonder she was so sad. Her opinion of Thomas had been clear – he was definitely not someone she would have willingly married. Lucy sank onto the bed, overloaded with the emotions and images of the past. She had to talk to someone or she would go mad. Picking up her phone she called Molly.

'Molly, I'm sorry to trouble you, but it's happened again...' She gave a breathless and slightly incoherent account of what she could remember.

'Oh, my word, Lucy! Are you okay? Do you want to come round and talk about it? Or I could come to you if you're not up to driving.'

Lucy heard the shock in Molly's voice, and saying it out loud brought home to her that what she had experienced couldn't, in theory, have happened.

'I...I don't know –'

'I'm coming round, go and make yourself a cup of tea or something and I'll be as quick as I can. All right?' Molly's voice was urgent.

'Yes, thanks.' Switching off her phone, Lucy ran downstairs to the kitchen and found Meg in the middle of preparing dinner.

'You okay? You're a bit pale,' Meg said, staring at her.

Lucy went over to the kettle, keeping her back to her.

'Fine, thanks. Probably overdid the gym today that's all. A friend's coming round soon for a chat and I just want some tea. Do you want a cup?' She managed to keep her voice steady as she filled the kettle.

'No, thanks, just had one. Your friend won't be round long, will she? Only dinner will be ready in an hour.'

'Should be enough time, but if not I can always warm it up, don't worry.' She made her tea and turned to face Meg with a tight smile.

Meg grunted and carried on chopping while Lucy drank her tea and flipped through the local paper. Meg must have sensed she was in no mood for talking and left her alone. The sound of the doorbell broke the silence and Lucy, swallowing the last drop, went to answer it.

Molly drew her into an enveloping hug and Lucy let out a deep sigh.

'Thanks for coming, Molly, I'm just so confused….' She sniffed.

'I'm not surprised. Is there somewhere private we can go in this great place?' she said, eyes widening at the grand staircase and marble floor.

'Think it will have to be my bedroom as there's no heating on in lots of rooms.' Lucy blew her nose and led the way upstairs, explaining that the help, Meg, was in the kitchen and her grandfather had his rooms on the first floor, not far from her bedroom.

'So Mary lived here after her marriage,' Molly said, softly, as she took in the family portraits lining the staircase.

'Yes, and Grandpa says it was her husband's father who had this house built from the fortune the family made from privateering.' She led the way to her room and opened the door. 'The…the portrait's over there,' she said, pointing. 'Should we remove it?' Lucy stood with her back to it, not daring to risk even a peak.

''Let me look at it first.' Molly moved to stand in front of it while Lucy tidied away her clothes, a little embarrassed by the state of her room.

A few minutes later Molly lifted the portrait down and took it outside to leave on a side table on the landing.

'Well, I have to admit the painting's a bit eerie, isn't it? I could have sworn her eyes were following me around. And her sadness is palpable, I'm not surprised you've had such a strong reaction to it – and her.' Molly joined her on the small sofa at the bottom of the bed and squeezed her arm.

'Can you pick up psychic stuff?' Lucy asked, not entirely convinced moving the painting would stop Mary taking over her mind and body.

Molly grinned sheepishly.

'I think I've become more sensitive with age, but wouldn't consider myself a real psychic. But I'm aware of some sort of energy around that painting so perhaps it's better if you don't have it in here. How are you feeling now?'

'Calmer, I think.' She rubbed her neck, the muscles taut under her skin. 'I'm beginning to feel like a split personality, but with one part of me living two hundred years ago and one now. A really weird sensation.'

'Do you feel scared?'

'Yes a bit. But I'm also intrigued to learn more about Mary's life, why she appears unhappy later in life. If that portrait was painted when she married Thomas, then it was only weeks after Nathaniel's death, so it's not surprising she looks sad. And she didn't like him. I feel something else must have happened later in the marriage. After all, she had two children, which should have been some compensation for losing Nathaniel.'

'I can understand your curiosity, but am concerned if you keep slipping back to a previous time, if this is what is happening, then your mental health might suffer. You're still dealing with your own grief, my dear, and shouldn't burden yourself with someone else's.' Molly's face was creased with worry and Lucy knew she was right.

'But what can I do? I don't deliberately try to make it happen, it…it just does. I can put the portrait back in the attic and see if that helps. And if it doesn't work?' She spread her hands.

'Why don't you move the portrait and let's see. No point

worrying unless we have to.' Molly looked around the room. 'It's possible this room, and this house for sure, played a part in Mary's life and is holding onto a genetic memory, just like you may be doing. I've been making rather a study of such phenomena over the past few years, after Natalie had a paranormal experience in her house and her friend Jeanne Le Page had something similar, but not as strong, in her grandmother's cottage. There is so much we don't understand and science can't explain,' she said, sighing.

'So it's possible unless I leave the house, which I can't because I'm committed to staying with Grandpa, then it could happen anyway?' Her initial reaction was fear. But what was she afraid of? So far she had apparently witnessed several events in Mary's life, but none had been life-threatening or remotely dangerous. Sad and upsetting, yes. Dangerous, no.

Molly gripped her hand.

'To be honest, I don't know. But remember, it's not your body or your innate self that is travelling back two hundred years, simply a small part of your mind. The real you remains here, in the present, and cannot be harmed by anything in the past. Can you accept that?'

'I think so, but it's hard to get my head around it. I'll move the painting anyway and let's see what happens.' A thought struck her. 'What's strange is although the past seems to last quite a long time, possibly hours, in reality I'm only away for a few minutes. Not even long enough to be missed.'

'Well, there is a theory that time is not linear, but forms a helix with the past, present and future running in parallel together. An interesting idea, don't you think?' Molly said, smiling.

'Now my head's definitely spinning!'

'No need to worry about it this minute, although it could explain so much we don't understand. How are feeling now? Do you want to talk more?'

'I do feel calmer, thanks. It was not having anyone I could talk to which was making me feel so wobbly.' She took a deep breath. 'Thanks so much for coming round, I'll be all right now.'

'If you're sure?' Lucy nodded. 'Okay, I'll be off. But promise me you'll ring if anything happens to upset or scare you. And give Natalie a ring, she had quite a traumatic experience with her ghost and vivid, realistic dreams of the past before making a complete recovery.'

'Okay, will do. It's good to know I'm not the only one having weird experiences.' She grinned.

As soon as Molly had left Lucy took the portrait up to the attic, stacking it among the other paintings. She whispered a quick 'Sorry' and sped downstairs before she could change her mind.

After supper Lucy spent time with Gregory who kept giving her intense looks.

'What is it, Grandpa? You keep looking at me as if I've grown a horn or something.'

'Not a horn, no. But there's something different about you this evening, can't put my finger on it, though. What have you been up to since I saw you earlier? More poking about in the past?'

Lucy gulped. If only he knew!

'Not exactly. Molly, the counsellor, popped round and we had an…an interesting chat about things. Brought up some stuff, that's all. And I'm going to try and catch up with her daughter, Natalie, who I haven't seen in years.'

'Now that does sound like a good idea. Go out and have some fun, it's about time. And then you can come back and tell me all about it. I like to know what's going on otherwise boredom sets in.' His expression was rueful and Lucy sympathised with him. Even though she had become a hermit herself, at least she could choose to go out and mix with people.

'I'm not sure two women catching up after twenty years will be of interest to you, Grandpa, but I will do my best to entertain you,' she said, smiling at the thought of the much more fascinating – and shocking – things she could tell him, but didn't dare. Not yet, anyway.

Chapter 8

The next morning Lucy skipped downstairs and greeted Meg with a cheerful 'Good morning' before pouring a mug of coffee.

'Morning. You're in a good mood today. Haven't won the lottery, have you?' Meg said, laughing.

'I wish! No, I'm simply in a good mood.' She sat down with her coffee and watched Meg cook the breakfast, the smell of fried bacon as alluring as ever.

'Pleased to hear it. Anything special you're planning today? Another gym session?'

'No gym, my muscles are aching from yesterday and the plan is three times a week to begin with. But I am going shopping for clothes this morning as I'm off to a friend's for supper tonight and need something other than jeans to wear.' She looked down at her jeans which, thanks to her weight-loss, hung off her body in an unattractive way. After a warm chat with Natalie the previous evening, during which she had been invited to supper, Lucy had run critical eyes over her clothes and figure. Time to make an effort.

'Sounds nice, I'll rustle up an omelette for Gregory to-night, his appetite isn't great at the moment anyway. So, tell me more about your friend.'

Lucy explained how they hadn't met for years but had used to be good friends and she was looking forward to renewing their friendship and Meg was all for it.

After a quick chat with her grandfather Lucy left, relishing the idea of a brisk walk down The Grange to the shops. She couldn't remember the last time she had gone clothes shopping and St Peter Port had a good selection of shops. The air was mild and a weak sun fought to break through the clouds as she strode along, hands thrust into her pockets. Walking past the stuccoed, elegant Georgian houses made her think of the families who had built them from the proceeds of privateering, like her own family. Their grandeur was somewhat tainted in her eyes now she knew the truth, but acknowledged it would be naïve to compare the moral standards of the eighteenth century with the present day. Instantly Mary's anguished face popped into her mind, startling her. Did her family have a house along here? When she had slipped back in time, Lucy had not noticed any clues as to where Mary lived before her marriage. The bedroom had been similar in style to her own in *Carreville* so was likely to be Georgian and definitely in Town, she guessed. Lost in thought, Lucy was brought back to the present when she stepped, without looking, into the road and the driver of a car coming into Vauvert sounded his horn at full blast. Shocked, she stepped back on the pavement and waited for the lights to change. Once safely across the road she concentrated on where she was going and it wasn't long before she was at the top of Smith Street and near the shops.

Lucy was a fast shopper. It wasn't long before she had bought not only a skirt but some smart trousers and new, better fitting, jeans. Pleased with her purchases, she headed to Dix Neuf in the Arcade for coffee. She had not long been seated at a table in the window when a familiar voice said, 'Hi, Lucy, how are you?' Looking up she saw a smiling Sam standing near her table.

'Fine, thank you. Would you, er, like to join me?' Lucy surprised herself by asking, normally fighting shy of inviting anyone into her space.

'Love to, thanks.' He pulled out a chair opposite, saying, 'Have you ordered? If not, let it be my treat.'

'No, I hadn't. A cappuccino would be great, thanks.'

When the waitress appeared Sam ordered two cappuccinos.

'Is it your day off?' she asked, fiddling with the menu. He shook his head.

'I'm in late today, starting after lunch and finishing – late,' he said, laughing. 'Are you coming in for a session today?'

'No, I'll be in tomorrow as planned.'

'Great. How did you feel after the session? Not too sore I hope?'

'No, I've been good, thanks.' Apart from travelling back to the early nineteenth century and becoming someone else. She couldn't tell him that, of course. Lucy noticed Sam glance at her left hand and for a moment was puzzled. Of course! She was registered as Mrs Lucy Stewart. He would assume she was married, wouldn't he?

'Glad to hear it. Wouldn't want to put you off coming back when you've just joined,' he said, with a grin.

She flashed him a smile in reply as their coffees arrived. A few moments were taken up with sipping their drinks and then Sam said, nodding towards the boutique's distinctive bag, 'Been enjoying some retail therapy, I see.'

'Yes, because of all the weight I've lost lately I've had to buy some new clothes.'

Sam's smile slipped.

'Sorry, that was stupid of me knowing we want to help you gain weight.'

Lucy took pity on him.

'That's okay. I'm meeting an old friend this evening and wanted to make a better impression than I would have in these ill-fitting jeans.' She nodded at her legs, still encased in the offending item held up by a belt.

Sam looked relieved and, after a sip of coffee, asked if she was going anywhere exciting. She told him about Natalie and how they had met as girls at Kings and they chatted for a few minutes about her memories of what had been such fun times.

Clearing his throat, Sam said, 'You returned to Guernsey on your own?'

Wondering if he was chatting her up, Lucy was hesitant about how much to say.

'Yes, my husband and I are separated and he's in Scotland. I'm...not sure about my long-term plans.'

'Sorry, probably shouldn't have asked such a personal question and if we were at the Club then I wouldn't. The staff aren't supposed to chat up members,' he said, with a rueful grin.

So he was chatting her up! Although flattered such a good-looking man could find her, a thin depressed time-traveller, attractive, it wasn't the right time.

'Well, it's no secret Hamish and I are having time apart to consider our...marriage.' Lucy caught the flicker of disappointment in his eyes and felt her own twinge of regret.

'Perhaps absence will make the heart grow fonder and you'll soon be back together,' Sam said, with a smile that didn't quite reach his eyes. Draining his cup, he stood and retrieved his jacket from the back of the chair. 'Right, I'll leave you in peace and hope to see you tomorrow at Kings. Thanks for letting me join you, Lucy.'

'You're welcome and thanks for the coffee.' She smiled at him, hoping he wouldn't cold shoulder her completely as she did enjoy his company. As a friend.

Lucy was thoughtful as she ate the lunch Meg had prepared. The events of the past few days were unsettling, to say the least. The apparent time-shift into Mary's life was leaving her confused and even less in control of her life than before. And now Sam was showing an interest in her. Could hardly be worse timing. She was barely aware of the homemade soup slipping down her throat as her head whirled. The afternoon spread before her and there was nothing she had to do. Realising this wasn't healthy, Lucy decided to go out for a drive around the island, looking for any changes made in the past twenty years. The decision made, she checked in with Gregory and then left.

At least Guernsey, unlike London, held no painful memories for her and Lucy found herself cheered by the familiar sights from her girlhood, particularly the expansive beaches of the west and north coast. The housing was denser than she remembered, but at least the beaches were untouchable, glinting under the spring sunshine as if to remind her of the summer pleasures of the past and those still to come. By the time she reached Pembroke Bay in the north, Lucy had a burning desire to run free on the broad sand exposed by the retreating tide and, after parking the car, stepped over the pebbles and onto the almost deserted beach. A gentle breeze rustled her hair and she took a deep breath of invigorating salty, ozone-laden air before running towards the waves lapping on the shore. For a moment she was a child again and raised her arms as a laugh escaped her lips, taking her by surprise. Oh, how good it felt to be away from the house and all her problems. Lucy had forgotten how healing the sea and the beach were. As a teenager she had ridden off on her bike, and then later her scooter, to a beach whenever she had rowed with her parents. Which happened quite a bit, she remembered. Living on an island, you couldn't exactly run away, but the beaches offered a kind of sanctuary and a chance to calm down and reflect. Now, as Lucy stood and watched the waves ebb and flow, she saw for the first time that she had not altogether enjoyed her childhood. Being an only child had meant all the focus was on her and it had been suffocating at times. And it wasn't easy to know your parents, or at least your father, had wanted a boy. Lucy had left Guernsey thinking the island was not a happy place to live, but it now dawned on her that the fault didn't lie with Guernsey, but her family. Even Natalie, who had been adamant she was not coming back after uni, had returned. Eventually.

Lucy opened her mouth and turned her face into the wind, tasting the salt sucked from the sea and which left tiny crystals on her skin. Focused on licking the salt around her lips, she didn't notice a small dog, ears flapping and tail wagging in its excitement, missing a thrown ball and colliding with her leg instead. Laughing, she looked down at the huge brown eyes of a dog the image of Storm, Mary's puppy.

'Oh', she gasped, shifting on her feet to keep her balance.

'I'm so sorry, has he hurt you?' an elderly lady puffed, hobbling on a stick towards her. 'He's only a puppy and has more energy than I can handle. I'm only looking after him while a neighbour's ill in bed.'

'No problem, I was just taken by surprise. And isn't he gorgeous?' She bent down to caress his long, silky ears and the puppy's tale went into overdrive. 'Is he a Bassett Fauve de Bretagne?'

The woman's eyes widened in surprise.

'Why, fancy you knowing that. I didn't think there are many on the island and I hadn't heard of them till my neighbour bought this little chap.'

'I only know of one and he's…not here anymore. I'd say your friend is lucky to have him, but he's a bit of a handful if you have a problem walking,' Lucy said, nodding towards her stick.

'It's only for a few days while she recovers from a heavy cold. But I think it's time he went back on the lead.' She slipped it on to his collar while Lucy had his attention. 'There, c'mon Basil, time we went home. Nice to have met you,' she nodded, before pulling the reluctant dog away from his latest admirer.

'And you.' Lucy stared after the retreating figures, but in her mind she was seeing Mary and Nathaniel walking with Storm at Havelet. She shivered. It was just a coincidence…

Back home she changed into the new skirt, pairing it with the red cashmere sweater. She took extra care with her hair and makeup, something which had not been a priority since losing Amber. But now, she wanted to present a more confident image to the world, or at least this small corner of it. Her grandfather smiled his approval when she dropped in to say goodbye.

'My, you do look nice, my dear. More feminine. Never have been a fan of women in trousers or jeans and your grandmother always made a point of wearing a nice skirt or dress when she wanted to look her best.' His eyes twinkled as he made her do a twirl.

'You sound like an old male chauvinist, Grandpa. Jeans and trousers are liberating for women; we can enjoy physical activities which are a bit tricky in skirts.' Lucy kissed his cheek and he laughed.

'I won't argue with you. Go and enjoy yourself and I'll see you in the morning.'

She gave a mock curtsy and left the room, smiling. The smile slipped when the image of Mary in her elaborate gown popped into her head. Now, why on earth did that happen? Pushing the question aside, Lucy hurried downstairs as quickly as her heels allowed. Trainers were so much more comfortable to wear…

The drive to Rocqaine, far down on the west coast, took her through the parishes of Forest and St Peters, past the airport and down towards the shady lanes leading towards Natalie's home perched above the bay. In the fading light Lucy found it hard to follow her friend's directions as country lanes were seldom signed and the area was new to her.

As she turned into what she hoped was the right lane and began to climb above the bay, she caught a glimpse of the sea with the sun edging towards the horizon. Soon after a sign for "Beauregard House" appeared on her left and she drove down a winding lane to arrive in what she guessed had been the old farmyard. Natalie owned what used to be the farmhouse, now completely rebuilt, facing the bay. A smaller cottage, the one-time barn, was off to the side and set at an angle, with a reduced sea view.

She parked and rang the bell on the solid oak front door.

'Hi, Lucy! Good to see you, come in.' A smiling Natalie flung the door wide and ushered her into a light and contemporary hallway with walls covered in artworks. Lucy was torn between admiring the house and taking in the changes in her friend's appearance. The once long fair hair was now pixie short and her blue eyes looked enormous in the slimmer, narrow face.

'You look wonderful,' Lucy said as they hugged, conscious the years hadn't been so kind to her.

'Thanks. I put it down to having found happiness.' Natalie's smile turned into a frown. 'I know you've had a rough time lately, but I'm sure life will improve soon. Now, let's grab a drink and join Stuart who's watching the sunset.'

Lucy followed her into a Grand Designs worthy kitchen and Natalie poured her a glass of wine before moving on to a huge sitting room at the back. A man with curly blond hair was sipping his wine while gazing out at the deepening red sky through a wall of folding glass panels. Turning, he smiled and kissed her cheeks.

'Hi, Lucy, good to meet you. Welcome to our home with a view.' He waved a hand to embrace what could be seen of the land sloping down towards the bay as the sun kissed the sea as the darkness deepened.

'Nice to meet you too, Stuart. And it must be quite something in daylight.' Reflected in the glass she saw Stuart and Natalie share a smile and with a pang recognised the glance of those in love. She took a gulp of wine.

'We're very lucky to live here, but it was a rocky start, wasn't it, darling?' Natalie paused, a shadow crossing her face. 'I hadn't expected to share my new home with an angry ghost and my dreams would be taken over by the haunting memories of a long dead woman.' He squeezed her arm while Lucy choked on her wine.

'OMG! Your mum mentioned a ghost but I hadn't known about the dreams. It must have been pretty scary.'

'It was and Stuart freaked out when I finally told him. After all, we'd only recently met as neighbours and knew little of each other and this used to be his family's farm.' Natalie glanced at her watch. 'Look, dinner's about ready so why don't you get settled at the dining table and we can continue chatting while we eat?'

Lucy agreed and followed Stuart into the adjoining dining room while Natalie headed to the kitchen.

'I assume it wasn't a coincidence you living in part of your family's old home?'

Stuart shook his head.

'No. My mother, after some years away, had lost contact with her mother, Olive. When she came looking for her she found Olive had been missing since the eighties and the farmhouse had been burnt down. Everyone assumed Olive had left the island. Mum inherited the farm, such as it was, and decided to rebuild the cottages, allowing me to buy mine at mate's rates.' He grinned. 'My father, who died some years ago, had run a property development company with Mum so she saw its potential.'

'How sad about Olive, though it's worked out well with you living here after all. Who lives in the other cottage now?'

'Oh, Mum and her new husband stay there a few weeks a year, spending the rest of the time in France.'

'Has Stuart been filling you in with the weird history of this place?' Natalie said, with a grin, coming in with a tray of dishes which she spread on the table. 'Please, help yourselves.' She waved her arm over the food.

'Yes, he has and it seems both our families have had the proverbial skeletons in the cupboard. In my case I've been taken back into the body and life of an ancestor from about eighteen hundred,' Lucy said, spooning fragrant rice and chicken onto her plate.

Natalie gasped.

'I can't wait to hear more! But perhaps after dinner, as Stuart has a pile of marking to deal with and you and I can share the more serious stuff then. In the meantime, shall we talk about what we've been up to over the past twenty years? Abbreviated, naturally.'

Lucy was happy to agree and while they ate they each shared bits of their past, including Natalie's experience of a violent boyfriend when she lived in London. Her disclosure and the admission they couldn't have children, brought home to Lucy how important it was not to assume other people were luckier than her. Natalie and Stuart seemed to have it all, but she saw the sadness in their eyes when they explained about the fertility problem and her heart ached for them. No-one could replace Amber, but at least she might have another child one day.

Supper over, Stuart retreated to the study with a glass of wine to ease the strain of marking and Natalie made a pot of coffee before ushering Lucy into the sitting room.

'I was intrigued by what you said about slipping back into someone else's life as it sort of happened to me,' Natalie said, pouring the coffee. 'In my case the woman, Olive, seemed to infiltrate my brain while I slept, taking over my dreams with memories of what had happened to her.' She paused, her brow creased as the unwelcome memories surfaced. 'I felt the blows when her husband beat her and…and raped her and woke up in pain for a few moments, wondering what the hell had happened. It took a while to realise what was happening to me and it totally freaked Stuart out.'

'Oh, that's awful! Must have been so scary for you. And there was a ghost as well?'

Natalie told her the story of Bill and Olive and how they had eventually solved the mystery of her disappearance and how a local vicar and the police had been involved.

'In some ways my experience is similar to yours. First I saw a ghost…' Lucy went on to describe her experience of slipping into Mary's life and her conviction that her ancestor wanted her to learn the truth of her sad life.

'It seems to me, Lucy, you might not be free of Mary unless you uncover what happened to her, just as I did with Olive. Could you cope with slipping back into her life again?' Natalie's gaze was intense.

'I…I don't know.' She chewed her lip. What was the worst that could happen?

Chapter 9

Lucy spent a restless night thinking of what Natalie had told her about Olive and the dream and ghost. It resonated too much with her own experience for comfort. Mary was getting under her skin as Olive had with Natalie. Short of leaving the house – and her grandfather – there appeared nothing to stop Mary making her presence felt in some way. Before finally drifting off to sleep, Lucy decided it would be better to take control of the situation by returning the portrait to her bedroom and "talking" to Mary as if she were present and telling her she wanted to learn what happened, but at times chosen by Lucy, not Mary.

After breakfast the next morning Lucy retrieved the portrait and hung it in her bedroom. Again, it was as if Mary's eyes followed her and for a moment she was unnerved. Remembering Natalie and how she had faced her fears, she took a deep breath and focused on her face.

'Mary, I've learned something of your life and understand there's more you want me to know.' She could have sworn there was a slight nod of Mary's head as she continued, 'but it's unsettling for me if I don't know when I might slip back to your life. If…if I tell you when I'm ready, are you willing to pull me back at only those times?' Lucy held her breath as she stared at the portrait, thinking she must be stark, raving mad to talk to it as if it were a real person. The ineffably sad eyes appeared to blink and she thought she heard a whispered "yes".

'Okay, then now is a good time for me.'

* * *

Within seconds Lucy experienced the now familiar feeling of falling as the floor changed beneath her feet, now shod in neat brown leather half-boots. Instead of jeans she was wearing a severe high necked black dress in a stiff fabric resembling moiré silk. And she – or rather Mary – was sobbing.

'I will not marry Thomas! I will not! How can you be so cruel as to suggest I marry a man who is known to be a drunkard and possessing no morals? He is the very opposite of my poor Nathaniel, who I loved with all my heart and is only recently drowned.' She raised her swollen eyes to her father who stood in front of her with a cold, implacable look on his face she had never seen before. Not given to emotion, he had always been a little distant, but never cruel as he now appeared. Her nervous mother, who usually took her side, had conveniently been called elsewhere. They were alone in her father's library and Mary's heart, already filled with grief over Nathaniel's untimely death, was ready to burst out of her chest at what he had proposed. She had read in her novels of people dying from a broken heart and sorely wished it for herself, as her life was effectively over without her beloved. And to be replaced by Thomas! Her body was shaking so hard she almost fell onto the nearby chair.

'Come now, girl, you forget yourself. Marriages are not about love, but strengthening the bonds between families and although I acknowledge it was an added bonus you and Nathaniel formed an attachment, I would have insisted the marriage went ahead without one.' He began walking up and down, picking up objects on his desk and putting them down again, all the time avoiding her eyes. 'I do concede Thomas has his…faults, but he assures me he holds you in the highest regard and swears he will be a good husband to you.' He coughed. 'Naturally, it would be unseemly to arrange a wedding so shortly after poor Nathaniel's demise and we propose a delay of three months.'

'Three months! I should not be out of mourning for Nathaniel then even if I agreed to this marriage, which I will not.' Mary's tears flowed freely as she curled up on the chair.

'You will do as I say, girl. You are honour bound to obey me and marry whomsoever I choose. It is ever the way for women, as well you know. Your head has been too stuffed full of romantic nonsense from those novels you read.' He towered over her, waving his arm in such a threatening manner she expected him to strike her and raised her own arm to protect her head. Instead of a blow, he shouted at her to leave and go to her room, where she was to stay until given permission to leave. Mary fled, her eyes blurred with tears and vowing she would die rather than marry Thomas.

* * *

Lucy came to, burdened with Mary's grief for Nathaniel and her shock at the proposed marriage to Thomas. She lay on the floor, stunned. Then images of a lifeless baby Amber bubbled to the surface and her tears came in gasping gulps until she was utterly exhausted and out of breath. Heaving herself up, she went to the bathroom for a glass of water and to splash her face. Taking deep lungful's of air, she began to feel calmer. Oddly, a feeling of release began to flow through her, of having let go a heavy burden. Puzzled, Lucy returned to the bedroom and stood in front of the portrait. She thought she saw a glimmer of a smile on Mary's face. Something clicked in her head.

'I don't know what's going on, Mary, or why I'm even talking to a painting like this, but is there any way you could be trying to help *me* in the same way I want to understand *you* and what you suffered?' She took a deep breath. 'Are we healing each other?'

The smile seemed to widen.

Lucy smiled back, feeling a fluttering in her heart.

'Good, then I'll let you know when I'm ready to learn more.' She turned her back on the portrait and sat with her notebook writing all she remembered of her experience as Mary. Her ancestor was becoming more real to her, a person of flesh and blood like herself, with emotions and feelings Lucy could relate to. Apart from the little matter of the two hundred years between them, they could be sisters, she thought, with an inward smile. Still not entirely convinced she wasn't going mad, she put away the notebook and went to see her grandfather.

He was gazing out of the window and appeared not to have heard her knock as when she said, 'Good morning, Grandpa,' he turned round with a dazed look.

'Oh, good morning, my dear. I was well away, remembering my youth. Or some of it. I was thinking of the time I met your grandmother and how I decided there and then she was the one for me and I told her so.'

Lucy laughed.

'And what did Grandma say?'

'Oh, she told me I was conceited, too big for my boots and I had to prove myself worthy of her,' he said, smiling. 'It was just after the Occupation and I'd been away fighting for King and country and came back to find a diminished island whose population had suffered much under the Germans and no-one was better than anyone else. Your grandmother, quite rightly, wanted to see what I would make of myself and didn't agree to marry me until some years later when I'd qualified as an advocate and bought us a little house in Les Buttes.'

'Good for her! Then you didn't live here after your wedding?'

'No, my father was still alive, but he died a year later and we moved in with my mother not long after, before we were expecting our first child.' His face clouded over and Lucy squeezed his hand.

'This house must hold so many memories for you, both good and bad. And you made a good choice with Grandma, she was a lovely woman.'

'She certainly took a shine to you, my dear. You were the daughter she had always wanted and she was delighted you struck out to do your own thing rather than becoming an advocate like me or an accountant like Dennis.'

'I never knew. Grandma didn't say anything to me but she did give me an extremely generous cheque when I went off to find myself.' Lucy remembered how overcome she had been at the time, even crying as her grandma had thrust the cheque for £5000 into her hand.

'Here you are, my dear, something to help with your travelling expenses. We didn't have the opportunities in my day to go off and see the world, thanks mainly to the war, of course. But it would never have occurred to us girls, anyway. Our sole purpose in life was to marry and bear children and only poorer women worked. At least in Guernsey.' She sighed and Lucy wondered if this was a sigh of regret. 'It was different on the mainland, after the war women felt they had earned the freedom to have careers of their own, but here…' she shrugged, 'we've always been a bit behind the times.'

'What would you have liked to do, Grandma?'

She laughed.

'Well, I loved clothes and fashion and when the war ended I dreamed of becoming a fashion designer in London. A silly dream for an island girl, but we all need dreams, don't we?'

'Did Grandma ever tell you she wanted to go off to London and become a fashion designer?' Lucy asked, recalling this conversation.

Gregory looked puzzled.

'What? Is that what she said? Well, I'm blowed! No,' he shook his head, 'she took a secretarial course and worked in an office until we married and then stayed at home to look after me.' His fingers tapped the arm of the chair as he seemed to think about it. Turning to face her, he went on, 'Makes me look quite the male chauvinist, doesn't it? Do you think she regretted giving up her dream for marriage?'

'No, I don't think so. She said it was a "silly dream" anyway and not something open to her at the time, unlike nowadays. Grandma always seemed a happy woman and it was clear she loved you even after all the years together.' Lucy squeezed his hand, worried she had made him sad.

He smiled.

'And I loved her. Best decision I ever made, as she reminded me frequently!' He chuckled and Lucy breathed a sigh of relief. 'Now, tell me how your evening went.'

She was only too happy to fill him in, describing not only the wonderful house Natalie owned, but the issues she had endured with her "ghost" and the bizarre dreams.

'It all sounds like something out of a book, but I can tell from your face you accept it as true.' He paused, his fingers tapping again. 'And the Reverend Ayres was involved, you say. So there must be some truth in it as I've heard he's a sound man and well liked in his parish.' His eyes locked on hers. 'Are you now convinced we could have a ghost here, as well?'

She cleared her throat. How much to say?

'Natalie's story has certain similarities to my…experience and in both cases there's a woman in an unhappy marriage and one was definitely murdered by her husband. We don't yet know what happened to Mary, but you hinted there was some scandal about her husband and with a missing date of her death, something must have happened.'

He pursed his lips.

'You're right, but I don't see how we can find out, do you?'

Lucy shifted in her chair.

'I told you Natalie relived some of Olive's life through her dreams and I...I've been having odd dreams too. About Mary. So perhaps she's trying to tell me what happened to her.'

'Umm.' He stroked his chin. 'All a bit far-fetched isn't it? What sort of dreams?'

She thought carefully before answering.

'In one dream I saw Mary being told her fiancé Nathaniel was reported missing, presumed dead just days before their wedding. And in another she learns his coat's washed up in the harbour.'

'Are you sure it's not your mind playing tricks, my dear? After all you've been depressed...' His face was creased with concern and Lucy decided to pull back.

'To be fair, Grandpa, I'm not sure either, but it was interesting to hear about Natalie's experience. Don't worry, I won't take the dreams too seriously.' She mentally crossed her fingers.

'Good. And what are your plans for today?'

'I'm off to the gym this afternoon and may have a swim as well.' She glanced at her watch, adding, 'It's almost lunchtime, I'll go and see what Meg's preparing for us. See you later.' She dropped a kiss on his cheek and left. Once outside his room she let out a deep breath, hoping her grandfather wouldn't worry too much about her "dreams". From now on perhaps she should steer clear of mentioning them.

The walk to Kings gave Lucy a chance to reflect on her latest trip to the past that morning. Setting aside the natural grief and despair Mary had shown, Lucy couldn't help but contrast how women, in particular, lived in the 1800s compared to now. Mary was totally under her father's control and, on marriage, would be subservient to her husband. Single or married, she was restricted in what she did and who she mixed with. Whereas now, here she was, free to do exactly what she wanted, go where she wanted and be whoever she wished to be. Okay, there were some restraints, like being manipulated into looking after her grandfather while her parents buggered off on holiday, but, generally speaking she, Lucy, wasn't subject to the onerous constraints of Georgian times. The most important difference, she mused, was being able to choose who she married. That thought led on to her marriage to Hamish and, for some reason then veered off to Sam. At this point she was walking up the drive to Kings and experiencing a slight frisson of anticipation. Giving herself a mental shake, she registered at reception and walked round to the changing rooms.

Five minutes later Lucy was warming up with stretches in the gym when Sam appeared and waved a hello. She smiled and carried on stretching before stepping on to a static bike for some blood pumping exercise. Out of the corner of her eye she saw Sam stopping to chat to each person in turn.

'Hi, Lucy, how're you doing?'

She pushed the hair out of her eyes, saying 'Fine, thanks. I'm beginning to look forward to the exercise and plan to have a swim today.'

'Good to hear, but remember not to overdo it. A slow build up is what we're after.' Sam's eyes were warm as he stood only inches away from her and Lucy could only nod her agreement. He smiled and moved on to someone else. She was left with warm cheeks and a determination to push down the feelings of attraction he arose in her. It simply wasn't the right time.

Later in the evening Lucy picked up the novel she had been reading but after a few minutes realised she wasn't concentrating and couldn't recall what she'd just read. With an exasperated sigh she closed the book and went up to her room to catch up on a much more interesting story.

Chapter 10

1800 – Mary

The wedding gown she had once been so excited to wear was now draped over the bed and her maid Jane stood twisting her hands nervously as she waited for the signal to dress her. Mary stood in front of the mirror, paler and thinner now and stripped of the black mourning dress worn for the past three months. After being locked in her room by her father for weeks while she refused to eat, she had given in and agreed to the marriage. Her mother had been her only visitor, wringing her hands and pleading with her to change her mind.

'My dear, your father is implacable and insists this marriage will go ahead even if he has to drag you to the altar himself.' She paced up and down and Mary saw the distress on her face. 'Will you not, as many women do, accept what is inevitable and look forward instead to having children and the joy they will bring? You will not need to spend much time in Thomas's company once you are a mother, and the house is large enough to keep you separate. He will have business to attend to and as a married woman you will be free to meet with friends whenever you wish, within reason.'

Her mother had repeated similar exhortations on each visit and slowly, Mary had come to accept the truth in what she said. A month ago she allowed Thomas to call on her once, when he made his formal proposal.

'My dear Miss Mourant, I am truly sorry you have been so distressed by the unfortunate death of my brother that you have been obliged to take to your bed until now.' He stood before her, attired in mourning, and as he bowed over her hand she caught the gleam of lust in his eyes and a whiff of stale brandy and tobacco. The shadows around his eyes indicated a lack of sleep the previous night or nights, and his un-brushed hair and stubbled cheeks were testament to missing the ministrations of his valet. Mary cringed inwardly as she allowed him to kiss her hand. The rumours of his carousing and womanising appeared to be true. And this was the man she was forced to take as her lawful husband and into her bed for the rest of her life!

'Mr Carre.' She dropped a curtsy, eyes downcast. Her parents had covered up their treatment of her by passing around the word she had become ill with grief. Her pale, waxy skin corroborated the story and Mary was so weak from lack of food, she sank into the nearest chair, leaving Thomas standing awkwardly in front of her. They were alone except for her maid, sitting a discreet distance away, her father having left as Thomas arrived. Etiquette decreed she invite him to sit, but Mary had no intention of complying. For perhaps the last time, she had the upper hand.

'Miss Mourant, I'm certain your father has advised you of my desire to request your hand in marriage, since my poor brother is no longer able to fulfil the marriage contract.' He coughed. 'Will you accept my proposal?' He made a slight bow, his thin lips curled in an expression of such confidence that Mary wished with all her heart she could refuse him and wipe that look from his face.

She hesitated, and his face was beginning to flush with annoyance, before she murmured, 'Yes, sir, I will.'

And now it was her wedding day. She had pleaded con-tinued poor health in order to avoid seeing Thomas again and her father had concurred, presumably relieved that the marriage would now take place. As Jane helped her into the gown, Mary took no pleasure in its beauty, seeing it more as a symbol of her subjugation to the men in her life. She knew dear Nathaniel would have not have acted as her master. They were to have been equal partners in their marriage, he had assured her. She had to force her mind to stop thinking of him, stifling a sob. Jane was as subdued as her mistress, barely saying a word as she completed the final touches to Mary's hair.

There was a knock at the door and Jane went to answer it, returning a moment later with a package.

'It's for you, ma'am, sent by Mr Carre.'

Mary opened it to find a velvet bag containing an emer-ald and diamond necklace.

'Oh, ma'am, what a beautiful necklace. Shall I help fasten it for you?'

Mary stood rigid, as if she had been sent poison rather than diamonds.

'No, Jane, I shall not be wearing it today. You may put it away, thank you.'

Jane tried to protest, saying it was customary for a bride to wear a gift from her groom, but Mary remained firm.

Her parents were waiting for her in the entrance hall and looked about to speak, but she focused her eyes on the front door which was swiftly opened by the butler who then dashed to open the carriage door for her. Once she was seated her parents joined her and as the carriage pulled away, Mary looked back at what had been her home until now and inwardly vowed she would never return. Her mother tried to engage her in conversation but she remained silent, nursing her inner misery.

There were few guests waiting in the Town Church, for

which Mary was glad. She had made clear to her parents she would only tolerate a quiet wedding, without fuss or ostentation, out of respect to Nathaniel. Her mother had been somewhat dismayed, having looked forward to celebrating the nuptials of her only child, but her father saw it in a brighter light, referring to the money he would save. Waiting at the altar were Thomas and his best man and Mary stifled a gasp as she saw Thomas was attired in a velvet coat edged with embroidery with matching velvet pantaloons, a heavily embellished waistcoat and an overblown white neck-cloth. Hardly the outfit for a groom mourning his brother.

Thomas turned towards her, his eyes raking her from top to bottom as if she were an object for sale. Which, she thought sadly, she was. His face darkened as he must have noted the absence of his gift before once again facing towards the vicar.

The service passed in a blur for Mary, only making the appropriate responses when required. It was as if it was happening to someone else, she was merely an observer. She only came to herself when the vicar said her husband could kiss the bride and he drew her to him and kissed her hard on the lips. It took all her willpower not to recoil. Thomas must have registered her unwillingness as his jaw tightened and he hissed into her ear, 'Why do you not wear the jewels I sent you? I will not be slighted in this way and you will pay dearly for it.'

Mary could only submit to him taking her hand firmly in his as they walked back down the aisle and out to the waiting carriage. It was a sombre group who followed behind, more reminiscent of a funeral than a wedding. Which, for Mary, was what it felt like. Once in the carriage Thomas grabbed her head with one hand, forcing another kiss on her mouth while reaching under her dress with the other to probe her intimate area. She gasped, trying to push him away, but he only laughed, saying 'Don't be so miss-ish, wife, you won't be a virgin much longer.'

By the time they arrived at her new home, *Carreville,* Mary was feeling sick and stumbled out of the coach into Thomas's iron grip. The household staff were lined up to greet them.

'Come, my dear, let me introduce you to our staff.' Gripping her hand, he added quietly, 'And smile, you're supposed to be a happy bride.'

Mary forced a smile to her lips as she met each member of staff, from the butler and housekeeper down to the cook and maids. Her own personal maid, Jane, was arriving later once she had packed up her trunks. By the time the introductions were complete, the guests had arrived for the wedding breakfast and after welcoming them with a fixed smile, she was led by her husband into the dining room. Mary had only been in this house once before, when she and Nathaniel had become engaged, and been invited for a celebratory supper with her parents. And Thomas. Her stomach lurched at the memory as he led her to the top of the table, laid out with the finest china, silver and glassware and helped her into her seat.

As with the wedding service, Mary drifted through the meal in a detached haze, making minimum conversation and barely touching the food. She avoided eye contact with her parents, seated either side of her and Thomas, although she could not miss seeing her father looked annoyed and her mother anxious. Towards the end of the meal there was a delightful diversion when the dog she had given to Nathaniel, ran into the room and straight up to her.

'Oh, Storm, how you have grown!' Mary cried, lifting him onto her lap and letting him lick her face while she laughed with pleasure. For a moment she forgot where she was and enjoyed their reunion. Although she had often thought of him, she had not dared to ask what had happened to the little dog.

'I had forgotten you had gifted the animal to my brother. It has been moping around the house these past few months and I had been about to send him packing.' Thomas's voice broke the spell and Mary clung tighter to Storm as she faced her husband.

'It's well that you hadn't, sir, as everyone here can see, we are happy to see each other again and I shall take him as my own dog. I'm certain Nathaniel would have wanted me to have him, do you not agree?' Mary held her breath, looking from the nodding heads of the guests to the pursed lips of her husband. Surely he could not refuse her so publicly?

Thomas must have thought the same as, with a tight smile, he replied, 'Of course you must keep him, my dear. Let us hope he will prove a good companion for you.' He signalled the butler, 'Jarvis, come and relieve Mrs Carre of her dog will you, and see he is settled with my own.'

Mary murmured her thanks and allowed Jarvis to lead Storm away, not made easy by the dog's attempts to return.

The diversion seemed to lighten what had been a stilted atmosphere and the guests began talking about the loyalty of their own dogs. Mary joined in, glad to forget for a while what lay ahead for her that night. She noticed that Thomas was drinking heavily, his speech becoming slurred as it became louder. At some point, her parents and other guest began to shuffle in their seats, making noises about leaving and carriages were called. Servants rushed to help and Mary found herself being congratulated once more as the guests paid their farewells. Suddenly, she was standing with Thomas in the hall as the door closed on the last guest. Her stomach lurched as he turned towards her with a wolfish grin.

'So, wife, we are finally alone and it is late. We must away to bed.' He turned to the butler hovering nearby. 'Send for the mistress's maid to attend her in her room.' Jarvis bowed and left. Thomas took Mary's arm, saying, 'I will escort you upstairs and join you shortly. Come.' To still the thoughts chasing around her head, she focused on her surroundings. The grand staircase wound up through the marble flagged hall and was lined with portraits and seascapes, referencing the family's ties to trade.

'My father had this house built ten years ago, when all the best families moved out of the old town, your father included. There he is,' Thomas pointed to the picture at the top of the stairs of a fierce looking man in his fifties, she guessed, staring haughtily ahead with steely blue eyes. She saw the likeness immediately.

'You favour him.'

'Yes, I like to think so. Henry was not well liked, but was much respected in the world of business.' He stood still, mirroring his father's stance, saying, 'I, however, have little interest in the mechanics of business and am only concerned with the fortune my father made and is now mine.' His eyes gleamed and Mary shivered, wondering how long the fortune, and her generous dowry, would last.

'You are cold, wife?' He tightened his grip. 'No matter, it will not be long before I warm that cold body of yours.' He pulled her along the landing and opened a door, pushing her inside. She was relieved to see Jane waiting for her near the ornate four-poster bed and moving forward, heard the door close behind her. Mary's legs gave way and she would have sunk to the floor had not Jane rushed to hold her and lead her to a chair. Pent-up tears flowed down her cheeks as Jane soothed and sought to calm her.

'There, ma'am, try to stay strong a little longer. I had cook make you a camomile tisane and once you've drunk it I'll help you change and freshen yourself.' She handed Mary the cup and as she drank, Jane removed her shoes and stockings and laid her nightgown on the bed. Slowly, she grew calmer, determined not to let Thomas know her true feelings. Once out of the confines of the gown and undergarments, Jane set the nightgown over her head and then proceeded to brush her hair till it shone. A quick wash and she was done. Only then did Mary examine the room in more detail. She had to admit it was beautifully furnished as befitted the mistress of the house. The bed linen was the best quality from France and the curtains were blue silk velvet, now pulled across the windows against the evening darkness. A wardrobe, dressing table and stool and an upholstered chair stood ready for her use. There were two doors other than the one she came through.

'Where do these lead, Jane?'

'That one leads to the master's bedroom and only he has the key, and the other goes to your sitting room. Let me show you.' Taking a candle, Jane led her to another beautifully furnished room set out with sofas and chairs and a writing desk. Mary went round touching her belongings unpacked from the trunk, thrilled to have her own room to relax in or share with friends. As she returned to the bedroom there was a loud knock on the communicating door to her husband's room. Before she could answer, Thomas entered, dressed in his night attire and a full-length dressing gown.

Mary froze as he ordered Jane from the room. Once they were alone he removed the dressing gown, throwing it on a chair and advanced towards her, one hand holding a riding crop and instinctively she shied away.

He grunted, his face dark with anger and grabbed her arm.

'You've made it clear to me and everyone at our wedding that you don't wish to be my wife, but the fact is you are, and you'll behave as such. You'll not make a fool of me again in public, woman. I'll teach you a lesson you won't forget.'

Mary bit her lips to stop crying out as he threw her on the bed and proceeded to beat her for what seemed hours, but was probably minutes. As she sobbed into the pillow he then thrust himself inside her violently while she remained on her stomach. The sharp pain melded with the almost unbearable pain she was experiencing from the beating and Mary was close to fainting when Thomas let out a deep sigh and rolled off her. Something sticky ran down her thighs.

He stood up, saying, 'Well, at least my dear departed brother didn't take your maidenhead, so I have the advantage on him at last.' Laughing, he left Mary still sobbing and hoping this was all a nightmare and she would wake up to find her beloved Nathaniel beside her. As she tried to move the pain in her body told her otherwise.

Chapter 11

2013

Lucy came round in her bed, crying out with the pain in her body. Then, as her eyes focused on the familiar furnishings of her own bedroom, the pain vanished and Mary was left behind. Except for the faint trace of Lily of the Valley and the sheer horror of what she had both experienced and witnessed. Shaking like a leaf she couldn't help checking herself for signs of a beating, but her skin was clear. God, did she need a drink! Padding over to the portrait, she stared at Mary, and saw a tear seep from her eye. Lucy reached up to wipe it away. Her fingers came away wet.

'I'm so, so sorry, Mary.' Turning to look at Thomas, his features untouched, she said, through clenched teeth, 'Bastard! And to think I'm related to you. I can only hope you got your comeuppance.' With that, she slipped her bare feet into slippers and went downstairs to raid the drinks cupboard. A stiff vodka later, Lucy returned to her room, threw a quick peek at the portrait – no more tears – and crept into bed. A glance at the clock told her the whole of Mary's wedding day had taken no more than ten minutes. She grabbed her notebook and wrote down as much as she could remember, the vivid images from the day crowding into her brain. She knew Mary's attempt to avoid marrying

Thomas and the brutality of their wedding night would stay with her forever.

'What's got into you this morning?' Meg asked, as Lucy stared at her untouched cooked breakfast. 'Not sickening for something, are you?'

She looked up to see Meg frowning as she stood ready to take her grandfather's tray upstairs.

'No, I'm fine thanks. Not much of an appetite this morning, sorry. Would you mind if I make myself some toast instead? I hate wasting food, but...' She shrugged, pushing down feelings of nausea, poor Mary's plight still clear in her head.

'Don't be silly. You must eat what you want and don't mind me.' She left with the tray and Lucy put a couple of slices of bread in the toaster before refilling her mug of coffee. Musing as she waited she now recognised Mary's bedroom and her own were the same room, separated by two hundred years of popular design and the invention of electricity. No wonder Mary's influence was so strong! Spreading the toast with butter and marmalade, Lucy pictured the room again. A four-poster bed with silk drapes and a matching canopy in a floral design picking up the blue of the curtains. A large French Aubusson rug at the bottom of the bed, Georgian furniture and walls covered in wallpaper bearing a delicate Chinese design of flowers and birds. Candles in wall sconces created a soft focus effect, like looking through a blurred lens. The Carres liked to display their wealth, she thought, and as international merchants they had easy access to the luxury markets of France and England. Now the sumptuous four-poster had morphed into a double divan topped with a duvet, a plain fitted carpet, faded curtains, a teak chest of drawers and cream painted walls. Part of what had been Thomas's bedroom was now the en-suite and the sitting room a further bedroom. In a way it was a relief to know she wasn't sleeping in Mary's bed after what she had seen…

'Better now?' Meg said, interrupting her thoughts as she returned with her grandfather's empty plate.

'Yes, thanks. Glad to see Grandpa's appetite's better than mine. I'll go and see him later.'

Meg nodded, giving her a keen look.

'Will you be wanting lunch later? I was planning on making chicken soup.'

'Lovely, thanks.' She finished her toast and helped load the dishwasher before leaving. In the hall Lucy stopped, taking a fresh look around as the image of its original incarnation popped into her mind. Surprisingly, it wasn't radically different, mainly because the tiled floor was the original and the staircase the same. The walls were now painted and covered with many more portraits, reflecting the succeeding generations. This prompted her to search out Henry Carre, Thomas's father, last seen at the head of the stairs. And there he was still, staring haughtily ahead as he had done for two hundred years. Lucy noticed a slight resemblance between Henry and her grandfather, but at least Gregory had proved to be softer hearted.

She lingered on the landing examining more closely the furniture and artefacts previously taken for granted. One piece, an antique side table, reminded her of one seen in Mary's time. It was a pretty, bow fronted table with delicate shaped legs and three drawers. Pausing to think, Lucy realised it had been in Mary's sitting room and the thought gave her a thrill. Perhaps there were other pieces around the house…knowing she could touch something Mary had owned strengthened their bond. Giving the table a gentle stroke, she walked on to Gregory's room.

'Morning, Grandpa. Did you sleep well?' As she moved over to his chair by the window, she couldn't help looking out for anything else she recognised.

'Good morning, my dear. Yes I did, thank you.' He examined her face. 'Meg says you're a bit peaky today, is that right?'

'Nothing to bother about, just didn't feel up to a fry up, that's all. I'm better now, thanks.' She gave him a kiss before sitting down, anxious not to have him worry about her. 'You know that portrait at the top of the stairs? A fierce looking middle-aged man? He reminds me of Thomas, and I wondered if they're related.'

He frowned, tapping his fingers on the arm of the chair. 'Ah! That's old Henry Carre, the father of Thomas and Nathaniel. Looks pompous, doesn't he? But as one of the most successful merchants of the day, I suppose he had a right to be.' He chuckled. 'Just as well he didn't know his fortune wouldn't last more than three generations.'

'Why, what happened?'

'Thomas happened! And his son after him, Mary's boy, named Henry after his grandfather.'

Lucy sat forward, a buzz of excitement flowing through her.

'But how do you know this? It's well before you were born.'

'Since we've been having our chats, my memory's coming back. Or at least bits of it.' He tapped his head and smiled. 'Your desire to know what happened to young Mary registered with me and I've remembered my grandfather, Albert, knew her son, who was *his* grandfather.' He slapped his knee in triumph.

'Wow! These guys must have lived to a good age.'

He nodded. 'Unusually for the time, the men in the family, apart from young Nathaniel and Thomas, all lived to their eighties or nineties, outliving their wives. You can see from the family tree you found.'

'So, did your Albert tell you anything about Henry?'

'He was only a lad, of course, but he wasn't impressed.

Seemed to think he was still the head of a flourishing merchant house, even though it had been failing for years. Still lived in this house, but struggled with the upkeep, including the servants' wages. It was his son, Samuel, my great-grandfather, who I never knew, who became an advocate to try and save the family name and fortune.' He frowned. 'And now I've lost it.'

She gripped his hand.

'I think it's amazing the family's lived in this beautiful house for more than two hundred years, so it's nothing to be ashamed of. And the family name dies with Dad, anyway. But what happened when Thomas ran the firm? You said he was the start of the decline.'

'Samuel told Albert Thomas had no interest in business, and rarely turned up at the office. He put a manager in charge of the day to day running and spent most of his time either drinking with visiting sailors or playing skipper on *The Mayflower*.'

Lucy digested this for a few moments, remembering Mary's concerns about Thomas's attitude to work and his extravagance. What a pity she couldn't share this with Gregory!

'It sounds as if Henry wasn't much better than Thomas when he inherited the business.'

'No, that's what I understand. But there was something else that may have had a bearing, and this is what I can't remember. Some scandal, as I told you.' He tapped his fingers in frustration.

'Don't worry, Grandpa, it may come back, and anyway what you've told me is fascinating enough.'

He smiled and touched her arm.

'Thank you, my dear, I'm glad I'm helping you with your little mystery "ghost". And it stops me becoming too self-absorbed. Now, what are your plans for the day?'

Lucy was restless and, after checking it was fine, made a coffee and went into the garden to settle her thoughts. April had supplanted March and the air was warmer with a slight breeze. She sat in a sheltered spot at the bottom of the garden and facing the house. As she sipped her drink it occurred to her that Mary might well have sat in a similar spot two hundred years ago, perhaps playing with her children. It seemed as though Thomas wouldn't have been around much, which would have suited her. Lucy shivered as the memory of Thomas beating Mary on their wedding night surfaced. What happened the next day? Did she really want to witness it, experience it? If she had had access to Mary's diary rather than reliving her life, it would be far less traumatic. Needing some advice, she rang Molly.

'Hi, Molly, sorry to bother you, but I had quite an experience yesterday when I slipped back to Mary's wedding day…'

After giving her the gist of what happened, Molly suggested she came round that afternoon instead of waiting until the next week's appointment. Lucy was only too happy to agree, the relief in having someone to confide in was instant. Still restless, she decided a long walk would help and went indoors to fetch a jacket before setting off towards Cambridge Park, the nearest green space to home. The exercise proved beneficial and she was much calmer on her return and ready for lunch. Meg nodded with approval when she asked for another helping of chicken soup.

'The trouble is, Lucy, you don't get out enough. I know you're starting at the gym, and that's good, but you're cooped up too much in the house and with nothing to do. It's not healthy, young woman like you.' Meg stood, arms akimbo, as Lucy drained the bowl.

'I know, you're right, but I am making some progress, you might not see it, but I know I am not as depressed as I was.' Lucy summoned up a big smile and Meg's face softened.

'Well now, perhaps you are, and after all you've gone through, it's bound to take time, eh?' She picked up the empty bowl, adding, 'Will you be home for dinner tonight? Gregory says he fancies some fish and I bought enough sea bass for both of you.'

'Sounds wonderful, Meg, and I'll be here. My social calendar's hardly filling up yet,' she said, pulling a face.

Meg looked thoughtful as she filled the dishwasher.

'If you wanted to invite your friends here for a meal sometime, like the ones who had you round for a meal, then I'd be happy to cook it for you and leave it ready to be served. That's if you're not up to doing it yourself yet.'

'Oh, that's very kind of you. I hadn't thought about asking people round, but it might be a nice thing to do.' Lucy was touched by the offer, typical of Meg's caring for others. 'And you're right, I don't think I'd be up to coping on my own. Never was a great cook.'

'There you are then. Just give me plenty of notice if you want to have a little dinner party. Nothing too fancy, mind, I don't go in for unnecessary sauces and suchlike. But I could provide three courses if you wanted.'

Lucy gave her a hug, saying, 'You're a treasure, Meg, and I know what a good cook you are. I'd happily serve your food to any guest. When I'm ready to entertain.' She wasn't sure when or even if that might be, but it was a worthwhile goal.

Arriving at Molly's, Lucy took a moment to breathe in the sea air wafting up the lane from the bay. Such a tranquil spot, without the noise of traffic she was used to in Queen's Road.

'Lucy! I thought I heard your car, come on in,' Molly said as she stood by the open front door, a warm smile on her face. After a quick hug they headed to the study where a tea tray stood waiting, complete with teapot and a plate of the ubiquitous gâche.

'I see you're all prepared,' Lucy said, grinning as she sat down.

'It gives us more time to talk, doesn't it?' Molly poured the tea and gestured to Lucy to help herself to gâche. Leaning back in her chair, Molly took a sip, looking thoughtful. 'I'm both excited but also anxious about your continuing forays into the early eighteen hundreds. From what you said, this Thomas is a violent man and you've already experienced the beating he gave poor Mary. I'm not concerned you could be *permanently* harmed physically, but rather there's a risk of *mental* harm. After all, my dear, you're still grieving for the loss of your child and the end of your marriage. Mary's story is beginning to sound a little too close to home.'

Lucy nodded.

'I've thought the same and,' she felt her cheeks redden, 'you might think I'm bonkers, but I had this sort of conversation with Mary, via the portrait. I suggested we were perhaps helping each other heal from our experiences and she agreed. Then I told her I needed to control the times when I went back.'

Molly's eyes widened and she gulped her tea, making her cough. She managed to say only, 'Oh!' before the coughing fit ended.

'It's as if we're telepathically communicating, and I "see" her smile or cry and she seems to hear what I say. There's definitely a bond between us, maybe the genetic link you mentioned the other day. She's like a younger sister and I care about what happens to her. And I think she's picked up on my grief, too.' Lucy sat, chewing her lip, aware how weird it all sounded.

'I see. Or rather I don't see, but I understand what you mean. Since we last met I've been researching more about regression and past lives and what you're experiencing could be explained by the phenomena. It's rare for it to be spontaneous, though. Usually there's a trigger, like hypnosis.'

Lucy gasped.

'You mean I could have been Mary in a past life?'

'It's a possibility. At least as likely as you slipping back in time into her life. You would still be two different people, living two hundred years apart, but the same soul.'

Lucy was silent for a moment, eating her gâche while she thought about Molly's suggestion.

'It's a lot to take in and I've never been convinced about past lives. Sounds a bit hippy-dippy to me.'

'It's one of the foundation stones of Buddhism, you know, and it's argued that you only stop having more lives once you've reached a state of Nirvana – "bliss", the ultimate goal.' Molly sipped her tea, then went on, 'I've been reading a number of accounts of past lives and it's uncanny how many have been found to be plausible. Personally, I find it quite fascinating.'

'Whether it's a past life or a genetic memory or whatever, the result's the same, isn't it? I still go back to the past.'

'Yes, but if it *is* your past life it might trigger more memories than you can handle now.' Molly leaned forward, a worried frown on her face.

'I take your point, but I don't want to stop. I need to know what happened to Mary and when I'm thinking about her or living her life at least I'm not worrying about mine.'

'That's something, I suppose.' Molly finished her tea, looking thoughtful. 'Why don't I teach you self-hypnosis now? You can use it for pure relaxation, or to control slipping into Mary's life and then bringing yourself back if you feel threatened or uncomfortable in any way. I shall feel happier if you have more control, as you said yourself.'

'Sounds good, thanks.'

Molly took her into a deep trance before explaining how she could easily take herself into a relaxed state and bring herself out again, whenever she chose. By the time she opened her eyes, Lucy felt as if she were floating on air, without a care in the world.

'Thanks, Molly. It's such a wonderful feeling isn't it? And I can see how it will be useful to manage the Mary situation. I wonder if she realises she's my five times grandmother or possibly an earlier incarnation of me!' She giggled at how absurd it sounded.

'I doubt it. Remember we don't actually know what is happening and I'm only proffering possibilities. The main thing is to be careful, Lucy. Don't put yourself at risk, please.'

'No worries there. I'm in charge of Grandpa and can't let him down, can I?'

Chapter 12

By the time Lucy arrived home she was desperate to catch up with Mary and find out what happened after the disastrous wedding night. She still couldn't get over the notion Mary might be more than an ancestor and wondered if it explained why she had been so horrified about the rape and beating Mary had endured. *She* had endured! After dinner she went to her room and stood for a few moments in front of the portrait, willing Mary to acknowledge her. When there was no response Lucy whispered, 'Mary, it's me. Can you hear me?'

A soft sigh stirred the hairs on her neck and Mary's eyes appeared to blink. It was like waking up someone from a deep sleep and Lucy held her breath, impatient for Mary to acknowledge her presence. Another blink. Then a soft murmur 'I'm here' inside her head.

'Mary, I was with you on your wedding day and night and am anxious how things were afterwards. May I join you again the following morning?' Lucy spoke out loud, watching for an expression on Mary's face to indicate if she had heard. A slight incline of the head. 'Now?' Another incline. Lucy lay down on the bed and closed her eyes.

* * *

'Morning, ma'am. I've brought your hot chocolate.'

Jane's voice broke through the deep sleep Mary had only enjoyed for what seemed like minutes. As she stirred pain shot through her body and she let out a cry.

'Oh, ma'am, whatever's happened?' Mary opened her eyes to find Jane gazing in horror at the bloodied sheets, testament to the brutal loss of her virginity. She tried to cover herself up but her maid must have caught sight of the livid bruises on her body and the dried blood on her thighs.

'My…husband was rather rough in his lovemaking last night, Jane. He…was angry with me and made me pay for it.' She tried to sit up but was too sore and Jane helped her to find a more comfortable position on her side, propping her up with pillows so she could drink her chocolate.

'I'm sorry to hear that, ma'am. Would you like me to bring you up your breakfast? The master's already left and gave instructions he wouldn't be back until this evening.'

Mary, worried Thomas could appear any moment, let out a sigh of relief. A whole day before she had to face him again.

'Please, Jane, but first let me finish my chocolate. I'm not sure I can leave my bed today,' she said, wincing at every movement. She looked at the rumpled bed and went on, flushing, 'the sheets will have to be changed, I'm afraid.'

'Of course, ma'am. I'll be away to fetch fresh sheets and we'll manage somehow.' Bobbing a quick curtsy, she left, leaving Mary fighting back tears of pain and anger. To think her parents had forced her to marry such a man, who was proving to be an even worse husband than she had imagined. Finishing her drink, she eased back against the pillows, feeling shame and embarrassment at what Jane must think of her. And the other servants, as they were bound to find out at some point. Her most intimate parts throbbed with pain and the thought of being subjected to further such treatment the coming night filled her with horror. Her body would take days to recover and her mind even longer. But she would not give Thomas the satisfaction of knowing how much he had hurt her – and how much she hated him.

The door opened with a bang and Mary looked up in alarm, only to be met with excited barking. 'Storm! I am so glad to see you.' She laughed as he jumped on the bed, but was too sore to cuddle him. Jane followed with a pile of fresh sheets and a jug of hot water, calling Storm to get down.

'Let me sponge you down, ma'am, before I change the sheets. I'll be as gentle as I can, but it'll sting, I'm afraid. I've brought some salve to apply afterwards.'

Mary gritted her teeth throughout the ministrations and when Jane was finished she helped her into a fresh nightgown.

'Now, ma'am, let's help you onto the chair, if you can bear to stay there while I make the bed.' While Mary eased forward a little, Jane took the pillows and placed them on the chair before helping her off the bed. Once the bed was made, Jane helped her back into it, supported by numerous pillows. Mary was exhausted but relieved to be nestled on clean sheets on which Jane had sprinkled lavender water.

'Right, ma'am, I'll bring you some breakfast shortly, cook's already been told.'

'Thank you, Jane. You've been wonderful. I'd be much obliged if you were to say as little as possible about what has occurred. It would be in everyone's interest to avoid tittle-tattle.'

'Of course, ma'am.' Her face, which had been pinched with concern, broke into a smile. She took the empty water jug and soiled sheets and left.

Mary allowed Storm back on the bed and he stretched out next to her, his head resting on her arm, his large brown eyes focused on her.

'You know something bad has happened, don't you, Storm? At least we're back together and I'll do my best not to let anyone part us again. Once I feel better I'll take you out for walks, but not today.'

The rest of the morning passed in a haze of pain, exhaustion and mounting hatred toward Thomas. Jane visited an apothecary and purchased some laudanum and after taking a few drops Mary was able to drift into a restless sleep as the pain eased. Late afternoon Jane arrived to say the master had returned and was changing for dinner.

'Do you wish me to say you are unable to join him, ma'am?'

The thought of having to face her husband after the events of the previous night made her stomach churn but what choice did she have? She would not give him the satisfaction of knowing how much pain he had caused her.

'No, I will dress for dinner, if you could help me, please.'

It took a while as her body was so stiff and sore, but at last she was attired in a satin evening gown with a matching shawl with her hair in curls framing her face. The butler arrived to escort her to the drawing room. Mary, rendered light-headed by the laudanum, was able to walk slowly into the drawing-room, looking around with interest. A carved marble fireplace dominated the room and above it hung a painting of a schooner. She recognised it as *The Mayflower*, bought by Nathaniel in partnership with her father. They had been walking near the harbour only two days before he drowned, when Nathaniel had pointed it out to her, a note of pride in his voice.

'We were lucky to buy her against stiff competition from other local merchants and it cost us dear. Fortunately she's proving to be a sound investment and has captured several French ships in only a twelvemonth. We may consider taking shares in another ship if our success continues. The latest French prize, moored alongside her,' he pointed, 'is turning out to be a particularly rich catch. It was carrying French emigrés to America with all their valuables on board. Naturally, all must be shared equally between partners and the crew, but everyone will be well rewarded.'

'Beautiful, ain't she? Can't fault my late brother for his eye for a good ship.'

Mary spun round, her heart thumping, to see a swaying Thomas nearby, clearly intoxicated as he slumped into a chair. He didn't appear to have washed away the lingering smell of the alehouse and she wrinkled her nose in disgust. Fortunately he would not have noticed as his eyes closed for a moment.

'Good evening, Thomas, I trust you had a good day?' She kept her voice cool, in spite of her churning emotions and physical pain.

Before he could reply, the butler arrived with a pot of coffee, setting it beside him and pouring a cup. Thomas opened his eyes, saw the coffee and sat up.

'Thank you, Jarvis. I'll ring when we're ready to go in for dinner.'

'Yes, sir.' He bowed and left.

Mary settled herself with care in a chair some feet away, hoping he would not notice her wince as she sat. The coffee appeared to clear his head.

'I see you are able to sit without discomfort, wife. Perhaps I was not firm enough with you last night.' Thomas sneered at her and she felt herself redden with shame at the memory. 'Do not be concerned, I shall not trouble you tonight.' He laughed. 'I have had my pleasure today with a lady much more willing and voluptuous,' he shaped such a figure in the air, 'and hardly wish to waste my time on such a scrawny body as yours. I only married you to give me a son and your dowry was more appealing than you ever were.'

Mary didn't know whether to laugh or cry. The insults warranted tears, but knowing he wasn't keen to bed her was a relief. She forced a small smile to her lips but remained silent.

'We must wish you will conceive soon to save us both the, er, trouble, must we not?' He rose and rang the bell and gestured for her to join him. As they waited for Jarvis to lead them to the dining room, Thomas said, 'I have engaged a portrait painter over from London to paint our joint portrait in celebration of our marriage. He will start tomorrow and we are to wear our wedding clothes so please inform your maid accordingly.'

'As you wish, but will it not take many hours to complete?' She felt sick at having to pose with him for hours on end in the now hated wedding gown and while in such discomfort.

'It will, but he works fast and am assured the details can be finished without our presence. I have better ways of spending my time than standing for hours like a tailor's dummy and only agreed to go ahead on that condition.' He frowned. 'It's not something to enjoy, but we need to be seen to be following the trend of family portraits among the wealthier local families.'

Mary was not entirely appeased but could hardly refuse. Privateering, in particular, had brought prosperity to the island and those benefiting were keen to ape London and Paris society with displays of their wealth. Her papa had also recently commissioned a portrait of himself and her mama. She had not thought it a good likeness but her parents seemed pleased with the result.

The dinner proved a painful experience for Mary, being forced to sit on a hard chair for hours exacerbated the effects of her beating. She was convinced Thomas had asked the kitchen to provide extra courses than normal and to take their time bringing them up. He made a point of asking her if she was well throughout the meal, accompanied by a sly look. It was two hours later when Thomas threw down his napkin, declaring he was retiring to his study for a brandy and she was free to return to her room. Jane applied more salve on her bruises and prepared a further dose of laudanum. Mary crawled under the covers trying not to dwell on the forthcoming ordeal of the portrait sitting.

After posing for the artist for three hours Thomas declared he had to leave on urgent business and would be available the following morning. Mary almost fell into Jane's arms and needed her help in mounting the stairs. Storm jumped around excitedly and it was clear to Mary he needed some exercise.

'I will rest for a while and after luncheon will take a walk with Storm. Please tell Cook I will eat in my room.'

After a light luncheon, Mary changed into a cream muslin day gown and a green velvet spencer. Jane helped her into brown velvet half-boots before fitting a green velvet bonnet adorned with feathers on her head. Clutching a reticule in one hand and Storm's lead in the other, Mary left the house accompanied by Jane. As a married woman she didn't need her maid, but wasn't yet confident enough to be out in public on her own. She set off, pulling hard on Storm's lead to keep him under control, heading towards the nearby New Ground, the place for a promenade favoured by the officers of the local garrison and the upper echelons of society. Nathaniel had escorted her there on several occasions and the memory caused a sob to escape her lips.

'Are you quite well, ma'am?' Jane hurried up beside her.

'Yes, quite well, thank you. I…was recalling how Nathaniel and I would take Storm here for exercise. It seems so long ago.'

Jane nodded in sympathy.

'It must be very hard for you, ma'am. And I want you to know you can depend on me for anything, anything at all. I serve you, no-one else.'

Mary saw the earnestness on her face and was touched. Jane, four years her senior, had been her maid for three years, and she had become fond of her. It seemed the affection was mutual.

'Thank you. I appreciate your loyalty and have much need of it now…now I am married.' Heaven knew what Jane had made of the sight she presented the morning after her wedding night, but at least she was likely to be discreet.

They arrived at New Ground where a well-trod path was lined with trees providing shade and some protection against any wind. Situated high above Town near open country it was vulnerable to strong easterlies. However, this spring day was calm and mild. It wasn't long before Mary was approached by a couple of officers who she recognised as friends of Nathaniel.

Raising their hats, they bowed.

'My dear Miss…ah, no, it is Mrs Carre now is it not?' The first, a Captain Yardley, greeted her, looking somewhat embarrassed. They had not met since Nathaniel's death.

'It is a pleasure to see you, Captain, and yes, I am married now. But of course not to the man we all knew and…liked.' He raised his eyebrows and smiled sympathetically.

'I understand, ma'am. My condolences on your loss. Ah, I see you have his puppy. What was the name again?' He bent to stroke his ears as the dog ran around excitedly.

'Storm, sir, and we have only been reunited for two days and he is proving hard to control. If you have any words of advice on the matter, I would be much obliged.'

'If you will permit us to accompany you for a while, between us I'm sure we could offer much advice, eh, Harry?' The other officer hastily agreed and the little group set off along the promenade earnestly discussing how to curb a young dog's overexcitement. Along the way they met other acquaintances who, taking their lead from the captain, treated Mary with courtesy and some sympathy. By the time she and Jane were ready to return, Mary was struggling to conceal how painful walking was for her and was glad her new home was only minutes away.

They arrived home to find Thomas had just returned and was in his study. Mary handed Storm to a footman and went upstairs to rest until dinner.

* * *

Lucy came to with a start. Her first thought was how she would hate having to wear the wedding gown again and pretend to be a happy bride. Then, opening her eyes properly, she realised she was safely back in the present and let out a deep breath. 'Oh, Mary, am I glad I'm not you!' she said aloud, although if Molly was right, she may have been once. Shaking her head at the thought, she grabbed her notebook and pen and added to the previous recollections of the past. Once done she stood once more in front of the portrait.

'Thank you, Mary, for sharing that with me. I obviously can't relive every day of your life, so perhaps next time you can choose what you feel is important for me to know. Will that be all right with you?'

Focusing on Mary's face for a response she caught a perceptible nod and smiled. It gave her an odd feeling now knowing the circumstances surrounding the portrait and the reasons for Mary's sadness. Needing to distract herself, Lucy went downstairs to check if there was anything interesting on television. She was in luck, there was a new crime drama called *Broadchurch* which sounded promising and she had time to pour a large glass of wine before it started. By the end of the first episode she was hooked and hadn't thought about Mary and her unhappiness once. Yawning, she switched off the television and went up to bed.

At lunchtime the following day Lucy had a phone call from Natalie.

'Hi, how're you doing? Seen any more of your ghost?'

'You could say that! I'll tell you more when I see you next.'

'Sounds intriguing, can't wait. In fact I hope it'll be soon. My friend Jeanne and her husband Nick have invited Stuart and me round for a kitchen supper on Saturday and I happened to mention you were back on the island. I know you've never met but know of each other through me and I think you'd hit it off. What do you say?'

'I'd love to meet them, I remember you telling me about Jeanne when we were teenagers. There was a family tragedy, wasn't there?'

'Yes, she had a rough time of it and left Guernsey for years. She's a successful writer now and Nick's a boat-build-er. They have two delightful children and live near my mum. It'll be fun and probably boozy so best to get a taxi. I'll text you the address. Brilliant! See you soon.' Natalie signed off and seconds later a text arrived. Lucy was left reflecting how kind her friend was to think of her and how generous of Jeanne to include her. She knew they had been best friends at school until Jeanne left for England at sixteen and now they were all back on the island, making fresh starts and finding husbands. Would she? Her mind flipped unbidden to Sam. Too soon. Perhaps when she was ready. But would she know when that was? Lucy sighed. She might see him that afternoon at the gym and the more she saw of him the more she fancied him. Forcing the idea aside, she went to the kitchen to see what Meg was preparing for lunch.

'There you are, I was beginning to think you'd lost your appetite again. It's lasagne with salad today if you'd like to help yourself. I'm about to take Gregory's upstairs.' Meg gestured to the pan on the side before lifting the tray set out with her grandfather's lunch.

'Thanks, Meg, smells delicious. And don't worry, I haven't lost my appetite.' Lucy smiled and opened the door for her before serving herself a large portion of the pasta and a small bowl of salad. She needed the fuel for the workout that afternoon. By the time Meg returned the plate was cleared.

'You were hungry right enough and I'm glad to see it. Can't abide food going to waste, though Gregory doesn't eat much these days. Reckons he doesn't feel as hungry as he did.' She started stacking dirty plates in the dishwasher and Lucy joined her.

'He's not sickening for something, is he? He seemed fine this morning.'

'No, don't worry. The carers keep a close eye on him. Which reminds me, have you heard from your parents lately?'

'Not since they messaged me before boarding the ship. Mum told me not to expect to hear from them for a while as mobile calls would be expensive and they can only email if the ship has WiFi.' Privately Lucy thought her parents preferred not to know how things were with them, so they could enjoy their cruise with a clear conscience.

A muttered 'humph' from Meg seemed to say she agreed.

'While I think, I've been invited out on Saturday evening, Meg, so please don't cater for me. They're friends of the couple I saw the other evening and if we all get on I might consider a return invite soon.'

Meg stretched her back and smiled.

'My, your social life is picking up! I'm pleased for you, Lucy. I look forward to the time you're out more than in, and your grandfather will feel the same, for sure.' She gave her a sly glance. 'Are they inviting a spare man to keep you company?'

Lucy flushed.

'No, I'll be the odd one out, but it's okay I'm not looking for a relationship yet. We're not even divorced, simply separated.' As she said it, a little voice in her head whispered, 'Are you sure?' And again Sam's face popped into her mind.

Meg simply nodded and began wiping down the worktop.

Thinking it better to avoid more on the subject, Lucy said cheerio and went upstairs to check on Gregory. He was reading the local newspaper and muttering under his breath.

'Hi, Grandpa, something annoying you in the paper?'

He looked up and smiled.

'Just the usual squabbles over too many road works and lack of co-ordination between the different services. I've always found it a mystery that the same problems keep repeating themselves. You'd think someone could have taken charge and created a giant spreadsheet by now.' He sighed. 'I know these things shouldn't bother me at my age and especially since I can't leave the house, but it's the incompetence I can't abide.'

'Were your clerks scared of you?' Lucy sat beside him.

He looked surprised.

'You know, I've never given it much thought. But you could be right, I didn't suffer fools gladly and we had the reputation as one of the best firms to uphold. My father drummed it into me that if you can't do a job properly then you shouldn't be doing it.'

'Pity that Thomas and his son Henry didn't follow the same precept and safeguard the family fortune.'

Gregory grunted.

'Even if they had, the days of wealthy merchants were numbered by the late nineteenth century. Steam ships took over from sail and the world became much smaller with goods traded without the need of entrepôts like little Guernsey, particularly after Peel brought in his free-trade policy in the eighteen-forties.' He paused. 'There was one trade, however, at which we excelled in Victorian times and I bet you'll never guess what it was.' He slapped his knees and grinned as she tried to think what it could be.

'Sorry, haven't a clue.'

'Marmalade!' Gregory chuckled as she gaped in surprise. 'Marmalade! But how, why…'

'Ah well, sugar duty was still extremely high at the time and Keillers of Dundee manufactured their still famous marmalade here in Town, to evade the duty. Fruit was imported from Europe and cheap female labour was employed to make it before exporting to the then British Empire. Interesting, eh?'

'Certainly is. You're proving to be a mine of information, Grandpa. It's better than being at school!' she laughed.

'Good. Talking to you is bringing back more of my memories so it's good for me too.'

'Then we must keep it up. Oh, and I'm invited to dinner with friends on Saturday so I might have something to share with you afterwards.' She stood and kissed his cheek. 'Off to the gym in a minute so I'll see you later.'

Lucy had been in the gym about fifteen minutes when she spotted Sam. Her heart rate increased which could only have been because she was pounding away on the Ellipse machine and not because she fancied him. So she told herself. As usual he nodded and smiled at her but before he could speak, was called away to answer the phone. Disappointed, she hoped he would return before the end of her session, but he didn't. Annoyed with herself for her contrariness, Lucy returned to the changing room and swapped her lycra for a swimsuit. A few lengths of the pool cleared her head and once she was changed, headed to the café for a drink. After ordering a smoothie she took a seat near the window as she checked her phone for messages and emails. She was reading through a short email from her parents when her smoothie arrived. Looking up to thank the waitress Lucy was surprised to see Sam grinning at her.

'Oh, thanks. What happened to the girl on the counter?'

'Had to dash off for a school pickup. As we're short staffed at the moment I'm covering for a while. Mind if I join you? I can keep an eye on the counter from here and I'm dying to sit down for a bit. Been full on today.'

'Sure, no problem.' Lucy made a point of focusing on her drink, trying to avoid eye contact.

'I see you had a swim today, how did you find our pool? Warm enough?'

Lifting her head, she let go of the straw and nodded.

'Yes, it was lovely. It's a great addition to the club and I plan to swim more often. The extra exercise will do me good.' She couldn't help smiling at his pleased expression.

'If you don't mind my saying so, Lucy, you're looking better already. There's a sparkle in your eyes now.' Sam's gaze was penetrating and she felt a flush flow up her neck.

'Yes, I'm…feeling better, thanks. Seeing old friends, getting out more. You know the kind of thing. It's like Guernsey is welcoming me back into the family.'

He nodded.

'I know what you mean. After uni I worked on the mainland for a few years and didn't think about coming back permanently, just for short breaks to see my family. Then,' he shrugged, 'don't know what triggered it, but I realised I missed the old place and came back and got a job here. Best decision I ever made.'

'At the moment I'm not sure if I'll stay forever, but it's becoming more of a possibility.' As soon as the words were out of her mouth, Lucy realised she meant it. Until now she had not looked beyond her enforced stay until her parents returned. There was nothing calling her back to England. And the island had its own attractions, including a grandfather she was getting to know and love, her old friends, the mystery of Mary's life and…she stole a glance at Sam, who was about to say something when someone entered the bar, and he stood ready to go. Perhaps add the attraction of a new man in her life.

Chapter 13

By Saturday, admitting her thoughts were too often filled with Mary's life, Lucy decided to take a couple of days break from time-slipping. Or whatever it was. She wanted to focus on the present and enjoy meeting new people, which was hard if her mind was two hundred years in the past. As she ate breakfast, Lucy dwelt on the upcoming supper party and what she should take. Remembering Natalie had mentioned heavy drinking the obvious choice was a bottle of wine. She knew her grandfather kept a good cellar as Dennis had boasted of it, saying it would last for a few more years. Lucy had been drinking the odd bottle kept in the kitchen rack. Looking at it now it was empty. By the time she finished eating Meg had returned from upstairs.

'Meg, do you top up the wine rack from the cellar?'

'Yes, and meant to go and bring up some more and then forgot. I can pop down before I leave –'

'No, don't bother, I'll go. I've never been in the cellars and wouldn't mind a quick look. Are the wine racks easy to find?' said Lucy as she helped stack the dishwasher.

'They're in the first room you come to and stacked according to whether you want red or white. Gregory still likes the occasional glass of burgundy so please bring up a couple of bottles as well as whatever you fancy. I'll write down the name of the one he likes. There's a wine carrier in the cupboard.' Meg pointed to a walk-in cupboard which

Lucy found to be a treasure trove of odds and ends. She quickly spotted a wooden wine carrier to hold twelve bottles.

'Right, I'll do it now. Grandpa won't mind if I take a bottle to my friends tonight, will he?'

Meg chuckled, handing her the slip of paper.

'I shouldn't think so! Even your father's hardly made a dent in what's down there.'

Lucy grinned and went off down the back hall leading to the cellar. Cool air hit her as soon as she opened the door and switched on the light. She was relieved to find the stairs solid and complete with a hand rail. Since a child she had not liked underground spaces but a large, well-lit room such as this should be okay. At the bottom she gazed in amazement at the stacks of wine racks in the room, although half looked empty. Remembering her family's history as merchants, it wasn't really surprising, she thought. In their hey-day, her forebears must have saved a fortune buying wine directly from France and other countries without paying any duty. Lucy was about to search for the burgundy when she became aware the air was turning oppressive and the hairs on the back of her neck stood up. A faint sound of sobbing seemed to come from a room behind a closed door and she hesitated. Instinctively, she knew someone had been in pain. Her breathing quickened as she debated whether to investigate. The air grew colder. Surely Mary hadn't followed her down here? Gulping, she took a few steps towards the door and tried to open it. Locked. Standing still, Lucy listened through the door, but the sobbing, or whatever it was, had stopped.

'Mary, is that you?' Not sure what to expect, she glanced around nervously in case Mary appeared. Nothing.

Overwhelmed by a sensation of sorrow, she turned and hastily scanned the racks for the burgundy. Luckily the racks were labelled with the names of the wines and she soon found the one Meg had written – *Richebourg Grand*

Cru Domaine Jean Grivot – and grabbed two bottles before searching for less exalted wines for herself. In a rush, she chose a mix of Merlot, Pouilly-Fuissé and Chablis and though desperate to get out, had to take the stairs slowly with the heavy carrier.

Back in the kitchen she found Meg preparing to leave.

'Here, let me help you.' Together they placed it on the worktop and Lucy let out a deep breath before slumping onto a stool.

'My, whatever's happened, my girl? You look as if you've seen a ghost?' Her eyes round, Meg clapped her hand over her mouth, adding, 'You haven't have you? Not the one you told me about?'

She shook her head.

'Not exactly. But I...I felt something odd. An atmosphere. Have you ever noticed anything a bit strange down there?' Lucy still heard the echo of distant sobs in her mind and shivered. What the hell had happened in the cellar? And when?

Meg frowned as she buttoned her coat.

'No, can't say as I have. Just bloomin' cold so I don't stay longer than I have to. Anyways, thanks for topping up the wine, saves me going down for a while. Unless you're planning on giving a party?'

'Not yet, and if and when I do, I'll fetch the wine if you like. I agree about the cold.' Lucy managed a smile, anxious to avoid Meg worrying about ghosts, again.

'Right, well, I'll be off. See you at lunchtime.'

Lucy transferred the wine to the rack, keeping back a bottle of Merlot to take with her to Jeanne's. Sitting down with an extra strong mug of coffee, she tried to clear her mind of what had occurred in the cellar. The past was taking too much of a hold over her and she needed to be firmly in the present if she wanted to make a good impression on Jeanne and Nick. Feeling calmer, Lucy went to see her grandfather.

'Morning, Grandpa. How are you today?'

'Not too bad, my dear. But you look a trifle pale. Anything the matter?' He patted her hand as she sat beside him.

'I've been down to the cellar to replenish the wine rack, including some of your favourite burgundy, by the way. And I…I found it unsettling. Did you ever notice something odd down there? Apart from being cold, of course.'

Gregory frowned.

'It's been a few years, but I don't recall anything out of the ordinary. Cold, as you say, but not unusually so. Why?'

She told him of her experience, including the sound of sobbing.

'I would have remembered that, for sure!' He shook his head.

'Yes, thought you would. I'm wondering if it's anything to do with Mary and maybe a bad experience she had down there. You're not aware of anything, are you? An accident, perhaps?'

'No, not that I recall. A lady in her position is unlikely to have visited the cellars, it would have been left to the servants. I suppose it's possible one of them had an accident at some time.'

'Um. Do you know what's behind the locked door? Our family treasure?' Lucy grinned.

'Ha! I wish! That boat sailed long ago, I'm afraid.' He rubbed his chin, thoughtful. 'I seem to remember there was a bit of a warren down there; storage areas for the overflow from the original warehouses in the old town near the harbour. Possibly tunnels connecting them, useful for keeping contraband out of sight of the Revenue officers. But any tunnels had been bricked up long before I was born.'

Lucy's imagination ran wild with the thought of smuggler's tunnels under the house, picturing sailors carrying casks of brandy and wine over their shoulders, in the best tradition of smuggling as portrayed in television dramas. It was hard to reconcile the image with her now respectable and somewhat dull family, and part of her was intrigued by those who had taken risks and led a more exciting life. Albeit illegally.

'Were any smugglers caught here in Guernsey and imprisoned or executed?'

'No, all the islanders benefited from smuggling to some extent and were only too happy to deprive the English king of tax revenue. Even the bailiffs, as head of the law, fought against any attempt to close down smuggling, until the Crown finally won in the early eighteen hundreds.'

'I wish we'd learned more about this at school. We only ever studied the boring bits about the French wars and the royal successions in England.' She stood and paced around the room, her mind returning again and again to the sound of sobbing and the nagging belief it was connected to Mary who, in spite of her desire to keep her at bay, wasn't playing along.

'So, how was your evening out?' Meg asked the next morning when Lucy arrived in the kitchen yawning.

'Great, thanks. Jeanne and Nick are a lovely couple and their children are so sweet, wanting to stay up to meet me.' She sat down, her tummy gurgling at the smell of fried bacon and eggs. It had been a good evening, with lots of talk, laughter and wine and Lucy was glad she had made the effort to go. Pouring herself a mug of coffee she smiled at the memory.

Meg nodded, sliding the food onto two plates and putting one down in front of her.

'I'm glad to see something's putting a smile on your face again. You've been looking a bit too serious lately. Will you be seeing them again?'

'I hope to. Jeanne's a writer and so interesting to talk to.

She said I could pop round anytime for a chat and a coffee while the children are at school and I might just do that. Oh, and everyone thought the wine was great and think I'm some sort of wine connoisseur!' she said, giggling.

'I did say your grandfather knew his wine. Right, I'm off to take him his breakfast. There's plenty of bread if you want toast.'

Having drunk more than usual the previous night, Lucy had a slight hangover and needed all the carbs she could get and after clearing her plate cut thick slices of bread and popped them in the toaster. Smothered with butter and marmalade and accompanied with more coffee, they did the trick and she perked up. As she was finishing the coffee her mobile rang. Glancing at the screen she was surprised to see it was Hamish calling. What on earth could he want?

'Hi, Lucy. It's me. Is it a good time to talk?'

'Hi, Hamish. I guess so. Is anything wrong?' They hadn't spoken for months and the last time she had ended up in tears, hurt by his lack of understanding of the pain she was in. She was stronger now, but her stomach clenched at the memory.

'No, not wrong exactly. But I want to tell you, or rather ask you something which you might not like. Might be upsetting.' She heard the uncertainty in his voice and her stomach tightened even more.

'You'd better get on with it then.' She forced herself to sound calm, detached.

He cleared his throat.

'I want a divorce.'

For a moment she wasn't sure if she'd heard right. Divorce? They had agreed to separate and give it up to a year to see how they both felt then. Admittedly, Lucy had hardly thought about him these past weeks, but…

'Divorce? Why now? We were going to wait –'

'I know, but I've met someone and…and we want to get

married. As soon as possible. You see we're…expecting a wee bairn.'

'Oh!' it was if the air had been squeezed from her body and instinctively she clutched her stomach. She took a few deep breaths before replying. 'I see. That was quick, wasn't it? We've only been apart a matter of months.' Her voice was scornful.

Another clearing of the throat.

'Yes, I know and I wasn't looking for someone else, I promise you, Lucy. But not long after I arrived back home in Aboyne, I bumped into a lassie I'd known at school and we got chatting. Over the weeks she helped me talk about losing Amber and…everything.'

I bet she did, Lucy thought, angry Hamish could talk to another woman about Amber, but not her. As the red mist of anger cleared, however, she realised she wasn't actually upset at losing Hamish, it was hearing he was to become a father again which hurt. A few more deep breaths.

'I don't need or want to hear any more, Hamish. You'd better start the proceedings for a divorce and if it needs to be soon you'll probably have to admit to adultery. I don't care either way. Just send me the paperwork. I'm in Guernsey at my grandfather's house, I'll text you the address. Good bye.' She clicked off the phone. Then she put her head down on the table and sobbed. Vaguely she heard the door open and then she felt Meg's arms around her, lifting her into a hug as she made soothing noises.

'There, there, whatever's the matter, my dear? It's not your parents is it?'

Lucy, worn out from the crying, shook her head and scrabbled for a tissue in her jeans pocket. After blowing her nose and wiping her swollen eyes, she told Meg about the phone call.

'Well I never! No wonder you're upset! Not exactly the sensitive type, is he, this Hamish? Now sit down and I'll find you a wee drop of Calvados to settle you a bit. You've had a nasty shock and I swear by it myself.' Lucy continued dabbing at her eyes as Meg produced what looked like at least a double measure and she took a welcome sip. The fiery amber liquid slid down her throat and made her gasp. It seemed to go straight to her head and after a few more sips she was calmer.

'Thanks, Meg. Sorry to be such a wimp. I…I was taken by surprise.'

'No need to be sorry, my dear. It's Hamish who should be sorry for phoning like that.' Meg's face was creased with concern as she sat and patted her hand. 'Are you going to let him have his divorce? You could make him wait, you know, and serve him right too, if you ask me.'

'I've already told him to go ahead and I won't go back on my word. It means I might be able to draw a line under our marriage and move on, as everyone's been telling me.' Lucy bit her lip. She knew now she was over Hamish, but baby Amber would always be in her heart.

Emotionally drained, Lucy visited Gregory to explain what had happened and left after agreeing to meet up later. She went to her room to freshen up before going out for a walk. The sunny April weather seemed to mock her inner torment as she headed towards Candie Gardens. However, the stunning flowerbeds full of daffodils, tulips and magnolia set among palm trees and shrubs of rhododendrons had a soothing effect and she found a free bench to sit and enjoy the view over the gardens as they sloped down towards the distant harbour. The spring flowers were a reminder this was a time of re-birth, of new beginnings and Lucy held onto that thought as she wrestled with the unwelcome news of Hamish's baby. He had embarked on a new beginning so why not her? An image of a smiling Sam came into her mind, accompanied by a frisson of excitement in her belly. As she twisted her hands together she felt the ring on her wedding finger and immediately pulled it off. Initially tempted to throw it into the bushes, Lucy took the more pragmatic decision to keep it and re-use the gold in some way. Once tucked into the pocket of her bag, she felt as if she'd taken the first step towards her new life and as she studied her left hand, showing the indentation left by the ring, her thoughts turned again to Sam. Could he be the one to help her move on? It was too soon to tell, but it might be worth getting to know him better. Pleased with the idea, Lucy went off to grab a coffee and cake at the nearby Café Victoria and think more about what she wanted from life.

Chapter 14

After lunch Lucy collected her gym clothes and set off to the Kings Club, buoyed by the thought of seeing Sam. She had no idea how to make him aware of her change of circumstances apart from the lack of a wedding ring, but was happy to see what happened.

By the end of her gym session Sam had still not appeared and Lucy's fledgling optimism began to disappear. As she left the gym another instructor entered and she asked if Sam was around.

'No, he was in earlier but he got a call about some emergency and left. Can I help?'

'Oh, no it's okay thanks. Will he be in tomorrow?'

'Sorry, I don't know. He's supposed to be, but...' he shrugged, giving her a smile.

Lucy nodded and returned to the changing room feeling deflated. She could only hope the emergency wouldn't keep him away for long now she had finally acknowledged she would like to get to know him better.

Back home Lucy made herself a cup of tea before calling on Gregory.

'Well, you're looking a lot better than you did this morning, my dear. What's changed?' His look was searching as she sat beside him.

Lucy told him about realising she no longer loved Hamish, but still grieved for Amber. And how she wanted to move on and hopefully find a new partner.

Gregory nodded.

'Glad to hear it. To be perfectly honest, I never did think Hamish was the right man for you, too taciturn and closed in. But of course it wasn't for me to say, and if he'd made you happy, then so be it.' He took her hand. 'What you need, Lucy, is a warm, people person who can make you laugh and there must be a few of them about on the island.'

Lucy felt her face flush.

'Yes, I'm sure, Grandpa and I'll look out for them, don't worry. If Hamish can move on then it's time I did as well.'

By the time Lucy had eaten her dinner she was overcome by a feeling of restlessness. Stymied from seeing Sam, her thoughts turned to the other overriding issue facing her. Mary. It had been some days since she had slipped back and now, particularly after the incident in the cellar, she was drawn to going back and learning more. At least it would save her from dwelling on the present – and future. After saying goodnight to Gregory she returned to her room and stood in front of the portrait, focusing on Mary, willing her to hear her.

'Hello, Mary, I…I'm ready to learn more of your story. Could you take me back to the next significant event of your life following your wedding?' She held her breath as she continued to hold Mary's gaze. There was the imperceptible nod she had seen previously and Lucy settled herself on the bed.

* * *

Opening her eyes, Lucy saw the now familiar furnishings of Mary's bedroom as she – or rather, Mary, – was being helped to dress by Jane. On a side table a vase of pink roses cast their scent into the room as Jane lifted a short-sleeved sprigged muslin gown over Mary's head.

'Oh, ma'am, the bodice seems tighter than when you wore it a month or so ago. Is it comfortable?'

Mary looked down at her bosoms seeming to push their way out of the pretty dress. She frowned as she lifted them in her hands.

'They do indeed feel heavier and somewhat tender but why should that be?'

'You've had infrequent courses for some time, since Mr Nathaniel died and you stopped eating. I don't recall you having one since your wedding unless I've forgotten.' Jane screwed up her face in concentration.

Mary was equally nonplussed. With the nightmare of her wedding night and other nights since, she had quite forgot about her courses which had indeed almost stopped while she was grieving and refusing to eat. And it was near three months since her wedding and she couldn't remember having to ask Jane for the rags used at such a time.

Their eyes met as realisation dawned on them both.

'Could it be I'm with child?' Mary's heart leapt at the thought.

'It's possible, ma'am. And you have been off your food a bit of late, have you not? That is often a sign of being with child,' said Jane, with a broad smile.

Mary clapped her hands in excitement.

'I can hardly believe it! I'm to be a mother! Oh, this will make it more bearable to be married to that…that bully.' Since her dreadful wedding night, Mary had taken Jane into her confidence about her feelings toward Thomas and could speak freely about him with her. As Jane had much admired Nathaniel and loathed Thomas, it had caused no issues with loyalty. Mary put her hands on her stomach, but it was as flat as ever. 'How can I be sure, Jane? Do I have to wait until my belly swells? I want to tell my husband so that he no longer needs to sleep with me.' The thought of not having to endure Thomas's attentions for up to a year made her almost dizzy.

'Your belly might not swell for a while yet, ma'am, and if you want I can ask a midwife my mother has used to attend you. She's proven to be reliable and will confirm whether or not you are with child. I can contact her today if you are eager to put your mind at rest?'

'I would be so grateful if you could. I don't want to risk any harm coming to the child.' She exchanged a look with Jane, who nodded her understanding. Thomas was known throughout the household as a violent husband and master. Mary had a thought. 'As long as she is of clean habits.'

'Mrs Sawyer lives in one of the old houses at the bottom of Fountain Street, ma'am, and although the house is almost falling down, she keeps it spotless and is known for being clean in her person.'

'Good.'

Once Jane had finished dressing Mary, she slipped away to find Mrs Sawyer and Mary, smiling, went down to breakfast, hoping Thomas would have eaten and left the house. Seeing him with a full plate of food in front of him caused the smile to slip as she took her place at the opposite end of the table.

'Good morning, Thomas. Do you have any plans for today?' she asked before giving her order to the hovering butler.

He looked up from his plate and frowned.

'You sound cheerful, wife. What's it to you if I have plans or no? Planning on a jaunt with those officer friends of yours, are you? Because if you are you can forget it. It's not seemly for my wife to mix with such men in public.'

Mary fought to hold her tongue. When Thomas had learnt she sometimes met, accompanied by Jane, with Nathaniel's old friends while out walking, he had lost his temper and forbidden her to see them again. The worst of it was, she knew, as did many others of their acquaintance, that Thomas spent a great deal of time in the company of low-life sailors or whores. But she was in no position to point this out if she wanted to avoid a beating.

'No, I have no such plans. In fact, fearing it may rain later, I shall stay at home today and finish some embroidery I began some weeks ago. Will you be home for luncheon?' She kept her voice neutral, even though she hoped he would be out for the day in case Jane was able to find Mrs Sawyer.

'Not that it's any of your business, but I will not. I have various…meetings through the day and don't expect to be home before seven.'

'Then I shall advise Cook accordingly.'

Thomas grunted and turned his attention back to his food. Mary looked away, even the sight of his plate of ham and eggs making her feel queasy. She had only requested toast and tea and when it arrived she barely nibbled at the toast. Knowing what she did now, she was surprised she hadn't wondered at her recent distaste for food, particularly in the morning. As she drank her tea she hugged to herself the wonderful thought she might be carrying a child. A pity the father was the brute of a man at the end of the table and not the man she had loved so deeply…

Mary was in her sitting room attempting to concentrate on her embroidery when Jane returned with a middle-aged woman with a heavily lined face and dressed in clean, though threadbare clothes.

'Here's Mrs Sawyer, ma'am. We slipped in through the servants' entrance and I made sure we weren't seen.'

'Thank you, Jane. Please do come in, Mrs Sawyer. Won't you take a seat?'

The woman hesitated, looking uncomfortable, and Mary realised she probably hadn't been in such surroundings before.

'No matter if you'd rather stand for the moment. I want to assure you there is nothing underhand about my request to see you, it is simply that I wish to have it confirmed whether or not I am with child. This is something both my husband and I greatly desire and do not want to get our hopes up unnecessarily. Are you happy to…to examine me?' Mary, for the first time, began to feel nervous about what this might entail.

Mrs Sawyer smiled, showing surprisingly white teeth for someone of her age and class.

'I don't need to examine you, ma'am, to know you are with child as the signs are there to see. But if you wish, an examination will enable me to be more accurate about when you will give birth.'

Mary gasped, surprised but pleased.

'Yes, let us proceed. My bedroom is through here.' She led the midwife and Jane to the bedroom where Jane helped her to lie on the bed with her stomach exposed. As the midwife gently pressed the flesh she asked her when she had last bled and Mary explained about the lack of her courses.

'It seems you can only have conceived since your wedding day which would fit with my findings.' Mrs Sawyer stood back while Jane re-arranged Mary's clothes. 'I think it likely you conceived either on or near your wedding night and the child will be due six months from now, about the beginning of December.'

Mary sat up, her eyes shining with delight.

'Thank you, Mrs Sawyer, I am indebted to you. How much is your fee?'

'Five shillings, ma'am. But, to be honest, your mother would have been able to advise you about your condition. Did you not ask her?'

Mary frowned.

'In truth, I did not want to trouble my mother as she has not been well of late.'

'Oh, indeed, ma'am. I'm sorry to hear it.' Looking around the beautiful room, she added, 'Thanks to your good fortune in marrying well you will be able to offer your child all they need,' she sighed. 'My man turned out to be a lazy, beer swilling good for nothing, leaving me to provide for us and the children. At least you don't have that worry.'

'No, you're right.' Mary asked Jane to fetch her purse. 'I am intrigued by how you knew I was with child as soon as you saw me. You're not a witch are you?'

Mrs Sawyer laughed.

'No, indeed I'm not. But there is something about a woman which changes when she is with child. A softness around the eyes, a flush to the cheeks and her bosom swells, straining against her dress, as does yours.' She nodded towards the bodice of Mary's gown.

'Oh, it is so simple when you know. If…if all goes well with me, I would like you to attend my confinement, if it would be possible.'

'I would be honoured, ma'am. I shall make a note of it. And now I must be off as another lady has need of my services today.'

Mary counted out ten shillings and handed them to her, saying, 'Please accept a little extra to help with your family.'

'You're most kind, ma'am. Good day for now.' She gave a brief curtsy and left with Jane.

Mary sank onto a chair, hugging her stomach as she contemplated her pleasure when she informed Thomas of the news.

Thomas arrived home an hour late and Mary, finding it hard to keep her temper, had had to inform Cook to keep the dinner warm. She hated having to put the servants out, something which never bothered Thomas, who acted as if they should be grateful to be employed at all. Mary was on the point of asking for her own dinner to be served when he burst into the dining room somewhat dishevelled. The butler, stony-faced, pulled out his chair before sending a footman to alert Cook. Thomas poured himself a large glass of wine before acknowledging Mary.

'Good evening, wife. Did you have a good day?' His speech slurred.

Supressing a shudder, she fixed a smile on her face.

'Yes, Thomas, I did. And I have news which I trust will please you.'

'Well, woman, spit it out.'

'It is something of a personal nature –'

He waved his arm, spilling wine on the table, hastily wiped by Jarvis.

'Ignore Jarvis, he doesn't count. Well, what is it?'

'I am with child and the baby is due in December.'

'I'm to be a father? To have a son? Hear that, Jarvis?' He stabbed a finger at the butler, who bowed and said, 'Congratulations, sir.' Turning to Mary, he added, 'Congratulations, ma'am.'

Thomas emptied his glass, promptly refilled by Jarvis, and leered at Mary.

'Well, well, you've finally managed it, have you? About time, too. I no longer have to force myself to share your bed, which will be a relief, I can tell you.' He belched and Mary felt her face flame with embarrassment, and kept her eyes averted from Jarvis. Suddenly no longer hungry, she rose, saying, 'I must excuse myself, I am overcome with the sickness brought on by my condition. Goodnight, Thomas.' She walked, her head held high, to the door, swiftly opened by Jarvis. She asked him to send Jane to her and he whispered, 'Do you wish for your meal to be sent upstairs, ma'am?'

She saw the sympathy in his eyes and nodded, 'But only a small portion, please, Jarvis.'

Once in her room she collapsed on her bed in tears.

* * *

Lucy came to with the same tears wet on her cheeks and she instinctively clutched her stomach. Ah, but she wasn't the one who was pregnant, although she had been. And become a mother, albeit for such a short time. Taking a deep breath, she went to look at the portrait.

'We have both been mothers, Mary, but my child died when only a baby. Your children grew to be adults, but something bad happened to you, didn't it? We will continue this journey together, never fear.'

Chapter 15

When Lucy woke the next morning she struggled to push down unwelcome feelings of grief. Amber. Hamish. Mary's pregnancy. Too many buttons had been pressed in only a few hours and, admitting defeat, she phoned Molly to make an appointment. Molly wasn't free until the following afternoon, but hearing her calming voice helped Lucy feel more composed. Molly reminded her to try some self-hypnosis and after her shower she had a go and it worked well. She imagined herself lying on a warm, sandy beach listening to the gentle lapping of the surf as her toes curled into the soft sand. If it had been later in the year, Lucy would have gone to one of the west coast bays for the true ambience, but had to settle with lying on the bed and picturing herself on the sand at Le Grand Havre.

If Meg noticed she was subdued, she made no comment, simply serving up her breakfast with a cheery, 'Good morning.'

Lucy returned the greeting and made an attempt to eat but only picked at it. Being calmer didn't remove all the painful memories. When she went upstairs to see Gregory she made an effort to appear more cheerful than she felt but he seemed to see through it.

'What's wrong? Still upset about Hamish?'

She spread her hands.

'It's a lot of things, Grandpa, but I'll be okay. What's more important is how you're feeling. You're the patient, not me.' She managed a grin.

'The usual aches and pains, but nothing to complain about. At my age I know nothing's going to improve so every day I wake up is a bonus, my dear. And I want to keep waking up until I see you happily settled with the right man.' He gripped her hand, adding, 'But try not to take too long as I might end up pushing my luck.'

Lucy, overcome, threw her arms around his neck.

'Oh, Grandpa, please don't think like that! I know you're no spring chicken,' she smiled as Gregory's eyebrows rose, 'but, being selfish, I want you around for a few years yet, even if it's just to spite my parents.'

He laughed.

'Now that's an incentive! They might even give up and return to their own home. I'd be happy as long as you were around to talk to.' He paused. 'Do you think you'll stay in Guernsey now? Or are you hankering to go back to England?'

'I'm warming to the idea of staying, as long as I can get a job and my own place, no disrespect to you, Grandpa. But I'd still visit you, no worries.' She smiled at the old man who had become so important to her and hoped she could fulfil his wish of seeing her with a new man. And she already had someone in mind…

'Hi, is Sam in today, please?' Lucy crossed her fingers as she waited for the receptionist's reply.

'Sorry, he's not back yet. Can anyone else help?'

'No, it's okay, thanks.'

Disappointed and now concerned for Sam and the family emergency, she went through the motions of her work-out on autopilot. She could hardly ask anyone for Sam's number and even if she had it, how could she phone without any idea what he was dealing with. They weren't even friends. By the time her session was over, Lucy was feeling anything but relaxed and after changing slipped into the bar and ordered a glass of wine. No healthy smoothie today, she needed alcohol and carbs, adding a pizza to the order. Taking her wine she found a window table and looked around, noting how many tables were occupied by two or more people. It seemed to emphasise her aloneness and Lucy was trying not to feel sorry for herself when the waitress arrived with the pizza.

'Thanks.' As the girl left Lucy spotted one of the gym instructors grinning at her from a nearby table.

'A naughty treat after your workout?' said the young woman, Diana, nodding at the pizza and wine.

'If you must know, Sam wants me to put weight on, not lose it. The work-outs are to improve my muscle strength.' Lucy smiled, tapping her nose.

'In that case, I apologise. I thought you were taking advantage of Sam's absence to indulge a bit. Hope I haven't offended you.' Diana looked contrite.

'No problem. I know it's not the healthiest snack, Diana. But sometimes…' she shrugged.

Diana laughed.

'Too right! I'm only jealous!'

Lucy had a thought

'I don't suppose you know why Sam's not been in, do you? He's such a nice chap I hope it's not something serious.'

Diana frowned.

'I only know someone close to him's in hospital and she's not expected to recover.'

'Oh dear, sorry to hear that. Must be a worry for him.' She bit her lip, wondering who the 'she' was. Mother? Sister? Grandmother? Girlfriend?

Diana stood, saying she had to get back to work, and

Lucy carried on eating the pizza, though with less appetite, thinking of Sam facing the loss of a loved one. Life could be such a bitch, she thought, draining the last of the wine before heading home.

That night Lucy's sleep was broken by a succession of disturbing dreams. In the first one Hamish was holding Amber and threatening to take her away with him.

'I'm leaving you, Lucy. I don't love you anymore and you're not a fit mother for Amber. She'll be better off with me in Scotland...'

Lucy was crying, trying to reach out to him but he was fading into the distance with Amber in his arms and she didn't seem able to move. As if she had been turned into stone.

She woke up with her heart hammering in her chest and a terrible feeling of loss. It took her a while to feel calm, the image of a gurgling Amber in her father's arms had been so real, so alive. She got up for a glass of water and then slowly sank into a fitful sleep. Sometime later Lucy was caught up in a dream about Mary and Thomas but was only an onlooker. It was a jumble of events that occurred when Mary was pregnant – her belly was growing larger and she was spending more time at home. Thomas appeared to be drunk and they were arguing. At one point Thomas raised his hand to hit Mary, but stopped and stormed off, leaving Mary to collapse, sobbing, onto a sofa. Lucy woke up, relieved it was a dream. Or was it? Had she witnessed something which happened or had she made it up? Either way, she was emotionally drained and her head throbbed. Her bleary eyes checked the time. Seven thirty. No point trying to go back to sleep and anyway she couldn't cope with any more such dreams.

Lucy's head had cleared after showering and dressing

but she was overwhelmed by a feeling of sadness. Luckily she would be seeing Molly later and she could offload onto her. The morning passed in a kind of daze. Gregory was bedridden with a bad cough and she wasn't allowed to visit him and although Meg assured her it wasn't serious, she couldn't help being concerned. Restless, she decided to visit the gym, now part of her daily routine, earlier rather than her usual time. The exercise helped her mood but she was disappointed not to see Sam.

After lunch Lucy drove off to Molly's, glad to have someone to talk to. All the mixed-up thoughts whirled around her head and she needed Molly's calm and level-headed approach. She was welcomed with the usual cup of tea and plate of gâche before bringing Molly up to date with the events of the past few days, including the time-slip and the unsettling dreams. Molly sat quietly, taking notes and not interrupting.

Once Lucy was finished, Molly topped up her cup, her lips compressed.

'Right, let's start with Hamish and his news. Are you sure you've now come to terms with this and are ready to move forward? After all, you admit it was extremely upsetting.'

She nodded.

'It was, initially. Then I began to see him in a different light and was more angry than upset. And I now know I want to meet someone else and hopefully have a family.'

'Good, it might be Hamish has done you a favour in forcing the issue. Your dream suggests you're still grieving for Amber, which is natural as long as it no longer overwhelms you.' Molly inclined her head.

'I find I'm thinking about her less these days, though Hamish's news, together with Mary's pregnancy, has brought it all back. But I'm not as overwhelmed as I was.'

'That's good to hear. Now, regards Mary. I'm concerned about the impact her life is having on you while you're not fully in control of your own life.' Molly frowned, adding, 'You're still vulnerable, my dear, and it's clear Mary was in an abusive marriage. Re-living this could put too much of an emotional strain on you.'

Lucy bit her lips.

'I understand where you're coming from, Molly, and appreciate your concern. But, and I know this sounds stupid, I feel *compelled* to keep going back. The dream I had about Mary and Thomas showed me events which must have happened after I last slipped back, and felt just as real.' She took a deep breath. 'I'm becoming convinced I *was* Mary in a previous life, so the connection is even stronger and I want to find out as much as I can about her life. If it's impacting on my life now then we could both find a kind of closure, I guess.'

Molly sighed.

'I can see why you wish to continue, Lucy, I'm only concerned about how well you cope with what you experience. I would feel responsible –'

Leaning forward, Lucy shook her head.

'No, I'll be responsible for my actions and any consequences, Molly. And if I struggle to cope then I hope you'll be here for me.'

'Of course I will! Now, shall we have a relaxation session? And I'd recommend you use the self-hypnosis technique before any more time-slipping.'

Lucy was happy to agree and when she left twenty minutes later, was looking forward to the next catch-up with her alter ego, Mary.

Chapter 16

When Lucy arrived home she found Meg in the kitchen.

'How's my grandfather? Any better?'

Meg shook her head.

''Fraid not. The doc's been back this afternoon and pre-scribed anti-biotics as he's running a temperature.'

'Oh, that's not good. He…he's not in any danger is he?' Lucy's heart contracted at the thought of losing him.

Meg shrugged, her face puckered in concern.

'I don't know. If the doc was really worried he'd have sent him to hospital, for sure. We have to see how he is in a day or two, I reckon. He's a fighter, is Gregory, and he's had more life in him since you've been here.' She gave Lucy a forced-looking smile. 'Let's be positive, eh?'

'Sure, but if he's so poorly, how come he's managing to eat?' She nodded at the chicken Meg was chopping.

'He's not so I'm making a broth to keep his strength up. I've prepared a pasta bake for you to pop in the oven when you're ready.'

'Thanks, I'll be down later.'

She went up to her room eager to connect with Mary. As she stood in front of the portrait, Lucy found it hard to avert her eyes from Thomas. He aroused her anger more than ever since she suspected he was once *her* husband and not simply Mary's. She told Mary she would shortly be ready to slip back to the next eventful time in her life. Again, an infinitesimal nod. Lying on her bed, Lucy breathed deeply and entered self-hypnosis.

* * *

'Jane! Come quickly, my pains have begun!' Mary doubled over as a vice-like pain ripped through her body, leaving her gasping for breath. She had been sewing a gown for the infant, not due for another two weeks, while Jane had gone to the bedroom for a shawl as the late November day drew in.

Jane rushed to her side, clutching the shawl. Mary gripped her hand, fear welling up inside her. All the horror tales of childbirth she had heard came rushing into her mind and she looked at Jane with wide, staring eyes.

'Don't worry, ma'am, I'll send for Mrs Sawyer directly, though it may be some hours yet before the little one makes an appearance.' Jane rang for a maid who was soon despatched for the midwife. Mary lay back against the sofa, trying to still her racing heart and mind. Although she had had months to prepare herself, it was still a shock to have her body overtaken with such pain without warning. Her pregnancy had been smooth, with little of the sickness experienced by others she had spoken with. Her nights were disturbed by the baby's kicks and frequent turning round, but she concluded it was a sign of his good health.

'Come, ma'am, let's make you comfortable in your bed and I'll make everything ready.'

Mary struggled to her feet with Jane's help and shuffled through to the bedroom. Her maid helped her undress down to her shift and wrapped a shawl around her shoulders. The pain had eased and she wondered if it was a false alarm, as she had heard it was not uncommon, particularly with the first child. On confiding this with Jane, her maid shook her head.

'No, ma'am, I saw my mother give birth enough times to know when the pains are for real. But there can be long stretches of time between them and you'll need to keep your strength up. I'll go and ask cook to prepare some broth for you and be as quick as I can.' After she left Mary felt the panic rising again and had to grip the sheets as she began taking deep breaths. For a moment Mary even thought of sending for her mother to give comfort and reassurance, but the memory of how she had kept quiet when she was forced into this marriage, stopped her. She would manage on her own, with Jane and Mrs Sawyer for support. And if she were to die, then at least she would be spared from her miserable marriage…

Jane burst into the room, carrying a tray with a large pitcher of water and a glass which she placed on the nightstand.

'Cook's preparing a pot of broth, ma'am, but I thought you might be glad of some water as well. Mrs Sawyer has sent a message to say she'll be here within the hour.' She poured Mary some water, which she drank greedily, her mouth dry from fear of what lay ahead. Some minutes later another pain gripped her belly and Mary cried out and she instinctively pulled her knees up, thrashing about on the bed. Sweat beaded on her forehead.

Jane soaked a cloth in water and eau de cologne and wiped Mary's face.

'There, ma'am, take deep breaths as I believe that can help with the pain. You're sure you don't want someone to fetch your mother? I know it's been a while –'

Clenching her teeth, Mary shook her head.

'No, I don't want her here.' She sank back on the bed, the pain slowly easing. Jane held the glass of water to her lips and she took a gulp. While Jane fussed about, fetching clean towels and sheets, Mary closed her eyes and let her mind drift to a happier time when she and Nathaniel had become engaged and life had appeared full of promise. They were both looking forward to having children and, in her innocence, Mary had pictured herself surrounded by adorable boys and girls hanging on her skirts. She had given little thought to the act of childbirth itself, having never witnessed anything more than a dog giving birth to puppies, seemingly without much trouble. Mrs Sawyer had hastened to dispel any romantic notions she may have had, advising her it would be painful. Mary's previous experience of bad pain had been the beating administered by Thomas and she could only hope childbirth would be no worse.

A noise at the door stopped her reflections and Mary was relieved by the arrival of the midwife. First divesting herself of a thick shawl, Mrs Sawyer, carrying a covered basket, approached the bed with a broad smile.

'Good day to you, ma'am. It seems your babe is impatient to be born. May I take a look?'

Mary nodded in agreement and the midwife pulled back the bedclothes just as a stream of liquid poured down Mary's thighs.

Blushing, Mary apologised, fearing she had lost control of her bladder.

Mrs Sawyer asked Jane for a towel before replying, 'Your waters have broken, Mrs Carre, nothing to be ashamed of. It means baby's getting ready to be born. Now, let's see…' She proceeded to prod and poke Mary before replacing the bedclothes and giving her a warm smile.

'Looks to me as if it won't be all that long, ma'am. Just a few more hours should see you delivered.'

A few more hours! Mary's heart sank, having hoped it would be much speedier.

'Do you have anything I can take to manage the pain, Mrs Sawyer? Laudanum or something similar?'

The midwife looked horrified.

'I'm sorry, ma'am, but laudanum would be dangerous for

the babe, although it would indeed greatly ease your pain. I do have a herbal tincture of my own, which includes willow-bark, known for the relief of pain and I have some with me.' She pointed to her basket.

'Then indeed I am willing to avail myself of such a remedy, thank you.'

Mrs Sawyer measured out a spoonful and Mary swallowed the bitter-tasting liquid with a grimace. Jane offered her a glass of water to wash it down and then went off to check if the broth was ready. Mary tried to make herself comfortable but the baby's movements made it difficult. Then she was once more gripped by pain only marginally less strong than before. She tried to stifle a cry but it was too much for her.

'Don't worry, ma'am, I'm used to the cries and groans of women in childbirth. You make as much noise as you need, it's to be expected. Remember, the Bible tells us women are to be punished for Eve leading Adam astray by suffering through childbirth.' The midwife rolled her eyes. 'Not that I agree with letting women suffer unnecessarily and we can keep topping up the tincture as needed.' She looked at the bedside clock, saying, 'I'll be noting the timing of the pains and keep checking progress down below to be ready.'

Mary nodded mutely as the pain began to ease. Perhaps it was better not to know how long the birth would take and simply try and cope as best she could. Jane arrived with the broth and Mary was grateful for the sustenance. It was delicious and, she suspected from the flavour, laced with Madeira. Catching Jane's eye, her maid winked.

'There be plenty more if you want, ma'am, Cook made a good pan full and can heat some up whenever you wish.'

'Thank you, it's very good of Cook.'

Mrs Sawyer now took out what looked like a part knitted jumper on circular needles from her basket and seeing Mary's quizzical look, said, 'I'm one of the women on the island who make the Guernsey jumpers favoured by sailors and fishermen. I've heard Admiral Nelson himself has requested his sailors be furnished with them and it's true we have been pressed to knit as many as we can. And with childbirth taking many hours, I have the time to knit many a garment.' She frowned. 'You would have no objection, ma'am? I assure you I shall remain vigilant to your welfare.'

'No, it's of no consequence. Indeed I am glad you could be helping valiant British sailors keep warm and dry while we await the arrival of my child.' Mary admired the woman's industriousness and the rhythmic clacking of the needles was soothing.

The next few hours passed in a blur of dozing punctured by bursts of pain across her back and stomach, helped somewhat by a combination of the Madeira laced broth and herbal tincture. At one point someone brought up the issue of informing her husband, but Mary said not to bother yet, knowing he was likely to be either drunk or with a prostitute, or both.

True to her word, Mrs Sawyer examined her at intervals, declaring all was progressing well, and administering further doses of tincture. Mary was by turns bored, although not wanting to undertake any distraction such as reading, and then bracing herself against the now more frequent pains. After enduring a particularly strong cramping pain, like an intense pressure down below, Mrs Sawyer examined her.

'Good, your body is ready now and it's time to start pushing. Take deep breaths and push down.'

Mary did as she was bid, willing to expel the baby from her womb. After pushing for what seemed hours, it was as if a boiling hot ball was being squeezed out of her and the midwife exclaimed, 'I can see the head! Not long now.'

Jane sent for hot water to be brought up and laid out the swaddling clothes in the crib standing ready for the new arrival. Mary continued to push and the feeling of intense stretching and burning below caused her to cry out. Leaning forward she saw the head appear and Mrs Sawyer eased the rest of the baby out.

'It's a girl!' cried the midwife as she wrapped a towel around the baby and handed her to Mary. Oh no! not the heir Thomas expected. But as she held the baby close and took hold of a miniature hand, she fell in love with her daughter regardless.

Mary was dozing later when she was woken by the door banging open and Thomas walked unsteadily towards the bed. The baby was wrapped in cloths and a blanket in the crib by her side and Mary was alone, the midwife had long departed and she had sent Jane away to rest.

'So, the brat's a girl, I've been told.' His flushed face loomed over her and she pulled the covers tight around her aching body. Thomas glanced briefly at the crib. ''Tis a pity for us both, wife, as it seems we will have to try again. I must have a son next time, do you hear?'

'Yes, Thomas, I hear you.'

Chapter 17

When Lucy opened her eyes she looked for the crib. It wasn't there. Panic. Where was her baby? She had just given birth – a girl – Amber. The memory of the birth was so vivid, but something was wrong – it wasn't her baby, was it? It was Mary's. Lucy lay back, drained as the memories swirled around in her head. Touching her body all felt as it should. But the memory of holding a baby girl had triggered another memory as tears fell. After a long and painful labour, supported by an anxious Hamish, she had been handed her daughter and experienced an intense emotion. Unconditional love. It was the happiest moment of her life. As it had been for Mary. For them both. They were entwined, connected. Sharing more than blood. Sharing a soul, a spirit. Lucy hugged her body, rocking back and forth on the bed as she cried. Tears for Mary. For herself. For Amber.

Eventually, exhausted, she stumbled to the bathroom for a glass of water. She drank greedily before catching her reflection in the mirror. Only there were two faces. Hers and Mary's. She blinked and they became one. Shivering, she filled the glass again and then went back into the bedroom to stand in front of the portrait. As she watched, Mary appeared to step down and come towards her, an arm outstretched. Lucy instinctively lifted her right arm and for a brief moment their hands touched. She felt a fizz like static electricity flow into her hand and then Mary was gone. Looking up at the portrait, she saw Mary nod.

Lucy slumped into a chair while she tried to make sense of it all. It wasn't possible. Yet it was. The air in the bedroom was suffused with Mary's perfume, mixed with the smell of blood of childbirth. Glancing at her watch she was amazed to see less than an hour had elapsed since she had gone into self-hypnosis and slipped back more than two hundred years. So much had happened…Getting out her notebook she settled down to write a full account of all she remembered. She couldn't help smiling at the idea of what anyone finding it sometime in the future might think. A pity she wasn't a novelist! Ah, but she knew someone who was. Maybe Jeanne could turn fact into fiction one day?

The following morning Lucy woke feeling energised, as if ready for a new start. She didn't know why this should be, but was happy to accept this shift in mood.

'Good morning, Meg,' she said brightly, as she entered the kitchen. Meg turned round, her expression serious.

'Morning, though I'm not sure as it's so good. Gregory had a bad night and the doc's with him now. I'm making him some tea and toast but not sure he'll be wanting anything.'

Lucy's stomach turned to lead as she pictured her grandfather struggling to stay alive upstairs.

'He…he's worse?'

'We won't know till the doc's seen him, but he's not getting any better, that's for sure.' Meg must have registered the shock on Lucy's face as she came and patted her arm, saying, 'But he's a fighter, so let's not worry too much yet, eh? What can I get you for breakfast? The usual fry up?'

'I'm not hungry, thanks. I'll make some toast and coffee.' All her earlier good feelings dissipated, together with her appetite.

'Coffee's made, just help yourself while I go upstairs.'

After Meg left she poured a large mug of coffee and

put two slices of bread in the toaster. While Lucy sipped her drink her thoughts were willing her grandfather to get better. She needed him. Selfish, she knew, but she also didn't think Gregory was ready to let go of life yet. He'd as good as said so, hadn't he? She buttered the toast as if in a trance and had eaten a slice before realising she'd forgotten the marmalade. She was spreading a thick layer on the second slice when Meg returned.

'The doc wants to have a word with you, he's in the hall now.' Her face gave nothing away and Lucy went out to meet him. A tall, slim man in his early forties, she guessed, he smiled and shook her hand.

'Mrs Stewart? Ben Tostevin, glad to meet you. I understand you're Mr Carre's closest relative here now?'

'Yes, I am. How is my grandfather?'

'Not too good, I'm afraid, it's developed into pneumonia, which I was afraid might happen.'

She gasped. 'Oh, no.'

'Only mild at the moment, though, and I've added another antibiotic and hope it will do the trick. To be honest, the next twenty-four hours are crucial as to whether he will get worse or begin to recover, which is why I wanted to talk to you. The carers can only stay for short periods as they have other patients, so I was wondering if you could stay with him to plug the gap? The housekeeper's offered to help out, but I know she has her husband to think of.'

'Of course I'll stay with him, though I'm not medically trained –'

'Not a problem, you can call the surgery anytime if you're worried about anything and someone could nip round. Handy being so close.' She nodded, the surgery was merely doors away. 'And I only live in Brock Road if you need me, also handy.' Lucy nodded as he handed her his card. 'Of course, the carers will be in as usual. I'm expecting your grandfather to sleep most of the time as I've given him strong painkillers, but to be on the safe side it's best he isn't alone.'

'I understand. Shall I go up now?'

'No, the carer's here for a while yet. I suggest you go up just before she leaves and she can explain anything you need to know. Is that okay? I'll call back this evening unless I hear from you before.'

'Fine, Doctor. Thank you.' She saw him out and returned to the kitchen to find Meg had made her fresh toast spread with butter and marmalade.

'Thanks, Meg. I'll be staying with Grandpa today once I've finished my breakfast.'

'Good girl. I'll make a flask of coffee for you and there are biscuits in the tin. And if you want something to read, your mother left a good selection of paperbacks in the sitting room.'

'Good idea, I'll take a look, thanks.' As Lucy chewed her toast she was both nervous and hopeful. She'd never had the care of a seriously sick person before and hoped she was up to the task. But the doctor seemed to think Gregory stood a chance of recovery and she wanted to do all she could to help. Finishing her toast, she went to the sitting room and scanned the shelves of books. Picking out an Erica James and a Nora Roberts, nothing too heavy or dark, unlike some of the gory crime her mother seemed to enjoy, Lucy made her way upstairs and knocked on Gregory's bedroom door. The carer, middle-aged with a cheerful smile, ushered her in and then explained she was only expected to sit near Gregory's bed and watch for any signs of distress or increase in temperature. He was allowed fluids if he needed them, but for the moment no solids. Lucy moved over to the bed where her grandfather appeared to be asleep and she heard his laboured breathing. Her heart contracted as she noted his pallor and how much thinner he seemed clad only in pyjamas.

As the woman left, Lucy settled in the armchair placed by the head of the bed. The bedside table held an array of medicines, tissues, glasses, a mobile phone, a jug of water and the flask of coffee and tin of biscuits as promised by Meg. She reached for his hand, resting on the bedcover, feeling the warm, paper-thin skin under her fingers. He didn't respond to her touch and, wanting him to know he wasn't alone, she said, 'Grandpa, it's Lucy. I love you and want you to get well quickly or I might be forced to ask my parents to return from their cruise. And we wouldn't want that, would we?' She then prattled on about going to the gym and meeting a nice man called Sam and how much more relaxed she felt about Hamish and his new relationship.

Mentioning Sam reminded her he was facing the loss of someone close and she hoped he was coping all right. Then, on the assumption Gregory probably wouldn't remember what she said even if he heard her, Lucy told him she was dreaming a lot about Mary, as if she had gone back in time and what an experience it was, without sharing any details. Gregory continued to lie there unresponsive so after sending up a heartfelt prayer for his recovery, she began reading a book while keeping a hand on his when possible.

Absorbed in the story, the time slid by broken only when she poured a cup of coffee and grabbed some biscuits. She stretched her legs while drinking the coffee, taking a turn around the room. Similar to the adjacent sitting room the light coloured walls were hung with local coastal scenes and the room was filled with antique mahogany furniture which seemed familiar. Definitely Georgian. Puzzled, Lucy stared at the matching dressing table, chest of drawers and chairs. Then it came to her, they had been in Mary's bedroom. As she trailed her fingers across the top of the chest a slight frisson brought her out in goose-bumps. Snatching her hand away she returned to the bedside, wanting to escape the past and focus on Gregory. As she sat down he became restless, his head tossing from side to side and a jumble of incoherent words fell from his lips.

'Hi, Grandpa, it's me, Lucy. Do you need anything?' She stroked his head, noting the beads of sweat on his forehead. Panic rose up inside her. What should she do? Then Gregory opened his eyes, blinking.

'Lucy? It is you, I thought…was dreaming…heard your voice…telling me…Hamish and…Mary…your dreams.' His voice was croaky and she leaned closer to hear him.

'I've been here all morning, as you've not been well. Would you like some water?' He nodded and she managed to prop up his head and hold a glass to his lips.

'Thank you, my dear. I'm so tired, think…sleep.' He closed his eyes and she eased his head back on the pillow. She found a damp flannel and mopped his brow. Holding her breath, she waited to see if he settled. Although wheezy, Gregory's breathing slowed and he seemed to be asleep. Lucy let out a deep breath as she clutched his hand, wondering how much he had heard and would remember.

Another hour passed and Lucy's stomach was rumbling when Meg entered with a tray of bread and soup. After asking after Gregory she asked if Lucy needed anything else and when she said no Meg left, saying she would be back at supper time.

During the afternoon Gregory had more periods of restlessness but never quite woke up and Lucy wiped his face with a cool flannel when needed. The book kept her mind occupied and it was six o'clock before she knew it and Meg appeared with her supper.

'I'll sit with him while you go and eat in his sitting room. The doc phoned to say he'll be round in an hour. So have a little break.'

Lucy stood and stretched her back, aching from sitting too long. Something she wasn't used to. She thanked Meg and took the tray next door and sat at the table in the window. The view of the garden, embracing spring with open arms as bushes and trees burst into colour with a mix of flowers and blossom, was a much needed change from Gregory's sick bed. She was surprisingly hungry after doing so little all day and soon tucked into the pork tenderloin with new potatoes and fresh vegetables. A slice of apple tart and Guernsey cream made a perfect finish to the meal and Lucy returned to the bedroom feeling full and ready for the night ahead.

'Thanks, Meg, the meal was delicious. Are you going home now?'

Meg frowned.

'Are you sure you can cope through the night? I could stay a bit longer, give you a chance for a nap.'

'I'll be fine, honest. It's not as if I have to do anything for Grandpa, is it? The carer's in later to do what's needed. I'd be glad of another flask of coffee, though, if it's no trouble.' She smiled at Meg, wanting to reassure her, who had enough on her plate whereas she, well she hadn't got much at all.

'All right then, I'll make a fresh flask of coffee and some sandwiches in case you're peckish later.' She huffed, 'I know from experience how hungry you can be during a night without sleep.'

Lucy couldn't envision wanting any more food after her lovely supper, but wasn't going to argue. After Meg left she sat by her grandfather who was still restless in his sleep. She kissed his hand and then held it between her own as she told him she would be there for him all night. She felt a twang of guilt for not informing her parents, but reasoned they must be in the Far East by now and at least two flights away so what was the point? Anyway, he was going to recover so no harm done.

She heard the front door bell ring and moments later Meg arrived with Doctor Tostevin.

Lucy described how Gregory had been and the doctor examined him.

'Although his chest is still rattling, I think he's slightly better. His temperature's down a little, which is good news. I'll give him another dose of the anti-biotic and hopefully he'll continue to improve.'

'Thanks, Doctor. What do I need to look out for tonight?'

'We don't want the fever or the chest pain to get worse. If it does, call me and it will probably mean he has to go into hospital. Which he's told me he doesn't want, so...' he shrugged. 'Let's hope it doesn't come to it.'

She sent up a silent prayer for her grandfather and Meg escorted the doctor out. Twenty minutes later she was back bearing a flask of coffee and a plate of cling-filmed sandwiches.

'Thanks, Meg, but please go home now and try and relax. You've been great.' Lucy gave her a quick hug, causing Meg to blush.

'Try and grab some sleep when you can. Here,' she said, pulling a pillow and duvet out of a cupboard, 'and I'll be back first thing in the morning. Good night.'

Lucy settled back in the chair, planning to try and rest after the carer had been, assuming her grandfather was peaceful. For the moment he was restless and she again took his hand to reassure him of her presence. By the time the carer arrived at nine, she was struggling to stay awake. She left her to attend to Gregory and took the flask of coffee next door for a few minutes break. Standing by the window she gazed at the night sky illuminated by a full moon and pinpoints of stars. The darkness over Town was broken up by pockets of light from buildings and street lamps. It was magical. As Lucy drank her coffee she couldn't help contrasting the beauty without with the suffering within. Her poor grandfather.

The carer appeared at the door. 'Hi, Lucy, I've finished and you can come back in.'

She swallowed the rest of her drink and followed her

into the bedroom. The woman had sponge washed Gregory and changed his pyjamas and he looked more comfortable, if still restless. They exchanged goodnights and Lucy regained her position in the armchair, propping her head against the pillow and snuggling under the duvet. Minutes later she was asleep.

'Lucy! Are you awake?'

The voice, little more than a whisper, stirred her from a deep sleep. Sitting up she rubbed her eyes and saw Gregory blinking at her. The bedside clock showed it was four in the morning.

She smiled and reached for his hand.

'Morning, Grandpa. How are you feeling?'

'Better, thank you. How long have you been here?'

She explained why she was there and about the doctor and medication and was relieved to notice his chest no longer rattled.

'It's been a bit of a blur to me. I remember having a cough which became worse and the doctor turned up looking concerned. Said something about hospital but I told him if I was going to die, I wanted to die in my own bed.' He smiled at her, adding, 'But it appears I'm not dying yet.'

'No, thank goodness! But I expect you still need to rest and you must drink plenty of water. Here, I'll pour you a glass.' Her hand shook a little as she held the glass to his lips, hardly daring to believe he was no longer in danger. But his skin was no longer clammy and his eyes had regained some of their sparkle.

'I'm very grateful to you for keeping watch over this old wreck, my dear, but I do think you should go to bed and get some sleep, as I plan to. I promise not to have a relapse while you're resting,' he said, dryly.

Lucy chewed her lip, not wanting to leave him even though he was clearly loads better, but also tempted by the thought of her own bed. Seeing his mobile gave her an idea.

'Okay, I'll go as long as you agree to ring me if you need anything.'

'Agreed. Now off you go and I'll see you later.'

She dropped a kiss on his forehead and left. Once in her room she threw off her clothes and climbed into bed, praying Gregory really was better or she wouldn't forgive herself.

Chapter 18

Waking with a start, Lucy was shocked to see the clock registering ten past eleven. Grandpa! Was he all right? After a quick shower, dressed in jeans and a sweater, she hurried along the passage to his bedroom and knocked. Answered by a croaky "come in", she was relieved to see him sitting up in bed reading the paper. Gregory's clear eyes and better colour confirmed his recovery.

'Morning, Grandpa, sorry I overslept. You're looking tons better, how do you feel?' She bent to kiss his cheek.

'Good morning, my dear. Meg and I weren't expecting you to surface for a while yet and she didn't want to disturb you.' He put down the paper and patted her hand. 'I'm feeling quite well, thank you, and the doctor's been and told me to finish the course of anti-biotics before he considers me fully recovered.'

'Brilliant. So you don't need babysitting anymore?' Lucy said, grinning.

'Ha! Don't be cheeky, young lady.' His eyes glittered. 'However, I do appreciate you keeping watch yesterday and no, you don't need to "babysit" any more. If you're around, by all means pop in and see if I need anything or for a chat.'

'Of course I will. I plan to go to the gym after lunch but otherwise will be here. Anything I can get you now before I go down for my breakfast?'

'No, I'm fine, thanks.' He hesitated. 'There is something

puzzling me, though. I seem to remember you talking to me while I was ill, and you mentioned Mary. Something about dreaming you were her, almost as if you were reliving her life. Did I imagine it?'

'No, I did talk about some vivid dreams I've been having, which appeared to be centred on Mary and Thomas. A bit surreal, but I've put it down to my fascination with Mary and what happened to her.' Caught on the hop, she didn't like lying, but could hardly tell him the truth, could she? He might have her sectioned.

'I see. Well, if your dreams do tell you what happened to our ancestor, please tell me, won't you? I don't like unsolved mysteries.' Gregory's eyes seemed to bore into hers and she felt the heat rise in her face. What exactly had she said when she thought he was unconscious?

'Sure, Grandpa. See you later.' She gave him a kiss and ran downstairs, suddenly feeling in need of food and coffee. In the kitchen she set up the toaster and coffee machine, drumming her fingers on the worktop while waiting. Her thoughts turned to Mary and what she might discover when she next slipped back. If Gregory continued to improve, she might do some time travelling that evening.

After lunch, spent with Gregory, Lucy collected her gym kit and set off for Kings. The warmth and brightness of the sun took her by surprise after spending so long indoors and as she stood in the drive she took lungfuls of air before striding along Queen's Road. By the time she reached the entrance to the club, her stomach was fluttering in anticipation at the possibility of seeing Sam again.

There were only a couple of people in the gym when she entered and, disappointed Sam wasn't there, she began her usual stretching exercises.

'Hi, Lucy, how are you?'

She turned to see a pale-faced Sam standing behind her and, instinctively, she wanted to hug him. He looked like a lost little boy rather than the confident, fit club manager she knew. Restraining herself, she said, 'I'm okay thanks. But what about you? I understand someone's been ill?'

His eyes clouded.

'Yes, my mother. She…she was in recovery from breast cancer, but started getting headaches and feeling dizzy a couple of weeks ago.' He drew a deep breath. 'She had a scan and…it showed several tumours, inoperable.' Rubbing his chin, he went on, 'it's all happened so fast. Mum collapsed last week and…died two days ago. I've been spending time by her bedside with Dad.' Tears glistened in his eyes and Lucy's heart went out to him.

'Oh, Sam, I'm so sorry. How awful for you and your family. If there's anything I can do…' she said, briefly touching his arm. But what could anyone do at such a time, she asked herself, knowing only too well he alone could deal with his pain.

'Thank you, it's been tough and will continue being tough, but life goes on and I'm glad to be back at work and keeping busy. And it's good to see you've been coming almost every day now.' He smiled, but it didn't quite mask his pain. They then spent a few minutes discussing her progress with Sam suggesting some minor changes to her programme. As he was about to move on, he hesitated, saying, 'I'm due a break in an hour, how about joining me for a drink in the café? If you haven't got to rush off anywhere.' The same tentative smile.

'Yes, I'd like to, thanks. Will meet you there later.' Her answering smile was warm.

'Great. Look forward to it.' He nodded and moved off to check on someone struggling with a rowing machine.

Lucy was left feeling sad for Sam and his loss, but pleased he wanted to spend time with her, if only for a very public coffee. It definitely wouldn't be appropriate to mention her newly-single status now, but at least they were still friends.

An hour later, showered and changed, she spotted him at a window table in the café and headed over. After asking what she wanted, he went to the bar and ordered her a coffee. Back at the table there was a momentary awkwardness as neither knew what to say.

'Are you settling back into life in Guernsey? Must be strange after London.' Sam broke the silence.

'Yes, I am. I've been in touch with old friends…' she went on to tell him about Natalie and Jeanne and how she was feeling more at home. 'I loved the buzz of London, but seems like the right time to start afresh. And after all, London's only a hop and a skip away if I need some of its buzz again.'

He nodded and she caught him glancing at her left hand before taking another sip of his drink.

'What about you? Planning to spend the rest of your life here?'

'Yes, for sure. Never been tempted to move away for longer than uni and holidays. My brother left years ago, for a high-flying career in Hong Kong and we've almost lost touch. He'll be back for the funeral, I guess.' Sam took a deep breath. 'And now…well, I need to be here for my dad as he's pretty lost without Mum. She always took care of everything, don't think he even knows how to boil an egg,' he said, his face pinched with pain.

'I'm sure it'll be hard for all your family. Look, you don't have to talk now if you don't want to, but I'm happy to listen any time you wish. I…I know how hard it is to lose a loved one suddenly and…how important it is to talk with some-one.' The words simply came out, with no thought. Was she really able to listen calmly if Sam needed to offload? Wasn't it too soon? Her own grief was still raw. As the thoughts tumbled through her head, Lucy reminded herself she only needed to listen, not tell him how to cope.

'I'm not ready to talk about it now, but thanks, I might take you up on your kind offer sometime. Coming from a mainly male family, I'm not used to sharing my feelings.' He smiled, and this time it did reach his eyes.

'That's okay, my husband found it hard to share as well.'

Sam seemed about to say something when his phone beeped. Looking at the screen he sighed and said, 'Sorry, I have to go. Might see you tomorrow?' He swallowed the last of his coffee and stood.

'Yes, I'll be in after lunch. Look after yourself, won't you?'

'Will do. Bye.'

After he had gone Lucy sat for a few minutes mulling over their conversation before grabbing her gym bag and leaving. Time to check on her grandfather.

After spending half an hour with a still tired Gregory, Lucy went to her room and was drawn like a magnet to the portrait.

'Shall we re-connect, Mary?' she whispered.

A voice in her head said 'yes'. Lucy made herself comfortable on the bed and closed her eyes.

* * *

Pain ripped through her belly as a voice shouted, 'Push! I can see baby's head!' Opening her eyes she saw Mrs Sawyer at the end of the bed and Jane hovering nearby. Exhausted and soaked with sweat, she summoned all her strength to push, clenching her teeth against the pain.

'Well done, Mrs Carre! Nearly there, another push should do it.'

Taking a deep breath, Mary pushed as the baby was gently guided by the midwife. Burning pain caused her to cry out and then she heard the welcome words.

'It's a boy! A beautiful, healthy boy, with strong lungs!' His cries rang out, filling the bedroom.

She collapsed back against the pillows while Jane wiped her face and Mrs Sawyer, after wrapping her son in a clean blanket, passed him to her.

'There, ma'am, a little brother for Miss Georgina to pet,' Jane remarked, with a wide smile.

Mary nodded, elation robbing her of speech. A son and heir to please Thomas, and now she could be left in peace to enjoy her children. No more having to endure her husband's unwelcome visits to her bed and the violent love-making. She kissed the baby's face before allowing the midwife to bathe and dress him in one of the white gowns she had sewn as part of the layette.

'There you are, Mrs Carre, time to suckle him to save our ears!' Mrs Sawyer grinned as she placed him in her arms. 'Has your husband been informed the birth was imminent?'

'No, he's away at sea, having urgent business in Cornwall, I believe.' Mary helped her son take her nipple in his mouth and experienced the slightly painful pull in her stomach as he sucked. It reminded her of when she had first started suckling Georgina, two years before. It made up for all the pain she had endured during the birth.

'He will no doubt be pleased to find you have borne him a son, ma'am. Do you have a name for him?' The midwife was engaged in dealing with the afterbirth and Mary averted her eyes. Not only was childbirth painful, it was messy and undignified in the extreme and she was glad to know this was the last time for her.

'He is to be called Henry, after his grandfather, who had this house built not long before he died.' She would have preferred him to be named after his late uncle, Nathaniel, but Thomas wouldn't hear of it. In fact he had become particularly angry at her suggestion, warning her not to mention Nathaniel's name again. She had assumed Thomas was still jealous of his older brother and her love for him, but thought it mean-spirited of him.

'A good manly name, is Henry. And how lucky he is to be born into such a family, ma'am. A bright future lies ahead, no doubt.'

'Yes indeed.' Mary stroked the thick, dark hair on the baby's head as he fell asleep on her breast. His future was assured as the heir to a thriving merchant's business, but what lay ahead for her beloved daughter? She couldn't bear it if she was one day to be "sold" in marriage as she had been.

'Jane, please ask Nurse to bring Miss Georgina to see her new brother.' Mrs Sawyer had completed her ministrations and with the bedding refreshed, there was nothing to indicate to her daughter how painful and messy childbirth was. Mary determined to shelter Georgina from the less pleasant aspects of being a female as long as possible.

'Mama! Mama!' A curly-mopped girl dressed in layers of cotton and lace hurled into the room followed by a harassed looking nurse calling, 'Miss Georgina, slow down!'

The girl came to an abrupt halt as she arrived by Mary's side, gazing warily at the baby asleep at her breast. She stuck her thumb in her mouth, looking from her mother to the baby.

'Georgina, this is Henry, your new brother. He's very small and I need you to help Nurse look after him for me, like you do with your dolls. Can you do that?'

'Yes, Mama. Me hold him?'

'No, not now. But you may stroke his head if you're gentle.'

Mrs Sawyer beamed as she watched Georgina slowly stroke her brother's head.

'What a sweet child, Mrs Carre, it's good to see how she's grown these past two years. She favours you, I see, in both looks and nature.'

'Thank you, she is indeed a good child.' Mary's heart was

filled with love at the sight of her two children together and knew she could bear anything which might happen to her as long as she had them. Children's lives were precarious, even those from wealthy families were subject to disease and illness with little help offered by even the best doctors. A busy harbour such as St Peter Port attracted ships from as far away as the Americas or India, bringing disease-carrying sailors and rats into the island. She vowed to keep her children as safe as possible.

Once Mrs Sawyer had left, Nurse took Georgina off to be made ready for bed and Jane helped Mary settle the sleeping Henry in his crib by her bedside. Exhaustion now caught up with her and she soon fell asleep.

The next two days passed in a blur of feeding the baby, feeding herself and sleeping when she could. Even when she had regained her strength, Mary was obliged to stay in bed for the requisite few weeks advised for new mothers, as she had after giving birth to Georgina. In some ways it was a relief to be detached from the goings on of the household and the world outside, although she was happy to see friends who came to admire Henry. With Thomas away, the atmosphere in the house was much lighter.

And then he returned.

It was Jane who alerted her, rushing into her room one morning looking flustered and bearing a jug of hot water

'The master's ship has just docked, ma'am, and word sent up to say he'll be home shortly. Shall I help with your toilette?'

Mary, not long awake after a night of feeds, gasped. Dishevelled and wearing a milk-stained chemise, she swung her legs out of bed and washed herself as Jane fetched a clean chemise and a shawl. Once dressed and with her hair brushed, Mary returned to bed to await her husband.

He would no doubt be impatient to meet his son and she wanted and needed to look her best in order to avoid criticism. Henry was sound asleep and his cheeks bore the slight rosy flush of good health. For a moment Mary considered sending for Georgina, but decided Thomas would likely ignore her as was his wont. To him girls were an expense and only of interest when of an age to be married, ideally forming an alliance beneficial to his business.

The door burst open without a warning knock, and Thomas strode in, bearing the salty tang of the sea mixed with sweat on his clothes and hair. His eyes gleamed with excitement as he approached the crib.

'So, wife, you have borne me a son? Good news for us both, do you not agree?' He peered down at Henry before glancing in her direction.

'It is indeed, Thomas, and happily he is thriving.' Mary contrived to remain calm and not betray her disgust at his lack of consideration for her in not bothering to change his damp, smelly clothes. She could only hope he did not want to hold Henry. 'And was your trip successful? You have been away longer than you expected.'

Thomas threw himself into a chair, a satisfied smirk on his face.

'I had gone to visit my agent and banker, a Zephaniah Job from Polperro. My father engaged him to manage our Cornish affairs some years ago and I deemed it useful if we met. It proved such an interesting diversion I was persuaded to stay longer than planned. I had no idea Cornwall possessed so many delights.' The smirk broadened.

She knew full well what he meant but did not care. From now on her only concern was her children.

'Well, I must be off. My friends will be expecting me to celebrate the birth of my son and heir and I must not disappoint. I will leave you to take good care of him.' As if an afterthought, he tossed a velvet bag to her. 'In payment for giving me a son.' Thomas rose and, after another peek at the baby, left as quickly as he had arrived.

Mary heaved a sigh of relief, glad to be rid of his presence. She opened the bag to find a ruby and diamond necklace and matching earrings. A generous "payment" indeed, and perhaps she should wear them at least once to avoid his anger. Thomas would probably drink himself into a stupor and need carrying home as had happened on numerous occasions. It turned out to be nearly three days before he returned, according to Jane, and then he took to his bed for more than a day. Mary thought it a shame he had returned at all.

Chapter 19

Lucy slowly opened her eyes, looking for the crib by the bed as the sound of Henry's cries echoed in her ears. Gazing around the room she took in the modern furniture and fitted carpet and for a moment was totally nonplussed. Memories flooded her brain. Holding Henry in her arms for the first time. Cuddling her daughter Georgina. Except they were not *her* children, they were Mary's. She remembered the smell of the room, a mix of blood, soap and Mary's perfume, Lily of the Valley. The semi-painful feel of the baby sucking her breast. Thomas returned from his nefarious trip, exuding an almost overpowering smell of sweat and unwashed body in his eagerness to see his son, but showing no interest in his wife. Except for the "payment" for her trouble.

Lucy groaned and shook her head, trying to draw back from the other reality. She must have been gone for days… Reaching for her mobile it was a relief to see the same date, only half an hour later. Would this be the norm now? Would she slip back for days – even weeks – at a time? Her head spun at the thought and thirst sent her to the bathroom for water. Back in the bedroom she forced herself to write everything down in her notebook, a lump in her throat as she described Georgina, imagining how Amber would have looked at the same age.

Closing the notebook, Lucy spent some moments thinking about Mary and how powerless she was, married to the loathsome Thomas, with no chance of happiness with another man. At least she, Lucy, had the chance of finding love again. It occurred to her if Mary was indeed a previous incarnation of herself, maybe she still carried around remnants of her life. Would this be influencing her life now? If so, in what way? The thoughts made her head ache and, needing to shake them off, headed into the shower allowing the hot water to wash away the residues of the past. Once dressed she went down to the kitchen to find Meg preparing supper.

'You're looking a little peaky, Lucy. Not coming down with anything I hope?' Meg frowned as she peeled the potatoes.

'No, I'm fine, just a bit tired after my session in the gym. Have you checked on my grandfather?' She switched the kettle on to make a pot of tea.

'Yes, he's improving by the hour and suggests you join him for supper if you've no other plans.'

'I'd love to, it's good to see him being more his old self. And what delights are you cooking up for us tonight?' Lucy made the tea and poured it into two mugs, passing one to Meg.

'Thanks. Pork chops and mash potatoes, as requested by Gregory. Always been one of his favourites, it has. Then sticky toffee pudding for afters, which shows his appetite's improving,' Meg chuckled. 'Why don't you go and keep him company now, and I'll be up with the supper later. Take a bottle of his favourite wine.' She nodded towards the wine rack.

'Are you sure he's allowed wine? He's been so ill…'

'Don't worry, the doc's said a small glass won't do him any harm. Off you go now.'

Lucy opened the bottle and collected a couple of glasses before going upstairs. Perhaps wine would do her some good as well. Gregory was propped up in bed engrossed in a book but put it down when he saw her and smiled.

'You come bearing gifts, I see. Well done. I've missed the old vino, acts like a tonic at my age. So I told the doctor and he was wise enough not to argue with me.'

'You're only allowed a small glass, Grandpa, so don't get too excited.' Passing him a half-full glass, she asked how he was.

'Much better, my dear, thank you. I'll definitely be up tomorrow and can't wait to look out at my garden again.' He took a small sip and licked his lips appreciatively. She sat down with her own glass, pleased to see him perking up.

'And what have you been doing this afternoon? Did you go to the gym?'

'Yes, I miss it if I don't go. I'd forgotten how important it was in my life and how good I used to feel after a workout. Thanks for giving me the nudge, it's made a big difference.' Aware it wasn't solely the exercise that was responsible for her improved mood, she thought it too soon to mention Sam. And she certainly couldn't mention the time spent as her alter ego, Mary. Lucy swiftly changed the focus back onto Gregory and they enjoyed a pleasant conversation while waiting for Meg to arrive with their supper. By the time they finished eating she could see Gregory was growing tired so after wishing him goodnight she took the empty plates and dishes back to the kitchen and loaded them into the dishwasher. She finished the bottle of wine while watching television and then went to bed, yawning her head off. It had been quite a day.

The next few days followed a similar pattern of Lucy spending more time with Gregory and only leaving the house to go to Kings. She and Sam exchanged greetings but he didn't seem to want a proper chat, which was fine. She knew how grief can make people withdraw into themselves. There was no rush. Natalie rang one evening to see how she was and

Lucy explained her grandfather had not been well and she wasn't going out much for the moment.

'Sorry to hear that, hope he gets well soon. We'd love you to come round again when you can. How're things with your ghost. Mary wasn't it?'

Lucy described the outline of her time-slips, punctuated by oohs and gasps from Natalie.

'My, this is absolutely incredible. Wasn't it scary going back into someone else's life? Not knowing what to expect?'

'The first time, yes, as it was unexpected. After that, I was better prepared though some of the experiences were pretty horrible. I could wish poor Mary had been happier, but then she wouldn't have drawn me into her life, I guess.'

'True, like my poor ghost, Olive.' There was a pause. 'You know, we should suggest Jeanne writes a book or books about our experiences one day. Changing the names of course!'

Lucy giggled. 'It's crossed my mind, too. She might have to fictionalise it, though. Who would believe it was real?'

'Oh, I don't know. Guerns have always been fascinated by the supernatural and it's not long since some locals actually believed in faeries and witches. Our stories are tame in comparison.'

By the time they had finished chatting Lucy's thoughts were turning towards Mary. She had made no attempt to connect with her over the past days, needing to reassert her own space. Her own self. But now, after talking to Natalie, she was ready to go back. At least she knew Mary had no more children so thank goodness she wouldn't have to endure another childbirth! There was time before bed for some time-slipping so she switched off the paused television drama which she'd been watching but not enjoying, and went upstairs.

Standing in front of the portrait Lucy found herself drawn to Thomas's face. It was a good likeness and the artist had also captured his personality in the icy blue of the eyes and the curled thin lips. He was as cruel and as arrogant as he looked, as she well knew. The last time she saw him Thomas had displayed the effects of his louche lifestyle; the wine-flushed cheeks, red-rimmed eyes and a thickening belly. The family tree noted his death in 1823, a mere forty-five years old. Not surprising, she thought. The lack of a date of death for Mary was puzzling. Was it connected to the rumours concerning her fate? Lucy switched her gaze to Mary and the heavy sadness in her eyes bore down on her like a stone.

'I'm ready to come back, Mary. Choose the next significant time you wish me to share.'

An imperceptible nod.

* * *

'Good morning, children, come and give your mama a hug.' Mary opened her arms wide as Georgina, looking, she thought, particularly grown-up for a four-year-old in a pale green sprigged silk dress, an exact copy of her own, ran to her. It delighted her to see Georgina, with her dark curls and eyes, look so like herself as a child. Two-year-old Henry, the image of his father with pale blue eyes and thin lips, followed behind, a finger in his mouth as was his wont. Mary embraced them both with equal fervour but in her heart she loved her daughter more. She had caught Henry on more than one occasion pinching his sister and pulling hair from her doll's head.

Mary sighed. He was his father's son.

'I have a surprise for you today, my loves. Nurse and Jane are taking you to the Midsummer Day celebrations at the Fair Field in Câtel and there will be much to enjoy, I'm sure. You are to have a picnic and Cook has included your favourites, with pies, jellies, cake and lemonade.'

'Are you not coming with us, Mama?' Georgina pulled at her sleeve.

'No, not today. My head cold is worse and I must rest. I shall look forward to you telling me all about it when you return. Now, kiss me goodbye and go with Nurse to get ready.' The children kissed her cheek and she watched them follow Nurse out of her bedroom.

'Are you sure you will be all right, ma'am? With you letting everyone have the morning off to enjoy the festivities, I don't feel I should leave you alone.' Jane stood frowning by the bed.

'It's only a head cold and all I need is rest and complete quiet. And with an empty house, this I shall have. Go and have fun with the children, Jane. But before you leave can you please bring Storm to me? He will be comfort enough while you are all out.'

Jane bobbed a curtsy and left.

Mary settled back against the pillows, wishing she was well enough to join her children on what promised to be a fun and sunny day. However, her head was pounding and a blocked nose was most uncomfortable. Jane had prepared a powder for her earlier and she trusted it would soon ease her discomfort. It was fortunate Thomas was away on one of his sea trips as he would not have countenanced giving all the staff time off today. He was a harsh master as well as husband and Mary wanted to show those who worked hard for them she at least appreciated them. Jarvis had been hard to persuade, feeling at least someone should have been left in the house, but she had pointed out there might not be another opportunity for all the staff to spend some free time together and he had relented.

'Here you are, ma'am, I found him in the kitchen with a large bone Cook had tossed him. Had to put him on the leash to get him away from it,' Jane said, pulling a reluctant Storm into the room.

'Come on, boy, jump up and keep me company. Thank you, Jane.'

Mary held out a biscuit and Storm leaped on the bed to take it, his leash trailing behind him. She chuckled, saying, 'So, you're happy to see me now I have biscuits!' As she caressed his silky fur the pain in her head began to ease and she became drowsy. Her eyes closed.

Some minutes later, stifling a yawn, Mary opened her eyes. She must have slept, the small carriage clock by the bed showing it was some minutes after ten o'clock. The household had left soon after nine. Storm was nowhere to be seen and she noticed the door was ajar. Muttering to herself about who had not shut the door properly, Mary pulled on a robe and, pushing her feet into slippers, left to look for her dog.

'Storm! Storm! Where are you, boy?' After checking all the doors on the floor were closed, she went downstairs, thinking he would probably have headed for the kitchen and food. She continued calling his name while checking the occasional room with an open door. No sign of him. The back corridor led to the kitchen and pantry but the doors were shut. Beginning to worry, she hesitated. Where could he have got to? It was then she noticed the door to the cellars, normally locked, was ajar. Opening it wider, she called out 'Storm!' and a faint answering bark confirmed he was down there. Needing a light she went into the kitchen for an oil lamp which she lit from the range. Retracing her steps to the cellar door she again called Storm, hoping he would come to her, but his bark was fainter still.

Clutching her robe and chemise around her Mary slowly descended the stone steps, the lamp casting a limited pool of light around her. This was the first time she had entered the cellars and had no idea what to expect, other than it was used for the storage of wine and spirits. As she grew closer to the bottom step, grotesque shadows played on white painted walls and her mouth turned dry with fear. Raising the lamp higher, she was relieved to see it was the serried ranks of wine racks causing the shadows.

'Storm! Come to me, now!' She stood still, waving the lamp to illuminate as much as she could of the room. A muffled bark came from behind a large wooden door and she moved across to pull it open. However, its sheer weight forced her to put down the lamp and use both hands to produce a gap of a few inches. Storm rushed past her, wagging his tail and barking furiously at the darkness behind the door.

'What is it, Storm? Is there something there?' Mary would have preferred to leave the cellar and whatever lay behind the door, but he kept barking and slipped back through the gap, forcing her to open the door wide enough to stay open and, picking up the lamp following him. The light revealed a narrow passageway littered with stacked boxes. It seemed to head downwards and she caught a glimpse of closed doors. Instead of racing off Storm stopped a few feet away before disappearing through a small gap in what appeared to be a doorway now sealed with wooden strips nailed across it. Within seconds he re-appeared, bearing something in his mouth, which he dropped by her feet. Bending down, she shone the light over his offering and recoiled in horror.

'No, no it can't be!' She cried out, staring wide-eyed at the human finger bearing a ring she recognised instantly. The ring she had given to Nathaniel on their betrothal.

Chapter 20

Before Mary could fully grasp the significance of Storm's find, he disappeared through the gap with a mix of barking and whimpering. Dread filled her. What else was hidden there? Distraught at the obvious conclusion, she began pulling at the lower wood panels with a strength she didn't know she possessed. Freeing them from the nails on one side, she pushed them upwards, creating a human-size gap. Pushing the lamp ahead of her she crawled through on her hands and knees. Picking up the lamp she was met with the sight of Storm, lying by a man's body and whimpering as he pawed at an arm. Her tears fell unrestrained as she looked in horror at the remains of the man she loved. His head, with hair intact, was mummified, the skin stretched taut over the skull while the hands were almost skeletal. Devoid of a coat, Mary recognised the waistcoat as the one he'd worn the day before he went missing and she gasped as the lamp illuminated a large rusty brown stain in the middle, over his heart. As she moved the lamp, it caught the glitter of a dagger, coated in what was obviously dried blood, lying nearby. Overcome with nausea, her legs buckled under her. As she crumpled onto the floor she fell against a dusty leather travelling case. Holding the lamp closer revealed the sparkle of jewels inside.

In the midst of her grief and horror, the awful truth was irrefutable. Thomas, her husband and the father of her children, had killed his brother in a fight about what were probably stolen jewels. He must have made up the story of a drunken Nathaniel going back to the ship, missing his footing, and falling into the sea. And he had removed his brother's coat and thrown it into the sea to provide confirmation of his drowning. Bile rose in her throat and she vomited up what little she had eaten that morning. Gasping, and with the sour taste in her mouth, Mary grabbed the case and lamp, pushing them through the gap then taking hold of Storm's leash, pulled him with her through it. Once in the corridor she took Storm back to the main cellar and tied him up before returning to replace the wooden panels as best she could and after wrapping the finger gingerly in her handkerchief, put it in the case.

With some difficulty, Mary managed to climb the cellar steps and peered out to see if anyone had returned. All was quiet. Back in the kitchen she replaced the lamp and then poured a large glass of brandy to take upstairs. Storm continued to whimper as she dragged him up to her rooms. Once safely inside, she removed his leash and collapsed into a chair, taking a gulp of the brandy. Her hand shook from the horror of what she had found and if it wasn't for the old case lying on the floor by her side, she could have convinced herself it was a bad dream. Storm began sniffing at the case and Mary, realising he could smell his master's finger, tried to close it but the catch was broken. With the case fully open she had a clear view of the jewellery within. Rubies, diamonds, sapphires and emeralds, all set in intricate gold necklaces, bracelets and brooches. Her eyes were drawn to an emerald and diamond bracelet which looked familiar. Lifting it out for a closer look she gasped and hurried over to her dressing table. The top drawer held all her jewellery and she found the necklace Thomas had given her on their wedding day. Intricately set emeralds and diamonds, it matched the bracelet exactly. More proof of his perfidy.

Mary flung the necklace back in the drawer with a shudder, and looked for the loose floorboard which always creaked when she stood on it, near the window. In her needlework bag she found a knitting needle to prise up the board and pushed the case into the void, before replacing the board.

Taking Storm into her arms, she said, 'I know, boy, you remember him and miss him as much as I do, and it's horrid to think of him lying there beneath us all this time. The man we both loved was…murdered and I…I don't know what to do.'

* * *

Lucy opened her eyes, expecting to feel the silky fur of Storm under her fingertips as he lay curled in her arms. Instead she was alone on the modern divan bed and dreadful images of what she had witnessed rushed into her mind. Overtaken by nausea, she dashed to the bathroom and brought up most of her supper. Then she started shaking as Mary's pain and horror reverberated in her own brain and body. After gulping down a couple of glasses of water, Lucy took deep, calming breaths and the shaking eased. Then, suddenly it hit her. She, with her father and grandfather, were descended from a vicious murderer! Guilty of fratricide and not only inheriting his brother's wealth, but his betrothed! Poor, poor Mary, what an impossible situation in which to find herself.

Reaching for her notebook, Lucy started writing, her hands still shaking. Not wanting to miss anything out, she forced herself to relive it all. Describing the jewels in the case, a memory floated to the surface. Mary had recognised a bracelet as being the partner of an elaborate emerald and diamond necklace given to her by Thomas. Lucy's mother had worn such a necklace years before. Could it possibly have been the same one? Thinking it too fanciful, she brushed the thought aside, and continued to describe the heavy cellar door which must have closed after Storm slipped through it. This in turn reminded her of the sound of a woman crying she'd heard in the cellar a few weeks ago. Could it have come from the boarded room where Nathaniel had died? Had it been a foretelling of Mary's discovery of her betrothed's decomposing body? Lucy shook her head, struggling to clear the thoughts and questions crowding her mind. One thing she was clear about was the priority to find the key to the locked door. She needed to see what exactly lay beyond it.

The next morning Lucy woke with a pounding head after a restless night filled with unsettling dreams full of men fighting in a darkened room lit only by flickering candlelight. They seemed to be arguing over a woman who was huddled in the corner, crying for them to stop. She was that woman. Items of jewellery, sparkling as they caught the reflection of candlelight, lay scattered on the floor. A knife – a scream – and Lucy opened her eyes. It hadn't been a time-slip, less real, more fluid, but it was disturbing to be haunted by such images. She resolved to see Molly again for some offloading and calm reassurance.

An hour later, having wolfed down a satisfyingly high calorie cooked breakfast, Lucy had managed to shake off the effects of her disturbed sleep and was ready to visit her grandfather. She found him in his sitting-room watching a couple of thrushes performing a mating routine in the tree outside the window. Their bright song filtered into the room.

'Good morning, my dear. Aren't they delightful,' Gregory said, nodding towards the birds as she kissed his cheek. 'Quite lifts one's spirits watching the little chap trying to woo the female. It's a good thing humans have a more sophisticated form of courtship, or the noise would be over-powering,' he chuckled.

'For sure. And all those with good singing voices would beat any competition.' They were both silent for a moment, entranced by the sight and sound of the vocal birds. Lucy couldn't help comparing what she saw with the horror she'd faced when slipping back into Mary's life. Had her ancestor enjoyed such simple pleasures as watching and listening to birds? She could only hope there had been some joyful times in her tragic life.

'You're looking a little distracted, Lucy. Is something wrong?'

'Not exactly, but I've been having the most weird dreams involving my ghost, Mary, and…and her husband Thomas. They've felt so real, as if I was actually *there,* sharing their experiences. Some of it was quite horrible.' There, she'd come out with it and it was nearly the truth.

Gregory's eyebrows shot up.

'Dreams you say? How long have you been having them?'

'A few weeks, but not every night. I admit I'm a bit obsessed with Mary and what may have happened to her, and I think she may be trying to tell me through the dreams.' Gregory waved his hand dismissively and was about to say something, but she rushed on, 'Something similar happened to Molly's daughter, and what she kept dreaming about turned out to be real events from the past. So it's not as far-fetched as it sounds.' She held her breath while he absorbed this.

'Hmm. And what does Molly say about your dreams?' His fingers tapped the table.

Lucy cleared her throat, thinking of how to answer.

'She agrees I seem to be sort-of reliving some parts of Mary's life, probably due to our genetic connection. We think something bad happened to Mary and she needs me to know so she can be at peace.'

'I remember my wife saying something about ghosts being restless spirits when she saw her ghost, but at the time

I thought it was nonsense. A figment of her imagination after the loss of the baby.' The tapping continued. 'I've remained sceptical about such things but have a less closed mind now. Might be to do with my own ever encroaching mortality and how little we actually *know* what happens after death.'

'To be honest, I've never given much thought to the paranormal, except this ghost I'm convinced is Mary. But these…dreams are powerful stuff. Can I share the latest and most dramatic one with you? Then see what you think.'

He nodded and she told him about Mary finding Nathaniel's body in the cellar and how he was supposed to have drowned, leading to her forced marriage to Thomas. Gregory listened in silence, his expression inscrutable. Drained by the effort, Lucy sat back in the chair, praying he wouldn't say it was a load of rubbish.

'Well, I wasn't expecting that, my dear.' He shook his head. 'Either you have an over-active imagination, or our Mary has somehow found a way to communicate with you. And what a tale she has to tell! But can it be proved, that's the question. As an old advocate, I'm focused on proof.'

'I may be able to provide some proof, Grandpa. Or at least some supporting evidence. If I can get past the locked door in the cellar, I might find the room where Nathaniel was killed. Obviously, his body will have been moved years ago, but the existence of the room would back up the possibility he was killed there.'

'Yes, it would. So, we need the key, don't we?' His face creased in thought. 'I can't for the life of me remember why that door's locked or where the key is, but a good place to start would be my father's desk.' He smiled and Lucy saw the twinkle in his eyes. 'I can see you're keen to solve this mystery, if indeed that's what it is, so feel free to look for the key and report back. We can't have your dreams being disturbed by a restless spirit, can we?'

Lucy smiled inwardly. If only he knew!

'Thanks, Grandpa, I'll start now,' she said, standing and leaning over to kiss him. 'Catch up with you later.'

She hurried downstairs to Gregory's study, relieved he was prepared to consider what may have happened to Nathaniel. Ultimately she didn't need to prove anything to him, only herself. For her own peace of mind. She shivered as the chill of the room hit her and went straight to the top drawer of the desk where she remembered seeing bunches of keys when she was looking for the family tree. Pulling them out she sorted through the attached labels. 'Blimey, how many keys does a house need?' she muttered, realising these must be the spares for every door, most going back to the time it was built. Heaving a sigh of relief, Lucy detached a bundle labelled 'Cellars' which included a couple of ancient, rusty keys. After returning the others to the drawer, she headed towards the cellar. The cold, slightly musty air reignited the memory of her last visit as Mary and she shivered as much for what she had seen then as the coldness. At least this time there was bright electric light to guide her down the steps.

Ignoring the rows of wine racks, Lucy went straight towards the far side of the room and the locked door. Painted white to blend in with the walls, only the old iron handle and keyhole identified it as a door. Her heart hammered as she tried to insert one of the oldest looking keys, but it was clearly too large to fit. Choosing another smaller key she tried again. This time it went in but she struggled to turn it. Taking a deep breath, she summoned all her strength and tried again. There was a click and Lucy pulled on the handle, the door slowly opening towards her and all she saw was blackness. Switching on her phone torch revealed a wall a few feet away and a short passageway to her left. Shivers ran down her spine. She'd been here before. Taking a hesitant step forward she shone the light on the wall, picking out the strips of wood nailed across an almost concealed doorway. Lucy drew a deep breath. So – the room did exist.

Chapter 21

After taking several photos on her phone, Lucy locked the door, tucking the key into her pocket and returned to Gregory's room.

'Hi, Grandpa, I found the key and here's what I discovered.' She showed him the photos, explaining how they fitted with her "dream". 'Apart from the corridor, which looks as if it's been blocked off. Didn't you say something about tunnels down to the original warehouses?'

Gregory squinted at the pictures, frowning in concentration.

'I do vaguely remember my father showing me when I was a lad and telling me it was no longer safe to use the area after a ceiling collapsed in the tunnels. That's why the door was kept locked.'

'Did he mention the sealed-up room?' She pointed to the photo showing clearly the nailed strips of wood.

He shook his head.

'I can't remember. It was only a quick look to explain why the area was no longer used. The rest of the cellars provided more than enough storage for our needs so it didn't seem important.' His eyes twinkled. 'But I can see it does add weight to the veracity of your dream.'

'Thanks, I'm glad. Mind you, Nathaniel's body will have been moved ages ago, so there won't be any proof of his murder. Perhaps further dreams will tell me more.' Lucy kept her voice neutral, while inside she was buzzing.

'Be careful what you wish for, my dear. You don't want to be plagued by nightmares.'

She rose to leave.

'No worries, Grandpa, I'll pretend I'm simply watching a film. See you later.'

Back in her room Lucy rang Molly and arranged to meet her late the following afternoon. She was keen to offload the traumatic events in the cellar, as it was increasingly harder to let go her *alter ego* – Mary. It was something Molly had warned her might happen, sending her spiralling back into depression. At least the gym sessions anchored her in the present and Lucy was eager to see Sam again, their friendship providing a much-needed antidote to her increasingly draining trips to the past.

After lunch Lucy packed her gym bag and set off for Kings, glad to be out of the house and its dark secrets. As April continued to show off its floral display of colour and scent, Lucy found herself smiling and walking with a lighter step. The message of hope and new beginnings helped to push aside the revealed tragedy of the past and her pulse quickened as she arrived at Kings. Five minutes later she was changed and in the gym, on the lookout for Sam. He was showing a new club member how to programme a rowing machine, but caught her eye and nodded. A few minutes later he joined her, smiling broadly.

'Hi, it's good to see you, but I can't chat now as I'm in the middle of an induction. Do you fancy a coffee when you've finished?'

'Sure, thanks.' He was looking brighter and Lucy hoped he was turning a corner, happy to support him if he wished. After her workout she showered and changed before heading to the café. He waved her over to a table and went to order their drinks.

'Here you are, I took the liberty of ordering a couple of Danish pastries in case you were peckish after the exercise.' He grinned as he lay down the tray, passing her a mug of coffee and a mouth-watering pastry.

Laughing, she said, 'I could never resist temptation! But you're hardly setting a good example to the members.'

'Ah, could it not be seen as boosting the club's profits? And I missed lunch and am absolutely starving.' He took a bite of his pastry.

Between mouthfuls Sam asked after Gregory and she asked after his family. Satisfied there was improvement on both sides, they both seemed unsure how to continue the conversation and concentrated instead on eating the sticky delicious pastries.

'Oh, that was so good, thanks. I'll have to work out twice as hard tomorrow, but it'll be worth it,' she said, licking her fingers. After wiping them on a napkin she sipped her coffee, content to be doing something as normal as sitting in a café with a friend, a world away from Mary's life.

Sam finished his pastry with a satisfied sigh.

'Definitely tastier than my usual homemade sandwich.' Picking up his mug, he looked pointedly at her left hand. 'I've noticed you've not been wearing your wedding ring recently. Has something happened between you and your husband?'

Lucy took a deep breath, and told him about Hamish, his new girlfriend and their baby. And his request for a divorce.

Sam's eyes widened.

'Oh, I'm sorry to hear that. Must be painful for you.'

'It was, initially. You see,' she paused, 'we…lost our baby daughter to a cot death eighteen months ago. It's what led to us splitting up.' She took a gulp of coffee, determined not to be overcome by the painful memories.

'Oh, my God! How awful, I can't begin to imagine what you went through. No wonder you became depressed.' Sam reached over to touch her hand, concern etched on his face.

His touch was warm and comforting and she managed a smile.

'It has been horrible, but I'm much better now. In an odd way, Hamish has done me a favour by making me realise I can't dwell in the past forever. I'll always mourn my daughter, but I no longer love Hamish and, like him, I'm ready to move on with my life.' Saying it out loud was cathartic, empowering and she hoped Sam would be the one to help her.

He nodded, his hand tightening on hers.

'It's not great timing, I know, for either of us, but I'd really like us to be friends and perhaps something more at some point.' His eyes locked onto hers. 'What do you think?'

'I'd like us to get to know each other better.' Her hand was tingling under his and she smiled, no longer feeling as alone.

Lucy almost floated home after leaving Sam at Kings. He was off the following day and they were going to have lunch together. She was happy to take it slowly, not wanting to spoil things by getting serious too soon. Which usually meant sleeping together. Sure, she was attracted to him and she sensed he was attracted to her, but they needed time to see how well they clicked together, if they shared common interests or hobbies. Looking back, Lucy saw how little she and Hamish had in common. They didn't even like the same music and had had numerous fights over holidays. Basically, he wanted to spend time in the Highlands and she had longed for a hot, sunny Greek island. They usually ended up in Scotland, wrapped up against the cool, misty August days. She wasn't going to make that mistake again!

Back at *Carreville* she dumped her gym bag and called in to see Gregory. He was sitting with his eyes closed and, not wanting to disturb him, she was about to leave when she heard him say, 'I'm not sleeping, simply resting my eyes.' She turned to see him grinning at her and, laughing, joined him at the table.

'You sure you're not too tired? I can always come back later.' She dropped a kiss on his forehead.

'No, relieve my boredom, my dear. Although the view of the garden is pleasant, it's not as stimulating as our chats.' She caught the flash of sadness in his eyes and felt a twinge of guilt at her own improved mood. Not that she should feel guilty, she knew, and Gregory would be the first to tell her so, but she did.

'Even talking about my weird dreams and bodies in the cellar?'

'Especially those! No matter how unlikely they might prove to be true, they have roused me from the contemplation of my own mortality to learning more about our shared ancestry. I shall rely on you to keep me updated on any new developments,' he said, patting her hand.

Lucy was relieved to note the sadness was now replaced by a twinkle.

'Of course I will, Grandpa, now I know you won't consider me off my head.' A sudden thought occurred to her. 'By the way, I think a necklace I've seen my mother wear was similar to one worn by Mary in a dream, before she found Nathaniel's body. There was a matching bracelet in the travelling case by the body. So they must both have been stolen by Thomas. Diamonds and emeralds? Could it have been Grandma's?'

Gregory frowned.

'A few family jewels were passed down the generations, yes, so it's possible. Your grandma was not keen on wearing them, said they were too ornate for her taste and I happened to agree with her. They were kept in the safe. However, I don't recall an emerald and diamond bracelet.'

'We may not know what happened to the jewels in the

case.' She paused, momentarily wondering what did happen to them. Did Mary keep them hidden? 'I only saw Mum wear the necklace once, when I was still at school, and Mum and Dad were going to a posh do at Government House. She was wearing a long green evening gown.' Lucy's pulse was racing at the possible connection to the stolen jewels.

'Ah, I remember now. We were all going to a ball welcoming the new Lieutenant Governor and my wife said something about lending Marian a necklace to match her green dress. I didn't pay it much attention at the time, but it may have been emeralds and diamonds.' He shook his head. 'Well, well well. The plot thickens, as they say in crime stories. Not only might we have a murderer in the family, but our women may have been unknowingly flaunting stolen jewels for the past two hundred years! What a family, eh?' His fingers tapped the table.

'We might never know which jewels were stolen or bought as I don't suppose anyone ever admitted something so scandalous. Where are Grandma's jewels now?'

He shrugged.

'All passed to Marian when my wife died. Didn't seem much point in making her wait until I popped my clogs and I remember she and your father were keen on her wearing them to balls and such like.'

'Ah, I know they've always liked socialising, but I haven't been around to see them for so long now. Did you or Dad have any idea of their value? Surely such antique jewellery must be worth a pretty penny?'

'You're right, they would be. Hate to think what it'd cost to insure them. We never did, just kept them in the safe. Looking back, we should have had them valued, might have raised some cash for my old age.' He smiled wryly.

'Oh, Grandpa! You should ask Mum for them back and then sell them. Who needs such expensive jewellery nowadays, anyway?' Her heart went out to him, seeing his beloved home decaying around him while her mother sported jewels she could live without.

'Don't worry about me, my dear. It's too late to make any difference now. I'm comfortable enough in these rooms and I can't see how shabby the rest of the house is.' He tapped his nose. 'Don't forget, the jewellery will be yours one day, so might be better not to say anything to your parents.'

She giggled.

'Honestly, for an advocate, you're not exactly being above board, Grandpa.'

'I only want to look out for my favourite grandchild. No harm in that,' he said, his eyes twinkling. 'If Marian hadn't already been given them, I would have bequeathed the jewels to you. Given you a few steps up on the property ladder. It's ruinously expensive here for young people, my dear, as bad as London.' His expression became serious. 'I believe you couldn't afford to buy a home there either.'

Lucy was touched by his concern and didn't want him worrying about *her* future.

'No, we weren't, but I'm sure I'll be fine. A small apartment's all I need, as I've never been keen on housework.' She smiled, waving her arms to encompass the large, elegant room.

Gregory laughed.

'I wouldn't have bought this house if I hadn't inherited it. Your grandmother thought it too large and grand and I had to agree to her having domestic help before she would consent to move in. Sensible woman, your grandmother. Think you probably take after her,' he said, looking pensive, 'though she came to love it after a while.'

'Of course she did, it's beautiful. I love it too, just a tiny bit oversized for modern families,' she said, adding, 'and must cost a fortune to run.'

'Which is why your father plans to sell it when the time comes. He's right, of course, but it's a pity after two hundred years in the family.'

'Perhaps it's time we made a fresh start, break away from the past and the nefarious goings on of some of our ancestors.' She shook her head. 'Poor Mary, I can't stop thinking about her.'

'We don't know for sure what did happen, my dear. Those jewels –'

'Jewels! Yes, I'll email Mum and ask her where they are. Hopefully she isn't gadding about the Far East while wearing them; she'd be a prime target for a mugger. Although maybe I shouldn't tell her they could be extremely valuable in case she panics.'

'Won't she wonder why you're asking about them now?'

Lucy nodded, thinking how to approach her mother.

'I'll tell her we've been talking about the past and the family and you mentioned the jewels passed down to Grandma and then to her and I'm keen to see them, if they're here in the house. Sound all right?'

'Yes, I think so.'

'Right, I'll go and email her. It's time we caught up with each other, anyway. Guess they've been too busy enjoying themselves,' she laughed, as she stood up.

'Remember not to say anything about my being ill. I don't want them rushing back and making a fuss.'

'Don't worry I won't. Bye for now.'

As Lucy left she didn't think for one minute her parents would curtail their cruise even if they did know about Gregory's illness. They were much too selfish.

Later that evening, having emailed Marian, Lucy was debating whether or not to re-connect with Mary when her mobile rang. She was surprised to see it was Marian calling on WhatsApp. This was a first since they left.

'Hi, Mum, how are you? Did you get my email?'

'Email? No, I don't know.' She sounded flustered. 'I'm

not ringing about any email, I thought you should know your father's been taken ill. He's in hospital for tests.'

'Oh, my God! Where are you? What happened?'

'Singapore. Lucky…ship…arrived in the port. We're in Raffles Hospital and waiting to hear what doctors say.' She heard her mother trying to catch her breath. 'He had…chest pain and trouble breathing. Possible…heart attack.'

Chapter 22

Shocked, Lucy took a calming breath before replying.

'Oh, Mum, I'm so sorry. How long before you know more? And how are you?'

'It could be a while as they want to do scans and things. But they say he's stable at the moment. I…can't see him yet but am okay, the staff's been wonderful. Supportive. It's six o'clock in the morning here and I've been up since two. Dennis woke with chest pain and couldn't breathe so I called ship's doctor.' Lucy heard her take a sip of something. 'We were just coming in to Singapore and the doctor said he needed to go to hospital. Ambulance was waiting by the time we docked. It's been a nightmare,' her voice caught on a sob, 'I thought he was going to die. Looked awful. Oxygen mask.'

Lucy's heart went out to her mother having to deal with something so serious on her own and thousands of miles away.

'Do you want me to fly out, Mum? It would take a while, but –'

'No, darling, let's wait and see what happens. The ship's here until tomorrow and everyone's so kind. I'll cope, just been a bit overwhelmed,' she sniffed, 'it must be late evening back home so why don't you go to bed and get some sleep. I'll ring early your time to let you know how your father is.'

'Okay, Mum. Try and relax and we'll talk later. Love to Dad. Bye.'

In the following silence Lucy went over what Marian had said. It was hard to take in that her father, although admittedly overweight and a lover of cigars, should suddenly be close to death in his sixties. Whereas Gregory had just beaten pneumonia in his nineties. She checked her watch – gone ten, too late to tell him now. He'd only worry. She sighed, wondering if she could sleep even though it made sense to try. If her dad didn't pull through then she would have to fly out to Singapore, she couldn't possibly leave her mum to cope alone. Deciding a glass or two of wine might help, Lucy went into the kitchen and found a half-full bottle and, grabbing a glass, took them upstairs to her room.

The wine didn't help after all. Lucy tossed and turned all night as her mind filled with images of a distraught Marian watching an unconscious (or was he dead?) Dennis lying in a bed hooked up to all kinds of bleeping machines. The odd times she slept her dreams were worse, involving coffins and bodies crawling with maggots. By six o'clock she gave up and went down to the kitchen to make a cup of tea. Back in bed she listened to the radio while drinking the tea, trying to keep unwelcome thoughts at bay.

At seven o'clock her mobile rang. Her mother.

'Hi, Mum, how's Dad?'

'Better. The good news is it wasn't a heart attack, but he has a coronary artery disease, called atherosclerosis, which, if not treated, could lead to a heart attack.' Marian sounded both relieved and tired.

'Does that mean he's still in danger?'

'Not exactly. He's on beta-blockers and other drugs to reduce his high blood pressure and cholesterol. We were lucky it was caught early and your father might avoid surgery if the drugs work.' Marian took a deep breath. 'He also has to follow a low fat diet and give up his precious cigars, which hasn't gone down too well with him, but he has no choice if he wants to live longer.'

'Poor Dad. So, what happens now? Does he have to stay in hospital?'

'Only until tomorrow. Luckily our ship's due to stay here tonight as part of the itinerary so, all being well, Dennis will be allowed to re-join it before it leaves at noon tomorrow. The ship's doctor and the hospital have confirmed they're happy for us to continue the trip and it'll be safer than flying home.'

'Thank goodness, I had visions of you both flying back as some sort of medical emergency.' Not only was Lucy glad Dennis was recovering, she was relieved her parents were not about to arrive home early. She wanted Gregory to herself a while longer and then there was Mary…no, it was good news her parents could continue the cruise.

'Yes, we've been lucky. With Dennis in good hands, I've returned to the ship to catch up on my sleep.' Marian let out a sort of bark. 'What *is* upsetting is we were both excited about visiting the famous Raffles Hotel and ordering Singapore Gin slings in the Long Bar. Instead of which your father ends up in Raffles Hospital on intravenous drips and I end up worried to death!'

'Oh, Mum, what a shame, but it could have been much worse, couldn't it? And at least you can have a cocktail or two on board.'

'Don't worry, I've already had a couple. Right, I'm off to bed. I'll ring you after your father returns tomorrow and you can speak to him then.'

'Bye, Mum. Give my love to Dad.'

Lucy released a long breath, echoing her frustration. She understood her mother had suffered an awful time with her father's near-death experience, but not once had she asked after her or Gregory. It appeared missing out on a visit to Raffles Hotel was of more concern. Shaking her head in despair, she nipped into the bathroom for a shower before getting dressed.

'My, you look washed out this morning. You're not going down with anything are you?' Meg greeted her as she shuffled into the kitchen.

'No, just tired after a bad night.' She told Meg about her father and his rush to hospital.

'Oh, I'm sorry to hear that. Sounds like he's had a lucky escape but won't be happy about going on a diet. Loves his rich food, does your dad. And I expect there's lots of it available on that cruise ship of theirs,' said Meg as she prepared a cooked breakfast for Gregory. For some reason Lucy didn't fancy a full English and slotted bread into the toaster to accompany her usual coffee.

'Please don't say anything to Grandpa, Meg, as I've not had a chance to tell him. Will go up after breakfast and fill him in.'

Meg nodded her agreement as she plated up Gregory's food then left with his tray.

Lucy drank two mugs of coffee in an effort to wake up and be ready to face Gregory. Thank goodness they knew her father wasn't in danger! She would have found it hard to relay bad news to her grandfather, particularly after his own recent brush with death. Although the father and son were not close, she knew they were fond of each other, in a semi-detached way. Their relationship was a reflection of hers with Dennis. She loved him but didn't always like him. Now her mother – she sighed. Yes, she loved her and liked her most of the time, except when she was selfish or snobbish. Ahh, families!

A while later Lucy called in to see Gregory.

'Morning, how are you today?' she said, kissing his cheek.

'A lot better than you look, my dear. Something wrong?' He gave her a keen look.

'Afraid so. Mum phoned last night and …' she went on to tell him what had happened.

'Poor old Dennis.' Gregory looked solemn. 'He was lucky the ship was near to the port instead of being far out at sea, far from a hospital.' Rubbing his chin he went on, 'I expect it was quite upsetting for Marian as well.'

'It was, for both of us, not knowing if Dad would pull through. I hardly slept last night.'

'I'm not surprised. When you talk to your parents, please pass on my best wishes and tell Dennis to follow doctor's orders. I know he never likes being told what to do.'

Lucy hid a smile. Talk about the pot calling the kettle black! They continued to chat for a while and then she left him to read his newspaper. Amidst all the upset over her father, she had almost forgotten her lunch date with Sam and needed to choose what to wear. But first she needed more coffee or she could end up falling asleep with her head in her lunch. Not a good start to their nascent friendship.

Upstairs after downing a mug of coffee Lucy surveyed her limited wardrobe. The only feminine item was the skirt she had bought for supper at Natalie's. The day she had bumped into Sam at Dix Neuf. Was it a good omen? Deciding it was, she matched it with the same cashmere sweater, adding earrings and a pretty silver necklace. Nothing flashy, but smart casual. If they were to keep seeing each other she would need to hit the shops again. Since losing Amber she had lost interest in clothes and her appearance, slopping around in joggers or jeans. No wonder things had deteriorated between her and Hamish. Even if she and Sam were only ever friends, she vowed to make an effort with her appearance. It would be as much for her sake as his. Her mother, always fastidious about clothes, hair and makeup, had often said "if you look good you will feel good" and she now saw she was right. Blessed with a good, if pale, complexion, she added a touch of blusher and lipstick before brushing her hair into a neat bob framing her face. Satisfied with the result, she grabbed a jacket and bag and ran downstairs.

Outside the front door Lucy filled her lungs with fresh air before walking smartly down the drive to the street. Sam had suggested meeting at the venue, Les Rocquettes Hotel in Les Gravees, a short walk away from Queen's Road, and not far from his house in Rosaire Avenue, meaning neither had to drive. She swung her arms as she walked, buoyed by the anticipation of the date that wasn't a date. What did friends of the opposite sex call it when they met up? She didn't know but did it matter? It was something to be enjoyed, and after the emotional intensity of both her time as Mary and dealing with her father's sudden illness, she needed some fun.

The sun peeped behind soft cotton-wool clouds as she arrived at the entrance and walked past rows of parked cars towards the hotel. The vibrant spring flowers spilling out of wall baskets and urns provided a warm, colourful welcome as she neared the entrance and spotted Sam waving.

'Hi, good timing,' he said, greeting her with a hesitant peck on the cheek.

'Only took me a few minutes, so a great choice.' She smiled, hoping she looked calmer than she felt.

'Right, let's go in. The bar's just here.' Sam led the way and once they had found a table he asked her what she would like to drink.

'A glass of dry white wine please.' As he went to the bar to order the drinks Lucy browsed the menu, which covered everything from sandwiches to tasty main courses. It had already been agreed they would split the cost as per their orders, as was usual with friends, making it easier to choose what she wanted. At the beginning of a new relationship, however, boyfriends had insisted on paying for her and she had felt obliged to choose cheaper options even when they had gone for the dearest.

'You're deep in thought. Anything wrong?' Sam said, arriving with their drinks.

She smiled. 'No, not at all. The menu offers such a great choice I was wondering if you have any recommendations?'

As Lucy picked up her wine he lifted his own glass in a salute.

'This has been my local for a few years and I've enjoyed everything I've tried. Not that I eat out very much, but if I haven't wanted to cook…' he shrugged. 'Fancy anything in particular?'

'The seafood mezze platter looks tempting if you're up for sharing.' She didn't want anything too heavy knowing that Meg was cooking a casserole for dinner.

'Great choice,' he beamed at her. 'Happy to share and there might be room for dessert after.'

She laughed.

'Hey, don't lead me down the slippery path to guilty pleasures! You're supposed to be encouraging me to regain weight by healthy eating.'

'I'm off duty now so what you eat doesn't count.' He grinned, standing up to return to the bar with the order.

By the time he returned, Lucy was more relaxed, helped partly by the wine but also by Sam's easy manner. The conversation flowed easily during the meal as they compared notes on their backgrounds and how they became interested in personal training.

'I've always been a sporty kind of guy and was never happier than when playing a game of footer or with my mates windsurfing or swimming. Although I did okay at uni, I knew after working a few months in an office that it wasn't for me.' Sam took a sip of his drink and grinned. 'Unfortunately, I was never going to make it as a professional footballer, so I looked into the fitness industry. I got a job at Beau Sejour initially and haven't looked back since.'

Lucy nodded.

'I'm with you on working in an office. My father wanted me to follow him into law, as he had followed his father. But to me it looked so dry and I knew I didn't want to spend four or five years studying to become an advocate and, like you, loved sport and any form of exercise. A no-brainer, except I'd have earned a lot more money as an advocate,' she said, laughing.

'For sure, particularly in Guernsey. But if something doesn't make you happy, what's the point? I had to live at home for a few years as my pay was too low for me to rent anywhere, but I stuck with it and now I not only love my job, but have been able to buy my own house. Win-win.'

'That's great, Sam. It's going to be tough financially for me starting again here when I'm ready and I might have to live at home. Not a happy thought.' She frowned.

'You don't get on with them?'

'It's a bit complicated now they've moved into Grandpa's house to supposedly look after him.' She rolled her eyes. 'My father and I tend to clash and Mum usually takes his side, although perhaps he'll be more mellow with his heart problem.'

'Heart problem?'

She filled him in with what had happened in Singapore and how he was supposed to make some life changes. He expressed his concern, but Lucy didn't want to dwell on her father while Sam was grieving for his mother. To her mind there was no comparison. She changed the subject by asking about Sam's house and the mood had lifted by the time they were ready to say goodbye.

'How would you feel about catching a film together sometime? It's something friends do, right?'

'Yes, I'd like that. As long as it was fun or uplifting, I'm not into horror or thriller movies.'

'Great, I'll check out what's on and get back to you. Are you coming to the gym tomorrow?'

'Yes, sure. We can discuss it then.' Lucy shifted from foot to foot as they stood together outside.

Sam leaned in and kissed her cheek.

'Good, I'll see you then. I really enjoyed our lunch today, thanks.'

'So did I, see you tomorrow.' Smiling, she turned towards the main entrance while Sam left the back way. Checking her watch, she would just make it home in time to leave for Molly's. What on earth would she think about her/Mary's discovery of the body in the cellar?

Chapter 23

Molly did not utter a word while Lucy described, in full detail, her latest "outing" as Mary. However, her face betrayed her shock and horror at the finding of Nathaniel's body and Lucy had to fortify herself with sips of water as the memories took hold. As she finished, at the point where Mary was back in her room with Storm and the jewels, there was complete silence for a moment or two.

'I hardly know what to say, except what a terrible experience for you and Mary. Life changing for her. What effect has it had on you?' Molly coughed and reached for her glass of water.

'I…have found it hard to let go, more than previous times. Mary's pain at finding Nathaniel seared through me, as if I'd lost a part of myself. Which in some ways I have. She and I are becoming one person, or more correctly I suppose, one soul. She's never far from my thoughts and I'm dreaming about her and the brothers.' Lucy took a large gulp of water surprised at what she'd said. It was the first time she'd acknowledged quite how much she was under Mary's influence.

'I was afraid this would happen and we need to take control now before you become subsumed in Mary's life and dissociated from your own.' Molly frowned as she glanced through her notes.

'But I don't want to stop going back in time, Molly. It feels even more imperative I find out what happened to

Mary if and when she told Thomas what she'd found. I simply can't leave it hanging in the air.' The mere thought made her feel sick.

'I'm not going to suggest you do stop, although I feel strongly there's a risk in carrying on, I think you would simply ignore me and go ahead anyway. Am I right?'

She nodded.

'Then what I do suggest is you perform an exercise to, in effect, close the door behind you when you return from the past. Using self-hypnosis you can suggest all the feelings, emotions and physical reactions to what you experience are left behind and can no longer affect you. You will still have the memories but will not retain Mary's reactions, physical or emotional. I'll take you through a session now to show you what I mean. All right?' Molly smiled encouragingly.

'Yes, sure, happy to try anything.'

Twenty minutes later, Lucy opened her eyes feeling as if she had enjoyed a deep, dreamless sleep. Molly's instructions for when she next slipped back were firmly rooted in her mind and she let out a sigh of relief.

'Thanks, Molly, not only do I feel great but I'll definitely be using that technique from now on. I had been worried about not being able to separate from Mary, and I think this will help.'

'Good, but if you do come back from the past struggling to release from Mary, promise you'll phone me. It's important for your own wellbeing you don't bring Mary's problems back with you, especially since you've been so much better lately.' Molly's eyebrows were drawn together and Lucy felt a twinge of guilt for going against her professional advice.

'I promise.'

'Hi, Grandpa, how are you?' Lucy slipped into Gregory's sitting room as soon as she arrived home, conscious she hadn't seen him since after breakfast.

'Ah, the wanderer returns,' he said, grinning as she kissed his cheek. 'I'm fine, what about you? Looking a little flushed. What have you been up to?'

'I had lunch with a friend then went to see Molly for one of our sessions. So, a good day.' She sat next to him and gripped his hand.

'A friend? Male or female?'

'Male. He's called Sam and is the assistant manager at Kings and we seem to hit it off. Neither of us is looking for a relationship just now as he's just lost his mother to cancer, but we both like the idea of being friends.' She found herself blushing as Gregory's eyes bored into hers.

'That's a shame about his mother, my dear, but perhaps starting out as friends is a good idea. You young people are too quick to rush into bed together instead of getting to know each other properly first.' He paused, his eyes becoming unfocused. 'Your grandmother and I courted for two years and, her parents being prudish Methodists, I wasn't allowed to kiss her on the lips until we were engaged. And we were hardly ever on our own, but we became such firm friends and knew we wanted to marry and spend the rest of our lives together.' He blinked, his gaze refocused on her. 'And we were very happy for more than sixty years, the best of friends.'

Lucy gulped, her own eyes moist.

'I'm glad it worked out for you, Grandpa, and maybe you're right, we do tend to rush into relationships these days. To be honest, waiting two years for a kiss might be a bit of a stretch, though.'

He laughed.

'I agree! Although I said we weren't allowed to kiss, we did manage to sneak a few whenever we could. Fortunately

Sarah didn't agree with her parents' religion, which also frowned on alcohol, and loved wine as much as me otherwise we might not have been so compatible.'

'I'd better ask Sam if he holds any religious or other strong views. At least I know he enjoys a drink. And it's too late to avoid kissing, though it was only on the cheek,' she said, grinning.

'Thought you had a sparkle in your eyes. I'm pleased for you, my dear, only do take it slowly. It's worth it. I assure you. Now, how did it go with Molly?'

Over the next few days Lucy's life returned to the usual routine of spending time with Gregory, going to the gym and occasionally snatching a coffee with Sam after her session. Choosing a film proved tricky but they finally settled on "Love is all you Need", a Danish/English rom-com starring one of her favourite actors, Piers Brosnan, the following week at The Mallard cinema.

'I know it's likely to be a cheesy romance, but it's either that or an apocalyptic sci-fi which doesn't sound much fun.' Sam said, with a wry grin. 'Or we can wait for another time?'

'No, I'm fine with cheesy romance and as it's been so long since I went to a cinema I'd almost have been tempted by the sci-fi.' Secretly she was pleased Sam was open to a film aimed more at women as this showed respect for her and her preferences. Whereas Hamish had refused to watch anything "girlie" as he put it.

Although not an actual "date", Lucy looked forward to spending more time with Sam and they'd agreed to have a drink after the film. When the day arrived she ate her supper quickly, ready to be collected at seven. The door-bell rang on the dot.

'Hi, Lucy. Hey, this is quite some place.' Sam's gaze swept the impressive stuccoed façade before kissing her cheek.

'It is and it's been in the family like forever, though not for much longer, I'm afraid.'

As he opened the car door for her he asked why and she said she'd tell him once they were on their way. As they headed out towards Forest and the cinema, she told him about her father's plan to sell once he inherited.

'I guess it does make sense as few of these old houses are still single dwellings. The upkeep must be horrendous, though it must be sad when your ancestors built it.'

'In a way, yes, but now I know it was built with ill-gotten gains…' she went on to tell him about the family involvement in privateering and possibly smuggling.

He chuckled.

'The island's finance industry's helping the rich avoid tax even today, so not much change there! Mind you, I've always had a sneaking admiration for smugglers and privateers, or legal pirates as they were. Must have taken a lot of courage and skill to outwit customs officers or to attack and overrun enemy ships.'

Lucy laughed.

'I feel the same. Must be all those pirate movies and the Poldark books I devoured years ago. They made it seem so romantic and heroic.'

They continued chatting about their favourite pirate films which included the more recent "Pirates of the Caribbean" series. By this time they had arrived at the Mallard and Sam hunted for a parking space. Once inside with their tickets the doors for their screen were opening and after buying two bottles of mineral water, they took their seats. Lucy took a while to relax, unused to sitting so close to a male friend in the confines of a cinema, but Sam showed no sign of behaving other than a gentleman and she was able to lose herself in the film. A tricky point was when the main female lead revealed she was being treated for cancer and wore a wig, which didn't faze Piers Brosnan, but Lucy was worried for Sam. Sneaking a glance at him, he seemed fine, smiling at the antics of younger characters. Fortunately there was humour amidst the sadness and the film ended on a positive note.

'So, what did you think?' she asked as they headed to the bar afterwards.

'I enjoyed it, though the story was a bit improbable, don't you think?'

'Yes, but that's nothing new with films these days. But I loved the setting of Sorrento and the Amalfi coast. I've not been to that part of Italy and it looks gorgeous. And the villa was to die for.'

Sam nodded.

'Makes you want to hop on a plane, doesn't it?' Pulling out a chair for her, he went on, 'Back in the real world, what would you like to drink? Perhaps a glass of Prosecco for an Italian vibe?' He grinned.

'Perfect, thank you.'

The rest of the evening went quickly as they continued talking not only about the film, but favourite movies from the past. The drive home passed in companionable silence and when they arrived at *Carreville* Sam switched off the engine and walked round to open the passenger door.

'Thanks for a lovely evening, Sam. It's so much more fun to see a film with a friend.' She stood near him as he closed the car door.

'No need to thank me, I enjoyed it too. Do you fancy going again if we like the look of a film?'

'I'd like that, thanks and we can try something less girlie next time,' she said, with a smirk.

Laughing, Sam kissed her cheek and said good night before getting in the car. She waved him off and went inside, aware of the huge grin on her face. Not ready for sleep, she made a cup of tea and took it upstairs to her bedroom where she planned to read for a while. But as she switched on the light her eyes were drawn, as if by a magnet, to the portrait. Mary. For an evening she had been able to forget about her but there she was. Those mournful eyes piercing her very soul.

'I will be back, Mary, I just need to have some fun in my own life. I think I've met my own Nathaniel. You do understand, don't you?'

The slight smile was her answer.

Chapter 24

During the next couple of weeks Lucy enjoyed spending time with Sam. As well as trips to the cinema they met for lunch or a coffee on his days off. She noticed how much readier he was to smile and laugh when they met, with only the occasional glimpse of pain in his eyes. Knowing from her own experience Lucy wasn't surprised when there were times Sam seemed lost in his own world. It was another good reason for taking their time getting to know each other as friends. Her own grief for Amber was no longer as sharp, but it wasn't far under the surface and even the picture of a six-month old baby in a magazine could prompt the familiar ache in her heart.

Around this time Lucy began having dark and troubling dreams which seemed to be connected to Mary. One dream caused her to wake one day soaked in sweat and gripped with fear. And with a vague memory of being somewhere cold and dark.

One morning, as she was finishing her breakfast, Marian phoned on WhatsApp. They had only spoken once since her father was taken ill.

'Hello, Lucy. Can you hear me all right?'

'Hi, Mum, it's a bit crackly but okay. How's Dad?'

'Not too bad. You can talk to him in a moment. Thought I'd better check how you and Gregory were getting on .Can't talk long as have a hair appointment.'

Lucy rolled her eyes. It had taken her mother weeks to ask after them and now…

'We're okay, thanks, enjoying each other's company and talking about family history. That's why I sent you an email about the necklace. We think it's very old and could be valuable.'

'Oh, the one which looks like emeralds and diamonds? I thought it was paste!' Marian's voice rose.

'No, we think it might be late eighteenth century and French. Do you have it with you?'

'No, it's in my jewellery box in my bedroom. Thought it was too elaborate for cruise wear – but what makes you think it's valuable?'

'I'll explain when you come home, Mum. I'm just glad it's safe for now. Shall I talk to Dad now? You don't want to be late for your appointment.'

'Right, I'll pass you over. Bye for now.' Lucy heard muted voices in the background and picked up the words "necklace" and "valuable". She grinned, knowing how excited her parents would be at such news.

'Hello, Lucy? It's Dad. What story have you been telling your mother about that old necklace?' Well, he doesn't sound traumatised by his brush with death, she thought.

'Hi, Dad. It's a long story and Grandpa and I will tell you more when you're back. What's more important is, how are you? Must have been a nasty shock, being taken ill so suddenly.'

'Yes, it was, though your mother was more worried than I was. Still, it could've been a lot worse and I was lucky with that hospital. First class care, and all that. Couldn't fault it.' She heard a deep sigh. 'Not as happy having to give up my cigars and booze and watch what I eat. It's mental torture every time we have a meal as there are only certain foods I'm allowed while Marian can eat what she likes. And after all the money this is costing!' He sounded disgruntled and

Lucy didn't think it appropriate to point out this cruise was supposed to have been an unmissable bargain.

'The main thing, Dad, is we're all relieved you're getting better and can enjoy the rest of the cruise. Where are you heading for now?'

'Sri Lanka and then the Red Sea, so several weeks left to go. I'm under doctor's orders to walk round the decks every day with the other old crocks and have to pass muster before I'm allowed ashore. Not what I signed up for,' he grumbled.

Gritting her teeth, she managed to listen to his moans without comment until he brought the conversation to an end. A quick goodbye and he was gone. Muttering 'Grr', Lucy made a cup of coffee as she considered how different Dennis and Gregory were in their response to serious illness. Her father, who until now had enjoyed good health, had become totally self-centred, be-moaning the doctors' orders whereas her grandfather had been grateful for his care and recovery. Once she had finished her coffee she went upstairs to tell him of the phone call.

'Good of your mother to ask after us,' he said, wryly, 'and your father doesn't seem to have taken well to his new regimen.'

'Well, hopefully he'll come to realise he has no choice if he wants to enjoy a longer life. It's Mum I feel sorry for as he's likely to take it out on her.' A thought hit. 'Do you think it would be all right if I looked for the necklace in her room? I didn't get the chance to ask and I'm dying to see it. Mum perked up when I said it might be valuable.'

'I don't see why not and remember, it will be yours one day. It's meant to be passed down through the females in the family so she can't sell it.'

'If I find any other jewellery which looks old I'll bring it to you in case you recognise what was Grandma's. Back in a minute.'

Lucy had not been in her parent's bedroom before and she felt uncomfortable invading their privacy, even though they were thousands of miles away. Their room overlooked the garden, like Gregory's, and was of similar size to her own. The décor was dull; insipid beige walls and heavy beige velvet curtains which did nothing to offset the heavy Edwardian furniture, including a half-tester bed. An open door revealed a modern bathroom in need of a refurbishment and Lucy could see why her mother would be keen to return to her own home, which had been continuously updated with each new latest "look". On the large dressing table stood Marian's old wooden jewellery cabinet which had provided Lucy with much entertainment as a child when Marian had allowed her to explore the contents of its various drawers. Her heart beat with anticipation now as she stood in front of it and lifted the mirror-backed top lid. Spread out on the velvet lining were two necklaces, neither of which looked particularly old or valuable.

Disappointed, Lucy pulled open the next drawer and found another two necklaces, one of which was the one she had seen her mother wear the once, and matched the emerald and diamond bracelet in the travel case. She lifted it carefully from its velvet bed and held it in her hands. It was heavy and the jewels sparkled in the light. It was exquisite, if over-elaborate for modern taste, and even to her untrained eye looked genuine in spite of her mother thinking it was paste. The other necklace was an elegant gold filigree choker chain of what appeared to be rubies and diamonds and nestled next to it were matching earrings. There was something familiar… As she picked up the necklace Lucy experienced a tiny electric shock. Of course, she had worn it! A present from Thomas to celebrate the birth of his son. Lucy had a fleeting flashback to the day Thomas arrived in her room after Henry's birth when she – or rather Mary – was propped up on pillows in her bed, still weak from the ordeal.

'Here, wife. Payment for bearing me a son,' he said, tossing a velvet bag onto her lap. Before she could reply he had turned on his heels and left. Opening the bag she had found the ruby and diamond necklace and earrings.

It took Lucy a few minutes to regain a sense of calm, unnerved by the sudden and unwanted visit to the past. Mary's past. She could only hope it was triggered solely by the handling of the jewels and not likely to be repeated. Looking quickly through the rest of the jewel box, she found nothing likely to be as old, although there were some Victorian pieces she remembered her grandmother wearing. There was no sign of the matching emerald bracelet found in the travelling case. The remaining jewellery was modern and probably bought by her parents.

She grabbed several paper tissues and wrapped up the two necklaces and the earrings to show her grandfather. Drawn to look at the portrait she went into her room. As she stood there holding them, a voice in her head whispered, 'The colour of blood…' A tear fell from Mary's eye and Lucy gently wiped it away. Looking at the stern faced man at Mary's side, she hissed, 'Murderer!' before leaving and returning to Gregory's room.

'Hi, Grandpa, look what I found.' She laid the jewellery on the table in front of him.

He nodded, picking up the emerald necklace.

'This is the one your mother borrowed but my wife never wore. And you think the stones are real?' He peered at it closely, picking up the magnifying glass he kept handy for small print. 'Umm, I'm no expert but you could be right. My mother inherited several pieces of jewellery, passed down over the years apparently, but no mention was made of value. Wasn't the done thing in those days.' He looked at Lucy with a grimace. 'Everything's about money nowadays, not how long something's been in one's family.'

She knew he was thinking more of the house and gripped his hand.

'I understand, Grandpa, but I think these pieces might have been stolen and cost Nathaniel his life.' She picked up the ruby necklace. 'In a dream I saw Thomas give Mary this and the earrings after she gave birth to Henry. It's likely they were among those he stole. Do you recognise it?'

'Yes, quite pretty and not as ostentatious as the emeralds. I think my wife wore it once. Again, we didn't think of it as being valuable. After the war, no-one liked to be seen showing off wealth, even inherited. Islander's clothes were little better than rags and everything was rationed.' He sighed. 'My mother's jewellery must have been kept well hidden to have escaped the Germans as they always took whatever they could find.'

'In my dream, there were quite a few items in the case and they aren't in Mum's jewel box. Would there be any in the safe?'

He shook his head.

'No, everything was given to Marian when my wife died.'

'Well at least we have these to back up what I saw in my dream, although we're missing the matching bracelet. Might have been sold or lost sometime in the last two hundred years, I guess.' She wondered if Mary had managed to keep them hidden from Thomas, along with the case. But if he had found them, then he would more than likely have sold them. They might never know.

'Your sleuthing is paying off, my dear, and I remain intrigued as to what happened so long ago. Keep me posted.'

Picking up the necklaces and wrapping them in the tissues, Lucy grinned. 'Don't worry, I will. See you later, Grandpa.'

Lucy was torn. Did she attempt to find out more about Mary and her fate, or did she put it off a bit longer and simply enjoy spending time with Sam? It wasn't as if they were mutually exclusive, but she sensed a darkness gathering around Mary and her ultimate fate. She didn't expect her to have died a peaceful, natural death, there being no record of her death in the family tree. And then there were the children. Mary's 'ghost' had been looking for them, but they had lived and grown to adulthood. Lucy could only conclude Mary had been separated from them in some way. And, she reminded herself, she had suffered along with Mary and reliving whatever happened would be doubly painful for her, a part of her psyche. Which was why Molly was concerned and had emphasised the need to leave behind her feelings, her reactions using the technique she had taught her. But could she be sure it would work?

This soul searching was taking place in the garden and Lucy had hoped for clarity, a sense of rightness. As she paced up and down, hardly aware of the colour and beauty of the shrubs and flowers opening up in the May sunshine, she realised she was afraid. Afraid of facing the past, even though deep down she desperately wanted to know what had happened. Taking a deep lungful of air, she took what she saw as the coward's path, and decided to stay away from Mary's life a while longer and build on her relationship with Sam. The present had to be the priority.

Chapter 25

'I was wondering, Meg, could I take you up on your kind offer to help me prepare and cook a meal for friends? I was thinking of a Friday evening if it suited everyone.' Lucy was in the kitchen making a cup of tea for them both while Meg was busy preparing that day's supper.

'Course you can, wouldn't have offered otherwise would I?' Meg put down her chopping knife to accept the mug of tea. 'Thanks. Were you wanting a posh meal in the dining room?'

'Oh, no, it wouldn't be much fun in there, it's too gloomy. As there'll only be five or six of us I thought we'd have an informal supper in the kitchen.' Her eyes flicked over the substantial pine table in the middle of the room, encircled by half a dozen pine chairs. With the right place settings and some candles, it would be perfect for a relaxed evening with friends. Her grandparents had had the kitchen updated before money became tight and the room was bright and airy with the cream Aga complemented by classic wooden units. Slightly shabby now, but warm and inviting, unlike most of the downstairs rooms.

Meg nodded.

'Good idea. And with the weather warming up you could have drinks in the garden first. The garden furniture will probably need a good clean first, mind you.'

'No problem, I'll take care of it.' For a moment, she hesitated, thinking of all the weeds and the general overgrown state of the garden. But, she reminded herself, the patio was large and flagged, providing plenty of room to walk about without going onto what should be the lawns.

'And what were you thinking for the meal?' Meg continued with her chopping as they talked.

'Something light. A cold starter and dessert but a cooked main. Nothing fancy and everyone eats meat and fish.'

'I'll have a think and let you know in the morning.' Meg gave her a sly look. 'And who might number six be? Someone you've met?'

Lucy felt her cheeks redden.

'He's a friend who works at Kings, nothing serious. Just thought it might be nice to have even numbers, that's all. Though I haven't asked him yet so…' she shrugged.

Meg pursed her lips and nodded, turning back to the pile of vegetables.

Lucy took the opportunity to go off to phone Natalie and Jeanne about the proposed supper. They both expressed delight at the offer and both couples would be free for the following two Friday nights. Now to check with Sam. Taking a deep breath, she called him, hoping he wouldn't see it as a "date". He was happy to accept but was only free on Friday 17th. After confirming the date with the others she returned to the kitchen to tell Meg there would be six for supper on the 17th. Receiving a knowing smile in reply, Lucy slipped upstairs to see Gregory.

'Hi, Grandpa, I'm planning a little supper for some friends in a couple of weeks, if that's okay?' she said, joining him at the window.

'Of course, bring some life into the old place,' Gregory said, looking up from his paper. 'And will this new friend of yours be among the guests?' He raised his eyebrows and winked.

'Oh, Grandpa, you're as bad as Meg! Yes, as it happens, but mainly to make up even numbers, and he's coming as a *friend.*' She went on to tell him about the two couples coming along and how Meg was helping her with the food. 'If you like what we choose for the meal, would you like the same? Seems daft for Meg to cook you something different.'

'I'd like that, then I can imagine I'm part of the dinner party without the bother of having to talk to anyone. All I need is good food and good wine.'

'Well, I was going to suggest you met Sam, as I could bring him up here first. But if you'd rather not...' She grinned at him.

'You know very well I'd like to meet this friend of yours and I promise not to ask embarrassing questions such as his intentions towards my granddaughter,' he said, his eyes sparkling.

'Grandpa! You're incorrigible. I'll ask Sam if he wants to meet you first, as he might have been put off by my descriptions of you.' She tried to keep a straight face but dissolved into giggles.

Gregory started to laugh and it was a few moments before they both calmed down enough to speak.

'I think that makes us quits, don't you?' he said, blowing his nose.

'Yep, it does.'

The next morning Meg shared with Lucy her ideas for the supper.

'I've been looking through my magazines for recipes, not being in the habit of giving dinner parties myself. My husband's never been one for anything other than simple food, and would be happy with either Guernsey Bean Jar or grilled mackerel every evening if I was daft enough to cook them for him,' she said, rolling her eyes. 'As you wanted something light, I thought this fennel and orange salad, served with wild rocket would make a good starter and you could prepare it yourself, no cooking involved.' She showed Lucy the recipe she'd pulled out of a magazine.

'This looks perfect, Meg, thanks. What about the main course?'

Meg held out another page.

'This is a one pot dish, so again easy. Salmon with roast asparagus, cherry tomatoes and new potatoes, so you could use Jersey Royals. Might even try it at home, as we like a bit of salmon as a treat.'

Lucy read through the recipe.

'Brilliant choice, just right for a kitchen supper. Can't wait to have a go at it.'

'I hoped you say that as it's really straightforward and I'll be around to help if needed, but it will boost your confidence if you do it.' Meg picked up the last recipe. 'If you don't mind a boozy dessert, this sounds and looks quite special, "Lemon syllabub with Peaches and Amaretti", made with white wine and brandy. What do you think?'

'Ooh, it looks scrummy and boozy desserts are fine by me! Thanks so much, Meg, I'm happy to try and do it all myself, but would appreciate you being on hand. And by the way, if Grandpa likes the sound of it, and I'm sure he will, he would like to have the same in his room.'

Lucy threw her arms around Meg, excited at the prospect of actually preparing a delicious meal for her friends. And Sam. Fingers crossed Mary wouldn't try to draw her back to the past and spoil everything.

The week before the planned supper Liberation Day, on 9th May, was celebrated in Guernsey, and the other Channel Islands and with most businesses closed for the bank holiday, Sam suggested they spend the day in Herm. Lucy thought it a great idea as it had been years since she had last been over the short stretch of water to the magical little island which always seemed to be sunnier and warmer than its big sister Guernsey. And sharing a day in Herm with Sam would be even more special. He booked the ferry tickets and a table at The Ship for lunch, and he reluctantly accepted she would pay her share.

After a couple of unusually hot sunny days, Lucy was disappointed to wake up on Liberation Day to find a strong breeze was pushing clouds across the sky. Still, it looked like it may stay fine and instead of the planned shorts she dressed in jeans and a lightweight top and packed a sweater and a waterproof in her backpack. After breakfast she popped upstairs to say goodbye to Gregory and then set off walking down to the Weighbridge and the ferry. With the whole of the front of Town closed to traffic because of the upcoming Liberation Parade she and Sam had no choice but to walk down and planned to meet at the Liberation monument by the Trident ticket office. The pavements became more crowded as she started down St Julian's Avenue and the noise level increased accordingly as islanders called out to friends or family intent on enjoying a day off work. Lucy picked up their infectious holiday mood and by the time she reached the monument was bubbling with excitement as her eyes darted around looking for Sam.

'Hey, Lucy!' Sam cried, waving at her from among the throng gathered near the ferry. She smiled and pushed her way towards him, sidestepping pushchairs and small children jumping up and down with excitement. Sam gave her a hug and a quick peck on the cheek and she squeezed him back.

'What a crowd! I'd forgotten how popular Herm is. Good job you booked tickets.'

'That's the Boy Scout in me, always be prepared,' Sam grinned. 'Hope you've got something warm to wear on the boat, it's likely to be a bit chilly as we get out to sea.'

Lucy patted her rucksack.

'Packed in here, I remember being caught out when I was younger and it took me ages to feel warm again. I was rather hoping it would be bikini and shorts weather today, but the sun seems reluctant to come out.' She frowned at the huddled clouds thwarting her desire for a hot sunny day.

'I'm sure it'll brighten up and walking will keep us warm. We'll grab some coffee at The Mermaid before we do anything else, okay?'

'Lovely. Oh, they're starting to board, shall we join the queue?'

Sam put his hand round her shoulder as he guided her to the queue of excited day-trippers waiting to board the ferry. Five minutes later they were settled in seats on the upper deck and Lucy fished out her thick sweater. Once they were underway what had been a gentle breeze ashore became stronger but, as if to make up for it, the sun appeared from behind the clouds and Lucy turned her face towards it.

'That's better,' she said, smiling and Sam leaned closer, giving her a hug.

'As a boy, a trip to Herm was always an adventure, like going to another country where everything was strange and different. And I still think of it in the same way now, with the same sense of anticipation. What about you?'

'Definitely. I'd heard so many tales about pirates and fairies in Herm that I kept looking out for them, even though my parents pooh-poohed their existence. They did acknowledge there may well have been pirates using Herm as a base two or three hundred years ago but there would be no trace of them now. But there was always something slightly otherworldly about Herm which makes it special.' Thinking of the pirates reminded Lucy of her ancestral privateers who were no better than pirates, and an unbidden image of Nathaniel's body made her shiver.

'Hey, are you cold? I can lend you my jacket' Sam's arm tightened round her.

'No, I'm fine, thanks. Someone just walked over my grave.' She managed a smile, determined not to let the past sabotage her day with Sam.

'Happens to me sometimes too, a sudden shiver. And I assure you there are no pirates on Herm today getting ready to jump out on us when we land. I believe they've all moved to Sark,' he said, straight-faced.

Laughing, she said, 'Remind me not to go there, then. Fortunately, I've always preferred Herm.'

The island was looming ahead of them and Lucy's stomach fluttered with excitement. What kind of adventure would she have today? She could hardly wait!

Miraculously, as often happened in Herm, the air became warmer and the sun shone more brightly as they walked the well-trodden paths around the island. And, in spite of a full ferry, the passengers had drifted off into various directions and they hardly met a soul, emphasising the impression of being alone on their own special island. Apart from The Mermaid, always a busy pub near the harbour and shops, the only groups they saw was when they arrived at Shell Beach on the far side of the island, renowned for its white sand made of crushed shells.

'How about relaxing and having an ice cream? I've brought a large towel to sit on,' Sam asked as they stood watching children building sandcastles while their parents lay stretched in the sun.

'Love to, thanks.'

They found a quiet spot and while Lucy set out the towel Sam went to buy the ice creams from the kiosk. Lying back Lucy loved the feel of the sun on her face and arms as she reviewed the morning so far. Sam was proving to be an ideal companion, kind, funny and a great conversationalist. The more she learnt about him, the more she liked him. In fact, if she was honest, she thought she was falling in love with him. Hugging the thought to herself, too soon to share, she sat up in time to see Sam arrive with the ice creams.

He joined her on the towel, releasing a satisfied sigh.

'What a perfect way to spend a day off. Nothing better than being on a desert island with a beautiful lady to keep me company.' He took a lick of ice cream and smiled at her.

Lucy felt her face flush.

'Thanks. Although I don't have a job, it does feel a bit like playing hooky and I'm loving it.'

After finishing their ice creams they packed away the towel and headed to the path signposted Manor Village taking them through the centre of Herm and then down the hill to the harbour and The Ship. And lunch. When Sam helped Lucy settle at a table in the small courtyard set for al fresco dining, she sighed contentedly. It was proving to be a perfect day.

When the ferry dropped them back in St Peter Port it had started to rain and as the roads were no longer closed they opted for a taxi rather than face the steep walk up the hill in the rain. Within minutes she was dropped off at *Carreville* and Sam carried on in the taxi. It was early evening and she found Meg in the kitchen preparing Gregory's supper.

'How was Herm?' Meg asked, with a sly grin.

'Great, thanks. At least the rain held off until we got back so we spent the day outside. I'm shattered, feel like I've been walking forever.' Lucy peeled off her waterproof and draped it over a chair near the Aga. 'Mm, something smells nice, is there enough for me?'

'It's tuna pasta bake with a side salad. I've made plenty as you said you'd not be late back. Your friend not joining you?' Meg continued slicing tomatoes for the salad.

'No, he's having dinner with his father. Actually, I think I'll eat upstairs with Grandpa and we can chat while we eat.'

'He'd love that. Why don't you go up now and I'll bring a tray for you both shortly?'

'Okay, thanks.' Yawning, Lucy went upstairs in a daze of happiness and exhaustion. The day had been full on, she hadn't enjoyed herself as much for years, and she felt drained both emotionally and physically. It would be an early night for her tonight.

She came to finding the room dark and cold and she began shivering, rubbing her arms to generate some warmth but with little effect. Where was she? What had happened? She sat up on the cold, hard ground, gripped by icy fingers of fear as realisation dawned and rocked backwards and forwards, clasping her knees up to her chest. The movement triggered a blinding pain at the back of her head and raising a hand she found her hair matted with something warm and sticky. Bringing her fingers cautiously to her lips she tasted something she recognised. Blood. She passed out again.

Chapter 26

Lucy woke with a horrible taste in her mouth. Instinctively she touched the back of her head. Nothing. Opening her eyes she was relieved to see her bedroom. Must have been a dream. But more than a dream. Shivering as the memory lingered, she was convinced it was a foretaste of something which had happened to Mary. Probably involving that bastard Thomas. Rubbing her eyes, Lucy squinted at the clock. Seven o'clock. With a sigh, she crawled out of bed to open the curtains then stood in front of the portrait.

'What happened, Mary?' she whispered to the mournful face in front of her. Mary's head seemed to move a fraction to the right, where her husband stood stony-faced beside her. Lucy nodded and moved away, enveloped in the waves of despair emanating from Mary. The leaden sensation was in utter contrast to how she had felt only hours before after the day spent with Sam. Thinking of him made her realise she couldn't let Mary's life, and fate, continue to intrude on her own life for much longer. There was no way a closer, more intimate relationship with Sam would work if she was experiencing spontaneous, unwanted forays into the past. Her extremely distant past. She promised herself once the supper party was out of the way, she would re-start the time-slipping and learn the final part of Mary's story.

The next few days slipped past as Lucy enjoyed spending more time with Sam when he was free, sometimes just for a coffee. They both acknowledged how much they had enjoyed their day in Herm and Lucy sensed they were drawing closer. His face lit up whenever he saw her and the hugs lasted longer. Her stomach flipped even at the thought of seeing him, but they continued to behave as friends only. Occasionally, her mind would drift off to Mary and her, as yet, unknown fate and she had to work hard to pull herself back to the present.

The day before the supper party Lucy went with Meg to the nearby Waitrose to buy what was needed. Meg knew exactly where to find everything and it amused Lucy to see her greeted by name by several of the staff. At the fishmonger's counter Meg insisted on the freshest salmon fillets before asking after the man's wife. Lucy was introduced as Gregory's granddaughter and received warm smiles in return. At the checkout, while Lucy paid, Meg chatted to the woman on the till. As she pushed the trolley towards the car, Lucy laughed.

'Do you know everyone who works here, Meg?'

'Most of them, for sure. I only live round the corner in Collings Road, see, and this has been my local supermarket for years. It was Besants first, then Safeway and now Waitrose. A bit more expensive but lovely quality and your grandfather insists on the best. And I went to school with some of the girls who work here and it's nice to keep in touch with old friends, isn't it?'

Lucy nodded, only too aware of how remiss she'd been over the years, but determined to change from now on.

On Friday Lucy was both excited and nervous about the upcoming supper party as she began the preparations. She couldn't remember the last time she had been a hostess as Hamish had not been keen on having people round, preferring to meet with friends in the pub or, on special occasions, in a restaurant. There may have been a couple of times the whole time they were married and none after Amber's death.

With Meg's help she moved the heavy table to face away from the main part of the kitchen and draped it with a plain white tablecloth from the airing cupboard. Once she had set out the cutlery and glassware it looked less kitcheney, but still informal. Lucy prepared the starters and desserts under Meg's watchful eye and set them in the fridge.

"You've done well, Lucy, and I'm sure you'll manage the salmon dish easily enough. I suggest you start preparing it about two hours before your friends arrive and once it's cooked leave it in the warming oven until needed. You'll be able to relax and enjoy yourself, which isn't easy for the host.' Meg gave her a pat on the arm.

'It's all thanks to you for finding such straightforward dishes. I was put off cooking by my mother as she would spend hours preparing fancy meals for us and they'd be gone in minutes. But it was what Dad expected, I guess. After all, I understand he was brought up with a cook and housekeeper. No wonder he loves his food!'

'Well, they do say the way to a man's heart is through his stomach, it'll be interesting to see if your young man enjoys your cooking tonight,' Meg said, cocking her head.

'Meg! He's just a friend, remember. I'm not trying to woo him with food or…or anything else. Naturally I want him to enjoy the meal, but I want all my friends to enjoy it.' She stood with her hands on hips, trying to look annoyed while ignoring the flush she felt creeping up her neck.

'If you say so.' Meg picked up her bag, saying, 'I'll be off now so see you later.'

After she'd gone Lucy concentrated on her To Do list which included selecting the wine and placing the chosen white bottles in the fridge. She was relieved not to need wine from the cellar, sparing her the accompanying feeling of dread. Once she was satisfied with the preparations she fetched her gym bag and set off to Kings for her usual session and a quick chat with Sam. After all her hard morning's work she also fancied a swim.

'Hi, Lucy, wasn't sure if you'd make it today. Thought you'd be busy in the kitchen.' Sam greeted her when she entered the gym.

'All under control, don't worry, and I needed a break. You are still coming aren't you?'

'Sure, I'm looking forward to it. It'll be great meeting your grandfather and your friends. If it wasn't for you, I'd not have gone anywhere for the past few weeks.'

'I've been almost as bad so maybe we've helped each other.' Lucy smiled, her stomach flipping at the nearness of him. Perhaps she'd better place him down the table at supper, or else she wouldn't be able to eat a thing.

The swim helped to clear her head and put her in a positive mood for the evening ahead. Before going to the kitchen to start prepping the main course, Lucy called in on Gregory.

'Hi, Grandpa, sorry I've been too busy to spend time with you today, but I'll make it up to you tomorrow.' She kissed him and sat down.

He chuckled.

'Meg was telling me how anxious you are it all goes well this evening, but I'm sure it'll be fine. Apparently you've not needed Meg's help with the cooking. Well done! Your grandmother couldn't boil an egg. Never needed to, of course. Her family was even wealthier than ours, but she abhorred ostentation, like that jewellery, for example.'

Lucy nodded.

'She was lovely, Grandpa, I always felt I could talk to her –'

'But not me, eh?' He patted her hand as she flushed. 'Oh, don't worry, Sarah used to tell me I had this hard shell with a hidden soft centre. I'm glad you've finally broken through to find it.'

Was that a tear he brushed away? Lucy's throat tightened. 'So am I, Grandpa, and I hope you enjoy your meal tonight.' She stood. 'I must be off or the salmon won't be ready in time. See you later.'

As she headed to the kitchen her own eyes were moist.

Sam arrived on the dot at six thirty, presenting Lucy with a bouquet of tulips and lilies as he kissed her cheek.

'Thank you, they're beautiful. Let me put them in water then we can go and see Grandpa.'

'Wow, this is some hallway! Those Georgians sure knew how to make a grand entrance,' he said, his head swivelling around. 'Don't tell me all those portraits are your ancestors?'

'Afraid so, but don't panic, my grandfather is not at all stuffy.' Not now anyway, she thought, smiling as she dashed into the kitchen, leaving him staring at what she now thought of as Rogues Gallery.

'Right, let's go up. Most of the house is unused since my grandmother died, but it must have been stunning once.' As she well knew, having lived there two hundred years before. Unbidden, images of how it was flooded her mind as she mounted the stairs and she pushed them away as Sam walked beside her. She must stay in the present.

'Here we are,' she said, knocking before entering.

'Grandpa, let me introduce my friend Sam Norman. He's been admiring the hallway. Sam, my grandfather, Gregory Carre.' She moved to one side as Sam shook Gregory's hand.

'Hello, Mr Carre, it's great to meet you. Lucy's told me so much about you.'

'She has, has she? Don't believe a word of it. Anyway, nice to meet one of her friends at last. She's been stuck with me most of the time. I hear you work at Kings?'

Lucy only half-listened as they chatted, keeping an eye on the time. After ten minutes they were deep in conversation about the pleasure of sea fishing so she excused herself to return to the kitchen, suggesting Sam follow when he was ready. She had scarcely finished transferring the salmon dish to the warming oven when the doorbell rang. Letting out a deep breath, she went to the front door, to be met with cries of 'Hi!' from all four friends.

'We shared a taxi,' explained Natalie, thrusting a bottle of bubbly into her hands. 'It's chilled, if you want to serve it now.' Among hugs and kisses Lucy welcomed them inside, to be met with more cries of 'Wow!' and 'What a fantastic house!'

'Thanks, everyone, but you do realise I'm not much more than a squatter here, don't you? I could be homeless at any minute,' she said, grinning, to be met with laughter.

'Thought you said Sam would be here?' Natalie whispered, as the others admired the staircase.

'He is, he's upstairs with Grandpa, who wanted to meet him. He'll be down… oh, here he is now.' Sam stood at the top of the stairs, with five pairs of eyes looking up at him. He smiled, then, although dressed in jeans and open-neck shirt, he assumed the stance of a man in a dinner jacket and strutted down the stairs à la James Bond, accompanied by clapping and laughter from those below.

'Marvellous! I've always wanted to shimmy down such a staircase,' said Natalie, as they introduced themselves. Stuart and Nick clapped him on the back and Jeanne rolled her eyes as if to say 'Men!' Lucy finally stopped giggling and ushered her guests into the kitchen, saying, 'I thought we could have drinks outside first, if everyone's agreed?'

'Lovely idea, Lucy, after being cooped up all day in an office I love nothing more than a glass outside. Though I must say, it looks very cosy in here.'

Deciding to open the bottle of champagne, Lucy set up the glasses on a tray and with the bottle in an ice bucket, led the way through the back hall to the garden and the newly cleaned table and chairs. In spite of the lawn being too long and the borders unweeded since her mother had been away,

Lucy thought it would pass. Was there such a thing as a shabby-chic garden?

'How nice to have such a large garden in town,' said Jeanne, 'and I expect there are great views from upstairs.' She glanced upwards and when Lucy followed her gaze she saw Gregory at his window, glass of wine in hand.

'Yes, you can see over Havelet to Castle Cornet. Look, my grandfather's up there with his wine, so shall we raise a toast to him as the true host?' Glasses filled, they all turned to face him and raised their glasses, saying 'Lucy's grandfather!' Gregory smiled and took a sip of his wine.

People began talking at once and Lucy simply smiled and sipped her champagne, enjoying the moment as the bubbles fizzed in her head. Sam caught her eye and joined her as the others wandered off to get a better view of the house.

'Enjoy your walk of fame, did you?' she said, her eyes dancing.

'Couldn't resist it. And it broke the ice, didn't it?' he said, with a cheeky grin

'Guess so. This house can be a bit intimidating.'

'I think your grandfather is great, we could have talked for ages. My own grandfather died some years ago and I still miss him. There's something about their generation which sets them apart.' He twirled his glass, looking thoughtful.

'I agree. Might have been living through the war, but whatever it is, I'm enjoying his company.'

A shout from Natalie caused her to look round and see her friend beckoning her to join them.

'Come on, I'm supposed to be playing host and there's a meal to serve.' Without thinking she grabbed Sam's hand and pulled him with her. Lightheaded with champagne and the company of her friends, she was happy to relax and enjoy what was turning out to be a wonderful evening.

Groaning, Lucy turned over, shielding her eyes from the sunlight peeping through the edge of the curtains. As she became more aware of the pain in her head, she remembered the cause. Lots and lots of wine. But what a fab evening it had been! In spite of the pain, she smiled as she reviewed the hours spent eating, drinking and laughing with her friends. The food had won compliments from all, including Gregory, and Sam had told her how much he had enjoyed himself when he said goodbye with a lingering kiss. A proper kiss. She sighed at the memory. Of course, they'd both had a lot to drink, but it had felt *real*. He was the last to leave and for a moment she was tempted to suggest he stayed, but he made the decision for her by saying, 'Good night, I'd better get going,' in a husky voice. When the others had left together, Natalie had whispered, 'Sam's lovely, go for it!' and winked.

As she stood under the shower, her head easing after taking painkillers, Lucy let her mind drift back to that kiss and her body's response. Could it be she and Sam were ready to move on with their relationship? She certainly was. But was he?

Chapter 27

'Good morning, how did it go last night?' Meg's cheery voice greeted Lucy as she entered the kitchen gingerly, unsure what state they'd left it in. It was pristine.

'Morning, Meg. Don't tell me you've cleared up after us? I wasn't expecting you to, in fact I planned to whizz through it after breakfast.' Guilt flooded through her, as if Meg hadn't enough to do.

'Don't fret, it didn't take long. There was no mess, just dirty dishes now in the dishwasher and empty bottles now in the recycle bin.' Meg grinned as she cooked Gregory's breakfast. 'Are you up for a fry-up? Supposed to be good for a hangover.'

'Thanks, the carbs should soak up any alcohol sloshing around.' Lucy poured a mug of coffee before slumping in a chair.

'So? How did it go? Did your man enjoy himself?' Meg's smirk was beginning to irritate her, but maybe it was her own fault. Too much wine. And, to be fair, she did want Sam to be "her man".

'Great, thanks. Everyone loved the food, so thanks again for your advice and encouragement. And Sam and my other friends all clicked and we had a fun time. Even Grandpa and Sam hit it off, so all good.' She took a sip of coffee, willing herself to become the proverbial bright-eyed and bushy-tailed version of herself before visiting Gregory later. Might take a few mugs of coffee.

Meg nodded.

'I told you not to worry, didn't I? And what beautiful flowers someone brought. Champagne too! You've got some good friends there, my girl, and you deserve them. You've lifted Gregory's spirits no end, you have.' She cleared her throat. 'Right, tuck in while I take up his breakfast.' She placed a full plate in front of her and left with Gregory's tray.

By the time Lucy finished she was feeling more herself and recalling how much fun the evening had been. Her life was turning around, thanks to the lovely people in her life. With her doctor's permission she was weaning herself off the anti-depressants which, she now realised, had been dulling her senses too much. The warm fuzzy feeling in her stomach when she thought of Sam showed they were coming alive again and she was now more in control of Mary. For the moment, anyway.

Half an hour later she visited her grandfather.

His eyes were twinkling as they exchanged greetings.

'You know, my dear, it made me so happy seeing you young people enjoying yourselves in the garden last night. And for the first time in years, I wished I could have come downstairs and joined you. I was reminded of the times Sarah and I entertained friends, which tended to be more formal, and probably not nearly as much fun.'

Lucy held his hand.

'You would've been very welcome, Grandpa. I know Sam enjoyed meeting you and I'm sure the others would have as well.'

'Ah, yes, now about your young friend,' he said, his face suddenly serious. She held her breath, wanting him to approve of Sam.

'What about him?'

The twinkle returned.

'Thought he was a charming young man, hailing from a good solid Guernsey family.'

She relaxed.

'That's more than can be said of our family, Grandpa. Bunch of pirates, thieves and murderers.'

Gregory laughed.

'I doubt if there are any old families here who can claim a complete lily-white ancestry. And to the best of my knowledge our family's been on its best behaviour for at least the past hundred years.'

'Pleased to hear it. And I'm glad you liked Sam because I quite like him too.'

He raised his eyebrows.

'I get the impression it's more than "like", but whatever happens between you, be assured you have my approval. Something, or someone's put the colour back in your cheeks, my dear, and I couldn't be more pleased.'

Lucy felt a rush of affection for the old man and gave him a big hug and a kiss.

'Whatever was that for?'

'To show how much I love you, Grandpa. Now, I suppose you want to know all about last night, don't you?'

After lunch Lucy made her way to Kings hoping the workout would see off the last remnants of lethargy. The other thing on her mind was Sam. Did he regret kissing her last night? Could be awkward if he did.

She had been on the cross-trainer ten minutes when Sam entered the gym and his eyes swept the room until he saw her. His big smile was encouraging.

'Hi, how're you feeling? You're looking great for someone who hosted such a smashing supper party last night.' He stood close to avoid being overheard.

'Thanks. I'm better than I was when I woke up but coffee, paracetamol and a full English sorted me out. And you?' The warm, fuzzy feeling was there again.

'Not bad. I came in early for a swim before work which helped.' Taking a quick look around, he shifted his feet before saying, 'Can I take you out for lunch tomorrow as a thank you for last night? I know we agreed on going Dutch but it would defeat the object, wouldn't it?'

'It would, so I'm happy to accept. Have you somewhere in mind?'

'Hotel Jerbourg does a great Sunday lunch and I thought we could walk along the cliffs after to work it off.'

'Sounds perfect.'

'Right, I'll book for one o'clock and pick you up at half past twelve. See you tomorrow.' He gave a quick nod and moved off to a woman waving for help. Lucy couldn't help a huge grin spreading over her face and spent the next ten minutes going hell for leather on the cross-trainer. If that didn't dispel her tiredness, nothing would.

Sunday arrived with a clear sky and warm sunshine and Lucy hummed to herself as she dressed in cotton trousers and a short sleeved top, smart enough for lunch and practical for walking. She would take a long sleeved sweater in case it turned cool on the cliffs. Meg simply pursed her lips when told of the lunch and later, Gregory, a twinkle in his eye, told her to enjoy herself. She planned to, with no intrusion from Mary.

Sam arrived right on time and, a little hesitantly, kissed her cheek. She smiled in return, hiding her disappointment it wasn't more passionate. Once in the car she avoided talking about the supper party and asked him about the Hotel Jerbourg.

'I don't think I've ever been inside, but I remember it's got marvellous views over the islands.'

'It has, one of the best positions on the island which is why I suggested it. I've booked an outside table so we can enjoy the view while we eat. I know the area well as Dad and I take the boat out fishing around Moulin Huet and Saints Bay.'

'So, is fish on the menu today?' she grinned.

Sam laughed.

'Probably, but not from us. We only fish for our own table and haven't been out for a while. Not since…' He bit his lip.

'Oh, I'm sorry.' She wanted to touch him but held back.

'No worries,' he smiled at her, 'I'm learning not to let it overwhelm me as it did. I want us to enjoy ourselves today, not be sad.'

'Agreed.'

Minutes later Sam drove into the car park at Jerbourg Point and they walked the short distance to the hotel. Lucy thought the hotel looked different to what she remembered and Sam said it had changed ownership and been extended. A waiter took them through the restaurant to the outside terrace and their table. Sam ordered a beer and a glass of white wine for Lucy.

She took a deep breath as her gaze took in the view of Sark stretched out in the sun-dappled sea, with the smaller island of Herm in the distance on her left.

'It's beautiful, isn't it? It's at times like this I wonder why on earth I left Guernsey to live in London.'

'Ah, but teenagers don't appreciate natural beauty, do they? It's something that's just there, and it's not exciting like the big smoke. But as we get older I think our perceptions and priorities shift, don't you?'

'Sure. Ah, here's our drinks.'

The waiter placed their drinks in front of them and asked if they were ready to order. Sam asked for a few more minutes and he left.

They sipped their drinks while perusing the menu, a three course set lunch with options for each course.

'I fancy the fish for the main,' she said, smiling.

'So do I,' Sam replied, with a grin.

Once their orders had been taken there was a short silence, eventually broken by Sam.

'Lucy, I know we agreed to see each other as friends, with no pressure about becoming…involved. But over these past few weeks I've come to realise you mean more to me than a friend.' He paused, taking a sip of his beer and Lucy's stomach flipped. Gazing into her eyes, he went on, 'I think I'm falling in love with you and I wondered how you felt about me.'

'It's funny you should say that, as I think I'm falling in love with you, too. So we're even.' She smiled and reached for his hand. He clasped hers in his and laughed.

'What a relief! I was afraid you'd tell me to back off, you weren't interested.'

'I very much am, but let's take it slowly, shall we? There's no rush.'

'Absolutely. And here's our starters, good timing. Suddenly I'm starving.'

Sam dropped her home about five o'clock. This time he kissed her properly, a lover's kiss. Coming up for air, he traced her face with his fingers.

'When can we meet again? You could come round to my place for dinner. I make a mean spag bol.'

'Sounds very tempting! I'm free any evening so it's up to you.'

'What about Wednesday? I finish early that day, giving me plenty of time to prepare.' His eyes were dancing.

'How long does it take to open a jar of sauce?' she said, laughing. 'Wednesday's fine by me.'

'Great. I'll text you my address but I can pick you up if you like?'

She shook her head.

'I'll walk, assuming it's not raining. If not I'll grab a taxi. In the meantime, see you at Kings tomorrow.'

'Yep.' Another kiss and he got back in his car.

Lucy floated into the house and up to her room, hardly believing how much things had changed in the past few hours. Once they had opened up about their feelings for each other, they had hardly stopped talking, and laughing. Wherever the path allowed, they had walked arm in arm on the cliff towards Muelin Huet, taking time to stop and admire the slowly changing view. It was as if they were old friends meeting up after years apart with an urgent need to share as much as they possibly could in the shortest possible time. They were sitting on a bench on the cliff path staring at the waves curling around the rocks when Sam said sheepishly, 'You'll never believe it, but as a kid I was afraid of the sea. Not great for an islander!'

'For sure. What happened?'

'Like most kids I learnt to swim at Beau Sejour and it was no problem. But when my parents took me to the beach I absolutely refused to go in the sea. Screamed my head off, apparently. Eventually, it came out I'd been obsessed with pictures of the sea monster in Victor Hugo's *"Toilers of The Sea"*, set in Guernsey and believed he really existed and would come and eat me if I went into the sea. It took ages to persuade me it was only a story and Dad had to go in the water with me before I gained enough confidence to go on my own. Now, it's hard to keep me out.'

'I never had a problem with the sea, but I hate underground spaces. My parents have a friend in Perelle who has an old German bunker in their garden and they had it restored to its original condition. When we were visiting one day they insisted on showing us round, but as soon as I went in and the door shut, I completely lost it. I couldn't breathe and thought I was going to die. As soon as they opened the door I rushed out, crying. Dad was pretty cross with me and kept apologising to his friend, but Mum kept calm and said it was fine, lots of people are claustrophobic. I'm not great in lifts either, but anything underground is far worse.'

Sam had cuddled her, saying not to worry, he would keep her safe.

Now, in her bedroom, Lucy thought about their conversation. Until then, she hadn't given any thought to what happened in the bunker. She'd only been about seven or eight. Something clicked in her head and she found herself standing in front of the portrait.

'The cellar holds the answer, doesn't it, Mary?'

Mary's head once again appeared to nod.

Lucy knew if she and Sam were about to deepen their relationship then time was running out for her to slip back into Mary's life to uncover what happened to her. Waking in a sweat from one of her "dreams" while he lay next to her, would be quite a turn off for him.

'I'm ready to learn more now.'

Another almost imperceptible nod.

Taking a deep breath Lucy settled on the bed and went through the technique Molly had taught her.

Chapter 28

The noise hit her first. Opening her eyes she saw Henry and Georgina shouting at each other as they both tried to scramble onto a beautiful, painted wooden rocking horse, which she had never seen before. Why, it even had a real horsehair tail and a leather saddle! She had just entered the nursery and the nurse and Jane were trying to calm them down.

'What is going on? I could hear your voices from my sitting-room below.' She moved towards them and picked up Georgina, who was red-faced and crying.

'Henry says it's his horse, a present from Papa, and I'm not to ride it. But it isn't fair, Mama, I'm the eldest!'

Mary looked at the nurse.

'Is this true, Lotty?'

The nurse, her hair escaping from her cap and looking flushed, shook her head.

'I don't know, ma'am. It's true 'tis a present for Master Henry from his father, but I didn't hear nothing said about Miss Georgina not being allowed to ride on it. All I heard the master say was he had brought it with him on the ship from London.'

Ah, so her husband was back from his travels and as usual had not had the courtesy of informing her. Mary only liked to know he was around so she could avoid him. The past four years since Henry had been born they had crossed each other's paths as little as possible. And since finding her beloved Nathaniel's body in the cellar the year before, she had scarce said a word to him for fear of saying what she knew.

'Georgina, darling, I'm sure you will have your turn so dry your eyes and remember big girls of six don't cry.' Turning to her son, standing silent with little fists clenched and a mutinous expression on his face, she sighed. He was too much like his father, displaying an arrogance unbecoming in a four-year-old. 'Henry, this is such a beautiful horse that I would very much like to have a little go myself. Would you allow me to? For I never had such a horse myself when I was a child, and think you're the most fortunate of children to have one.'

For a moment the room itself seemed to hold its breath.

Henry appeared to be weighing up his answer, looking first at the splendid horse which was at least twice his height, and then his mother, giving him her best smile.

'Yes, Mama, you may have a go. Then it's my turn.'

'Thank you, Henry. You are very kind.' In spite of his faults, Mary loved her son and hoped with her influence he would indeed grow to be kind. Unlike his murderous father.

A little later, Mary was alone in her rooms sewing a blouse for Georgina when Thomas barged in without knocking, his face puce.

'How dare you tell Henry he has to share his rocking horse with his sister! I bought it for him only, she can play with her dolls. It's all girls are fit for.' He stood in front her, his legs spread and hands on hips.

Mary could feel the blood rush to her head and before she could stop herself, burst out, 'And how dare you treat our sweet daughter as if she were of no account? And how would you like it if our children were to learn their father is a murderer? Who killed his own brother!' She took a deep gulp of air to steady her racing heart.

Thomas staggered back, as if she had slapped him, his face drained of colour.

'What? What did you say?'

'You know what I said. I happened on poor Nathaniel's body twelve months ago while chasing after Storm. And…and your bloody dagger was by his…body and there…was a case…jewels. Recognised a bracelet…matching my wedding necklace.' Tears fell down her cheeks onto the blouse as she struggled to speak, recalling the hideous vision of Nathaniel's decaying body.

For a moment she wondered if Thomas would strike her dead on the spot, but even he would know he might have trouble hiding such an event. She watched as he stomped around the room, looking unsure of what to say. It felt good to have the upper hand for once, but in her heart she knew it could only rebound on her.

'I will move the body and you won't be able to prove a thing. After all, Nathaniel was declared drowned years ago. There will be nothing to connect me to his death.' His colour began to return as he must have thought he had out-smarted her.

'True, you can dispose of what is left of your brother, except for one thing.'

'What? The case of jewels? That means nothing on its own.'

She shook her head.

'I have Nathaniel's finger, bearing the ring I gave him on our betrothal. It…it had broken off his hand.'

He grew pale again.

'His finger?' he whispered.

'Yes, and your dagger and the case of jewels.'

'You must tell me where they are hid or I will make you sorry you were born.' His eyes blazing he lunged towards her, but she had picked up her scissors and held them in front of her.

'Come any nearer and I swear I will stab you. Leave me alone and I promise not to tell the world what you have done. Not for your sake, but for our children's. I do not wish them to be branded the children of a murderer, much as I would love to see you hang for what you have done. You not only took your brother's life but you robbed me of a life of happiness as his wife.' She spat the words out, grief for Nathaniel making her past caring.

Thomas swayed on his feet, glaring at her, but staying back.

'I never planned to kill him. He came upon me in the cellar where I was hiding the Frenchman's jewels and I stuffed some in my pocket and was about to leave when he arrived. He became angry, berated me for keeping part of the spoils for myself, told me they must be shared by all.' Thomas spat on the floor. 'Easy for him to say, he had inherited everything from our father. I had debts to settle and needed money. We fought…and he was dead. It was his fault, if he had let me keep the jewels he would still be alive.'

Mary gasped.

'You dare to blame him for his death? You are beneath contempt. I shall never reveal where everything is hid.'

His eyes blazed at her.

'You haven't heard the last of this, wife. That's a promise.'

He turned on his heels, slammed out of the room and left her sobbing. What had she done?

Lucy opened her eyes, the sound of crying echoing in her head. Taking deep breaths, she sat up on the bed. At least this time, although she had vivid recall of what had happened, she was more detached emotionally than on previous occasions. The only reminder the faint aroma of Lily of the

Valley. Just as well, she thought, reaching for her notebook. Hearing Thomas describe how Nathaniel met his death was chilling. It was Thomas's greed which had killed his brother. And poor, poor Mary! And still she took on Thomas. Once she had written it all down and thinking it was a shame she couldn't take a voice recorder back with her, Lucy knew with sickening certainty that Mary would have paid a heavy price for telling Thomas what she knew. Shivering, as if someone had walked over her grave, she stood again in front of the portrait.

'Oh, Mary, you were so brave and I really admire you for wanting to protect your children. It will soon be time to tell me the final part of your story.'

A tear fell from Mary's eyes and Lucy wiped it with her finger. Putting it to her lips she tasted salt.

Less than twenty minutes had elapsed since she had arrived home so Lucy went along to see Gregory before his dinner arrived. She had already told Meg in the morning she wouldn't need dinner herself; Sunday lunches were known for keeping you full for longer.

'Well, my dear, I don't need to ask if you enjoyed yourself today,' Gregory said, with raised eyebrows.

'Yes, it was lovely, Grandpa.' Some of it, anyway, she thought, pushing aside images of Mary confronting Thomas with a pair of scissors.

'Come on then, tell me more. It's clear there's more to it than "lovely". Did Sam tell you he loved you?'

'Grandpa! How did you guess?'

'He didn't say as much when we had our little chat on Friday, but reading between the lines it was obvious he had strong feelings for you and hoped you'd be more than friends.' He coughed. 'I may have hinted you were more than fond of him, too.'

'You're incorrigible, Grandpa,' she said, trying and failing not to laugh.

'Old people are allowed some leeway in affairs of the heart, my dear. If we push things on a little bit, it's only because we care.'

'All right, you win. And yes, we both admitted wanting a closer relationship and today was our first official date. Sam's invited me round for dinner on Wednesday and we'll take it from there.'

Gregory beamed.

'Excellent! Now tell me what you had for lunch and where you walked so I can imagine myself there with you.'

The next morning Lucy phoned Jeanne to see if she was free to meet for coffee and some shopping in Town. Jeanne was happy to accept, saying she needed a break from her writing. They arranged to meet at Dix Neuf at ten thirty and Lucy, arriving first, was able to get a table by the open window. Although they were ostensibly meeting to shop, Lucy's mind was never far from Mary and her story, and what she wanted to ask her friend. Jeanne joined her five minutes later and after a hug sat down with a contented sigh.

'Such bliss! With the children at school I feel obliged to write even when I don't feel like it, so it's lovely to have an excuse to get out and chill with you. I think we could be good friends, don't you?'

'Yes, I do. We have several things in common for a start. But first, what would you like to drink?'

Once they'd ordered two cappuccinos, Lucy told Jeanne she and Sam were now dating and she needed to shop for new clothes.

Jeanne clapped her hands.

'Great! I saw there was a spark between you, and told Nick you'd make a great couple. We both liked him a lot and will happily have you both round whenever you're free.' She leaned closer, grinning. 'What sort of clothes do you need? Sexy undies?'

'Er, well, I admit it wouldn't hurt to buy some new undies too, but I actually need nice clothes for everyday wear and evening. I lost a lot of weight due to my depression and didn't care what I wore. But now –'

'You want to look nice. Of course, no problem. This will be fun! Better than shopping on your own as shop assistants always tell you something suits you, when it may not. Though I must say, Lucy, you've always looked nice when I've seen you.'

'Thanks, I've been making an effort lately.'

Their coffees arrived and when they were alone again, Lucy went on to say she wondered if Jeanne might be interested in writing about Mary's life. She told her about slipping back in time and what she had witnessed and there was still more to learn.

Jeanne's eyebrows rose and her jaw dropped.

'Blimey! There's much more to it than I'd realised when we first met. It's hard to take it all in. And how traumatic for you, poor girl.'

'It has been and I know it sounds far-fetched, but some of it can be proven to have happened. As it doesn't show my family in the best light, perhaps fictionalising the story might be better?'

Jeanne nodded.

'I see your point. Though as it all happened so long ago, I don't think it would be a problem. Anyway, you've given me lots to think about and I could be interested in developing a book, fiction or non-fiction.' She grinned. 'If I'd known what you were going to tell me, I'd have ordered something stronger than coffee.'

Two hours later they returned to their cars in North Beach car park carrying the proceeds of their shopping trip. Lucy had several carrier bags while Jeanne had one. Flushed with the success of the trip, they embraced, promising to keep in touch. Lucy drove home smiling, looking forward to Sam's reaction when he saw her wearing one particular purchase.

The rest of Monday passed pleasantly enough and her enjoyment of the gym session in the afternoon was heightened by the change in her relationship with Sam. They'd agreed to continue behaving as friends in the Club, to save them both any awkwardness, but if anyone had watched them closely they would have seen the mutual desire in their eyes as they discussed a change in Lucy's workout regime. Walking home afterwards, she thought about Gregory's advice to get to know each other as friends first, and she fully agreed with him. Even though it had only been a few weeks, she couldn't wait to take it to the next level. Wednesday couldn't come quick enough. But before then she had to go back and learn the rest of Mary's story and planned to do so the following day.

Lucy was on edge on Tuesday, despite telling herself nothing bad could happen to *her*. She was a different person in this life, not Mary anymore, and she had proved she could detach herself, to an extent, from anything she experienced. But it didn't stop her feeling scared. At one point she considered asking Molly if she would be with her, but then thought it might inhibit her slipping back if a non-family member was present. And what could Molly do until she came back, anyway? Deciding the best time would be after the gym session, when it was still afternoon, Lucy stuck to her usual routine of visiting her grandfather after breakfast, finding it hard to relax with him.

'Anything the matter, my dear? You're very quiet today. Not had another of those awful dreams, have you?' Gregory's face was pinched in concern and she decided this was a good time to offer her latest time-slip as a dream.

'Actually, I have, Grandpa…' She went on to describe the confrontation between Thomas and Mary, including his admission of Nathaniel's death. And his threat to Mary.

Gregory's eyebrows could hardly have risen any higher.

'My word, Lucy, I can hardly believe it. Although it does seem to fit with your earlier dreams, and we know at least some of the jewellery exists.' He shook his head, his breathing becoming erratic.

'Grandpa, are you all right? I'm sorry if I've distressed you,' Lucy panicked. Please don't let him have a heart attack or something.

'No, I'm fine, my dear. My old heart has blips occasionally. I'm not upset, simply shocked and somewhat intrigued. It's hardly a normal situation is it? It's you I'm concerned for, having such a dream must have been awful for you,' he said, gripping her hand.

She nodded, stuck for words. How could she tell him what was actually happening? Either way, he was right, it was awful for her.

'It seems we do have a villain in the family, and I wonder what became of poor Mary?'

'I might learn more in another dream, Grandpa, and then Mary can finally rest in peace.'

'Yes, it's a little unnerving having a restless spirit around the place, don't you think?' He chuckled, adding, 'Dennis might not get so much for the house if it's known to be haunted. Serve him right, expecting me to pop my clogs when I was ill three years ago. I'll hang on for as long as I can, thank you.'

Lucy smiled.

'You go, Grandpa, I don't mind being here for you.'

'It's very sweet of you to offer, my dear, but I dare say you'll want to spend your time with a certain young man who will be much better company for you.' His eyes were twinkling and she felt the heat rise in her neck.

'Oh, Grandpa!'

Back from the gym Lucy went to her room, placing a glass of water and her notebook on the bedside table. And a box of tissues. In case.

She stood once more in front of the portrait, which she had come to see as a travesty of both the wedding day and marriage. Were any other portraits hiding equally bleak truths, she wondered. Probably best not to know, she thought.

'Mary, I'm ready to learn the final part of your story. *Our* story. Will you help me, please?'

The virtually imperceptible nod.

'I'm hoping once I've learned all there is to know, you will find peace and be able to join your children – and Nathaniel – wherever souls go. You understand?'

A glimpse of a smile this time.

Lucy nodded and made herself comfortable on the bed. She didn't know where the words she'd spoken to Mary had come from, but hoped with all her heart they would prove to be true.

Chapter 29

What was that sound? Mary opened her eyes, pulled from her sleep by a noise she couldn't place. Her heart was beating fast and her fingers trembled as she lit a candle on the night stand. Ever since the day, some months ago now, Thomas had threatened her if she didn't reveal the whereabouts of what he wanted, she had slept but fitfully. Alert to the slightest sound, her sleep was often disturbed by the innocent creak of the floorboards as they settled into the drop of temperature of the winter air. But this hadn't sounded like a floorboard.

Mary lifted up the candle, spreading the light into corners where someone might hide. Nothing. As she moved away from the bed, the candle flickered somewhat, as if caught in a draught. The door! Her heart beating loudly in her ears, she moved towards the door and was horrified to see it stood ajar. Storm! Mary looked around for her dog, usually asleep at the foot of her bed and the most reliable of guard dogs. He was gone, but he could not have opened the door himself. Had Jane not closed it properly? Or had someone opened it deliberately?

She wrapped a shawl over her thin nightgown, pushed her feet into slippers and opened the door wider, to be met with darkness. No candles were allowed to stay lit in their sconces once the household were in bed, for fear of fire. Mary clutched the candle-holder tightly, shielding the candle from any draught which might blow it out. Not being able to call out Storm's name without waking anyone, she hoped he would come to her unbidden. After going up and down the landing without any sign of him, Mary approached the staircase leading downstairs. Again, complete darkness, no sliver of light from under a door. Where is he? Oh, Storm, why did you leave? Part of her wondered if it could be a trap set by her husband, but Thomas was away at sea and not expected back for another two days. Taking a deep breath she descended the stairs slowly, the carpet runner absorbing any sound. Reaching the bottom she turned towards the back hall where the kitchen lay in case he had gone there looking for food. A faint bark came from nearby, but before she could decide from where something hard struck her head. All went black.

She came to finding the room dark and cold and began shivering, rubbing her arms to generate some warmth but with little effect. Where was she? What had happened? She sat up on the cold, hard ground, gripped by icy fingers of fear as realisation dawned and rocked backwards and forwards, clasping her knees up to her chest. The movement triggered a blinding pain at the back of her head and raising a hand she found her hair matted with something warm and sticky. Bringing her fingers cautiously to her lips she tasted something she recognised. Blood. She passed out again.

'Come on, wife, wake up. I need to talk to you.'

Mary felt herself being shaken, when all she wanted to do was sleep. Rough hands grabbed her body and forced her into a sitting position when icy cold water was thrown into her face.

Gasping, she cried out, 'No, leave me alone.' Opening her eyes, all she could see was Thomas, one hand gripping her arm the other holding a lantern. The light cast shadows on his face, giving him the appearance of a demon, which to her, he was. 'Where am I and where's Storm?' she said croakily, her throat as dry as parchment. 'And what are you doing here? You're supposed to be at sea.'

'Your dog is safe, I only used him to lure you downstairs and I lied about my return.' He waved an arm. 'You don't recognise your new chamber, wife? Then I'll show you.' Thomas lifted the lantern and cast the light around the small now empty space where she had discovered Nathaniel's body. Mary moaned, realising his intention towards her.

'I see you remember now, don't you? But the body you thought you saw is now gone and will never be found. As for you, well that's in your hands now. Not only do I wish to recover the case and the jewels to eliminate any evidence against me, but I now need the jewels to raise money.' He laughed humourlessly. 'You see how it has come full circle, has it not? Now we have had the damned Smuggling Act forced on us, I have lost a steady supply of income which leaves me short of funds. So, wife, where are they hid?'

Mary felt sick and dizzy and could feel blood seeping from the wound in her head.

'I'm not telling you.' Closing her eyes, she drifted off, hearing the distant sound of Thomas's voice saying, 'Pah, let's see if a few more hours down here in the dark and cold will make you change your mind. I'll be back later.'

Mary drifted in and out of consciousness as her life's blood slowly ebbed away. She sensed she was dying, and although sad to be parted from her children, found a sense of peace washing over her. Opening her eyes, although it was dark, she saw her beloved Nathaniel standing in a beam of light and beckoning her toward him, his face suffused with love.

'My beloved!' she cried, rising up and leaving her broken body behind as she moved into his embrace.

* * *

Lucy came round, tears streaming down her face. Poor, poor Mary. And what a bastard Thomas was to treat her like that. The tears were her own, not Mary's this time. Tears for herself, for a life so cruelly ended. Sitting up, she drank greedily from the glass of water, as if she too, had been deprived of water for hours. Picking up the notebook and pen, Lucy began the painful task of recording the last hours of Mary's life. Her previous self. It was an odd and disturbing thought. As she wrote, she realised it wasn't clear whether or not Thomas had meant for Mary to die. He had certainly meant to frighten her into saying where she had hidden the jewels and the other evidence. But kill her? They would never know. The image which stuck most in her mind was that of Mary and Nathaniel joining together at last. If she was an artist she would paint it, but, unfortunately she could barely draw let alone paint. The image would have to remain in her own mind alone for ever.

Lucy closed the notebook and was about to get up when it hit her. What happened to Mary's body? She drew in a sharp breath. Could it still be in the blocked up room in the cellar? It was certainly possible. Thomas would have no need to move it, probably giving out some story of Mary having left in the middle of the night, no longer wanting to stay with him. It was no secret she was deeply unhappy in the marriage. He could have packed a bag of her clothes and dumped them in the sea, to give the impression of her running away. There were sure to have been questions asked, but what could anyone have done? No-one knew Thomas had killed his brother and had no need to suspect him of killing Mary. Anyone close to her would have known she could never have left without her children, but she was estranged from her parents. Jane would have been suspicious, but who would have listened to a maid?

Lucy had started pacing around as these thoughts surged through her brain, and she ended up in front of the portrait. She blinked. It wasn't possible.

But it was.

Where Mary had stood there was nothing, simply the background of the fireplace. It was as if she had never been in the painting.

Lucy felt the blood drain from her face. How the hell? As she lifted the painting off the wall she felt a soft touch on her cheek, and heard a whispered, 'Thank you.' Startled, she nearly dropped the painting and could only nod in acknowledgment. Relief flooded through her as it dawned on her she was no longer tied to Mary and her deeply unhappy life. Wondering how on earth her grandfather was going to react, she went along to his room with the painting.

'Grandpa, I think we've seen the last of our ghost.'

Gregory looked up from his paper and smiled.

'And what makes you think so?'

She turned the painting to face him.

'What! But that's impossible!' He looked at Lucy more closely. 'Oddly enough, you look as if you've seen a ghost not lost one. Has something happened? Another dream?'

She sat down, trying to compose her thoughts as Gregory continued to study the portrait, his brow furrowed in concentration.

'Yes, I've had another dream. I only dozed off briefly after the gym, but I…I think Mary wanted us to know the rest of her story so she could be free.' She paused. 'Sorry, Grandpa, but do you have any wine up here? Only I could do with a glass and I think you may be glad of one too when you hear what I have to say.'

'In that case, yes, there's a bottle by my bed which is nearly full. Bring a couple of glasses from the bedside cupboard, will you?'

Lucy went through and fetched the wine and glasses and poured them each half a glass. For now. She touched Gregory's glass with a 'Santé' before taking a quick gulp.

'Are you sure you're ready to tell me what's happened, my dear? I'm willing to wait if you're not.'

She shook her head.

'I have to tell you now, Grandpa, it's too important to wait.' Fortified by sips of wine, Lucy described what happened between Mary and Thomas leading to Mary's death in the cellar, and her reunion with Nathaniel.

By the time she finished, they'd both emptied their glasses and Gregory topped them up, saying, 'My God, Lucy, this is unbelievable. And any sane person could rightfully conclude we'd be mad to believe it.' He took a healthy swig of wine before adding, 'if it wasn't for the portrait and the jewellery and the room in the cellar.' His eyes widened. 'The cellar! You don't think – '

She nodded.

'Exactly, Grandpa. If Mary's body is still there, then no-one can accuse us of being insane. At least, not you. There may be some doubt over me and my apparent ability to connect with someone who died two hundred years ago.'

'Do you feel up to the task of checking the cellar? I'm only sorry I can't help, under different circumstances I wouldn't dream of letting you do it, but...' he shrugged, looking frustrated.

'At least if I do find her, it won't be a shock, will it? And if it proves what we think happened did happen, then I'm willing to do it. We can't ask anyone else, can we?'

'I suppose not. Mind you, if there's a body down there, we'll have to inform the police and there will be an inquest. I'm not sure how we're going to explain how we found her.'

'We only have to say I came across this boarded up room and out of curiosity decided to take a look. No problem.'

He laughed.

'There's no doubt you're my granddaughter! Pity you didn't go into the law, you'd have made a good advocate. Right, when are you going to explore?'

'I'll go down after Meg leaves this evening, don't want her involved with the fuss if we have to call the police. But I'll need a crowbar or a claw hammer, if you have them, Grandpa?'

'No idea about a crowbar, but all tools should be in a cupboard just inside the cellar at the top of the steps. And you will need a powerful torch. I kept one in the kitchen under the sink, if your father hasn't moved it.'

'Great, I'll take a look.' She stood, eyeing the portrait. 'What on earth are we going to do with this? I hate seeing that awful man.'

'He can go back to the attic for now. Your father might end up selling the family portraits one day and someone might be daft enough to buy the portrait of "A Georgian Gentleman from Guernsey".'

'I'll take him up now and then it'll soon be time for dinner, if I may join you?'

Gregory smiled.

'I'd love you to. And we'll need another bottle of wine.'

Lucy shot up to the attic to find a dark corner for Thomas and found a watercolour of a rustic scene to replace it. She wasn't going to risk any more ancestors with a sad past sharing their stories with her. Next she went downstairs and found Meg in the kitchen preparing their dinner and when Lucy asked about a torch, pointed to a cupboard.

'I make sure the batteries are always up to date as you never know when there might be a power cut. Do you need it for something particular?'

'Yes, Grandpa's asked me to check out an old part of the cellar. I'll put it back when I've finished. And I'm eating with him tonight so will help with the trays when you're ready.'

Meg nodded, saying, 'Will be about twenty minutes.'

Lucy went back into the hall and opened the cellar door cautiously, waiting for the usual feeling of cold and fear to overtake her. But there was nothing except the usual chill, Relaxing her shoulders, she switched on the light and noticed the cupboard hanging on the wall. Inside she found a large heavy claw hammer but no crowbar. Leaving the torch there she returned to her bedroom to hang the watercolour. There, much better. She was looking idly round the room when a vague memory stirred in her mind. Something she had seen. What on earth was it? She stood still trying to make it clearer. An image of Mary. The leather case. Jewels. Yes, she remembered now, Mary hiding the case under the floor. This floor! Her breathing quickened as she moved to the spot near the window, recalling Mary lifting up a floorboard. A void between the beams. All now concealed under a fitted carpet. Surely it wouldn't be there after two hundred years? Lucy tried to stem her feelings of excitement, knowing the chances were low. Might be worth a look, though.

Lucy waited until she and Gregory were on their own eating dinner and told him what she remembered from one of the "dreams".

His jaw dropped, his fork left halfway to his mouth.

'Goodness, my dear, I hadn't thought about the where-abouts of the case, assuming it would have been found at the time.' Gregory put the fork down and took a deep swallow of wine. His eyes shone. 'We mustn't get too excited, but it would be marvellous if we found it. Not only for the value of the jewels, but it would provide more confirmation of what happened, wouldn't it?'

'Yes, it would. I'm still going to check out the cellar first though and then, depending on the outcome, may have to leave lifting the bedroom carpet until tomorrow. Can't have too much excitement in one evening, can we?'

Chapter 30

Lucy picked up the torch and the claw hammer and made her way down the cellar steps. As she got closer to the closed heavy door, her heart hammered loud in her ears, but there was none of the unusually cold atmosphere she had experienced before. She opened the door and kept it wedged open with an empty wine crate, allowing some electric light to brighten the passage beyond.

Standing in front of the shuttered doorway she switched on the torch and left it on the floor while she started on a board at shoulder level. It took a while, but with the claw hammer she was able to ease one nailed end away from the door frame and she let it fall away, still nailed at the other end. Picking up the torch, Lucy shone it through the gap. She thought she saw something on the floor, but couldn't make it out and needed to prise open the next board. Once she had done that, she again shone the torch into the dark, musty space.

In the corner was what looked like a bundle of rags.

Lucy's heart nearly stopped. The memories flooded back and tears welled in her eyes as she pulled away all the lower boards so she barely needed to stoop to enter. Gripping the torch so tight her knuckles turned white, she took the few short steps to the corner and shone it down.

The skeletal head, with wisps of hair, peeped out of what once had been a colourful shawl covering a dirty white nightgown.

Lucy bowed her head and whispered, 'I know your spirit has long gone, Mary, but I promise your body will be given proper burial. Goodbye.'

Brushing the tears away, she left the torch and hammer and sped through the cellar and up the stairs to Gregory's room. He looked at her face and nodded.

'I'll call the police.'

A couple of hours later, Lucy sat in the kitchen nursing a glass of wine while she waited for the police to finish whatever they were doing in the cellar. With them was a forensic pathologist who had appeared quite animated at the prospect of examining a possible two hundred year old corpse. Her grandfather had handled the police questions beautifully.

'It appears, Inspector, we may have solved an old family mystery. A young woman, named Mary Carre, and married to a Thomas Carre, whose house this was, disappeared suddenly about eighteen hundred and seven. Her death was never recorded and it's been a bit of a puzzle as to what happened to her. We do know her marriage was not a happy one.'

'I see, Mr Carre, this could be most helpful.' The inspector scratched his head. 'Has someone been keeping a family history or tree? After all, it's a long time ago, isn't it?'

Gregory produced the document Lucy had found.

'Yes, my father was interested in genealogy and filled in this family tree. Please, take a look.'

The policeman read the section dating the early 1800s and nodded.

'Interesting, sir, thank you.' He turned to Lucy, sitting quietly nearby after giving her own statement. 'Mrs Stewart, it must have been a terrible shock to come across a body like that. I hope you're feeling better now?'

'Much better, thanks. What happens now?'

'We will take away the remains to be examined more thoroughly by the pathologist and then, if you believe them to be those of a family member, you may arrange a burial after an inquest. From what you've said, sir,' turning back to Gregory, 'it seems the most likely outcome. Of course, if you wanted more proof, we could compare DNA if one of you were happy to provide a specimen.'

'Thank you, Inspector, but we are quite happy to accept the remains are those of Mary Carre. It's such a pity we'll never know how she came to die in such circumstances.' Gregory shook his head sorrowfully and Lucy had to smother a grin.

The inspector rose, wished them a good night and went downstairs to see how his team were progressing in the cellar. After whispering 'Brilliant' to a smiling Gregory, Lucy followed to wait in the kitchen.

A quick knock on the door and the inspector came in to say they were finished and the remains were being brought up to be taken to the mortuary. Lucy escorted them all out, bowing her head as the black bag was carried to a waiting van. The police had only just driven off when Gregory's carer arrived to ready him for bed. Suddenly overwhelmed with exhaustion, Lucy decided an early night was in order and went upstairs. As she got into bed, her gaze was drawn instinctively to the area of carpet near the window. Would there be any hidden "treasure", or had Thomas or someone else beaten them to it?

The next morning Lucy told a bemused Meg about the discovery of the body while she had been checking out an old store room for Gregory.

'Ooh, glad I wasn't here when you found it. And all them police nosing about would have given me the willies!

Wonder if it was the poor ghost you mentioned not long after you arrived. If it was then she won't be back, will she?' Meg was twisting a dishcloth in her hands, looking around the kitchen as if at any moment a ghostly figure might appear.

'No, she won't be back, Meg. The story will probably end up in the Evening Press, and we'd be grateful if you'd be as discreet as ever. I'm sure you don't want Grandpa and our family to be the subject of wild rumours or speculation. You know what it's like here.' Lucy knew Meg liked a gossip as much as the next islander, but hoped her loyalty to Gregory would encourage her silence.

After breakfast, and checking that Meg had left, Lucy went up to her room armed with the claw hammer. She had to move a dressing table and a couple of chairs in order to roll the carpet back after freeing the edge from the grippers along the skirting. Then there was the underlay to roll back. Finally the floorboards were visible and Lucy checked if any were loose. All were nailed down and she used the edge of the claw hammer to prise up a board in the right area. Nothing. She prised up another two and was beginning to accept the case had been found, when she spotted a small piece of linen caught in a corner. Gingerly, she pulled it out. It was a scrap of a folded lacy handkerchief and Lucy recognised it immediately. Gently opening it she saw once more Nathaniel's skeletal finger bearing Mary's betrothal ring; a signet ring of gold with an onyx centre engraved with his entwined initials, NC. The final proof.

'Sorry, Grandpa, no fortune in jewels, someone got there before us. The good news is I don't think it was Thomas as I doubt he'd have left this behind.' She opened the linen handkerchief to show him the finger and ring and passed it over.

'Well I never. A bit creepy isn't it? All that's left of Nathaniel. Pity about the jewellery, it would have been part of your inheritance. Made you a wealthy woman, my dear.'

'It was always a long shot, but I'm pleased I found the finger. Why don't we bury it with Mary? Seems fitting, somehow, don't you think?'

'An excellent idea.' He gave her a keen look. 'This whole business must have been extremely upsetting for you. I do hope you will be able to put it behind you and have some fun now. I've just remembered, aren't you going to Sam's for dinner tonight?'

'Yes, I am and don't worry, I'm fine. It's been…interesting, but it's over now and I've got lots to look forward to.' The last couple of days had been so taken up with Mary's story Lucy hadn't been able to think about the upcoming dinner with Sam. She would have to tell him about the body as it would be public knowledge soon, but it could be brushed off as ancient history. Maybe one day, if they were to remain a couple, she could offer the version she'd given Grandpa about her "dreams". 'Right, I'll go and re-lay the carpet. See you later.'

Back in her room she pushed the carpet back into place. It wasn't perfect, but at least once the furniture was back in place, no-one would know she had been searching unsuccessfully for a fortune. But, with a bit of luck, she had found love.

With that comforting thought Lucy picked out the clothes for the evening ahead. One which she hoped would lead to years of shared happiness with Her Man.

The End